Domino Effect

Also by Karen Lee Field

The Land of Miu Series
(for young readers)

The Land of Miu
The King's Riddle
The Lion Gods

Cat and Mouse Adventures
(for young readers)

House on the Hill

A Dark Novel

Domino Effect

Karen Lee Field

Website: www.karenleefield.com

ISBN: 978-0-9943362-3-1 (pbk)

Front cover design by goonwrite.com
Text design by karenleefield.com

Dedication

Barry
You are in my heart and in my thoughts, always.

Introduction

Suicide was a word I associated with stories in books and magazines. I suppose I thought it was fictitious in many ways. I believed it could never affect my family. What I didn't realise is that it could happen in real life ... and then in May 2006 my eighteen-year-old son took his own life.

In my darkest hour, I could not concentrate on anything. My memory failed me. I couldn't function in everyday life. I saw things that I *knew* could not exist. Lack of sleep played with my mind and feed the depression. Fear for my eldest son consumed me so much that I could not rest unless he was in the same room as me. The pain, guilt, fear and grief I felt claimed the whole of me; changing my entire life.

At the time of my son's death, I was suicide unaware and remained that way until it was too late. I don't want another mother to find herself with the same regrets I have. I don't want another family to experience the uncertainty, fear and pain my family has suffered. It's important for me to know that young adults have the knowledge needed to recognise when a friend is in despair and, more importantly, know how to deal with it.

Be suicide aware. Know the signs. Know suicide can happen to anyone. No matter how rich or poor they are. No matter how educated they may or may not be. No matter how popular they are. Be forewarned and equipped to deal with what could happen and maybe that knowledge will help save a life.

Twelve years later, I feel the need to help raise suicide

awareness to prevent others from going through what my family and I have experienced. This book is the result of that need. Please remember, however, that I am not a counsellor or a doctor, and I have no degree in medicine. I am a mother who lost her son to suicide. This is not our story. This is not a true story. The characters in *Domino Effect* are fictitious. Their story is fictitious. But what they go through—their emotions, their actions and their feelings—and what they experience are based on reality.

I want to thank my family for the love and support they gave me during the worse years of my life. Thank you for showing me life is worth fighting for. Thank you for the long walks on beaches, through botanical gardens and wildlife parks; because the sight of native animals, the aroma of wild flowers, and the touch of the warm sun helped the healing process for me. And, finally, thank you for proving to me that memories can still be made and treasured.

Tuesday, 30th May

"In grief at your death, but in gratitude for your life, and for the privilege of sharing it with you, we commit your body to be cremated."

Kirsti Fowler stared at the oak coffin, tears blurring her vision, a lump causing pain in her throat. Was her twin brother really in that wooden box? How could it be possible? She turned to her parents and found them huddled together. Her mother sobbed uncontrollably and tears rolled down her father's cheeks. She had never seen him openly cry before and it made her feel uneasy. Kirsti's older brother, Tim, stood ashen-faced on the other side of them. He stared at something above the coffin. Kirsti had seen that look many times before and knew he was a million miles away.

Her gaze returned to the framed photo of Owen, which sat amongst the beautiful array of flowers on top of the coffin. His smiling face stared back at her and a small sob escaped her throat. How could he be dead? A mistake. It was all a horrible mistake. It had to be. She swallowed and turned her attention back to the grey-haired minister.

"Earth to earth, ashes to ashes, dust to dust."

She didn't hear the rest of his words. Nothing seemed real. It had to be a bad dream. She shook her head, knowing it wasn't, but wishing with all her heart that she would wake up anyway. In fact, she would be quite happy to be woken by Owen's overly loud rap music in the next room. How she would love to hear that dreadful music right now and catch her brother dancing in the middle of his room.

9

Movement caught her attention. Her parents stepped away from the pew and walked towards the coffin. They each carried a single yellow rose in their shaky hands. Yellow was Owen's favourite colour. A hand nudged her shoulder and she looked up to gaze into Tim's eyes and saw pain and sleepless nights, but something else too that she couldn't name at that moment. No smile touched his lips or his eyes, but he squeezed her shoulder gently and indicated to her silently that she should follow their parents. She gulped and looked down at her own rose before taking a step forward. She had not accepted that Owen was dead, so how could anyone expect her to say goodbye to him? She didn't want to say goodbye. She wouldn't!

She walked slowly towards her parents, the coffin looming on the other side of them. As she drew closer, she could hear her mother whispering something. Pain stabbed Kirsti's chest, she gulped and tried not to listen as she knew they were private words between mother and son. Her father silently stared at the coffin, one hand caressing the polished wood. She looked at the photo, at her parents, at the coffin. What does a person say at times like these? Words meant nothing. A tear slid down her cheek.

As she stood fiddling with the rose she still held in her hands, Kirsti heard Tim breathe a swear word. He pushed past her and dropped his rose at the base of the photo.

"Goodbye, Bro." He turned and walked away.

At that moment, Kirsti was aware of the church filled with people behind them. The sounds of grieving family and friends washed over her. An eerie silence filled the air as they watched the deceased's family mourn at his side. Kirsti twirled the rose stem between her fingers and she saw her mother reach out and touch the coffin for the first time. Her fingertips brushed tenderly against the wood and an image of her mother touching her face in that same way flashed in Kirsti's mind.

"I love you." Her mother's voice sounded like a little child's.

Now, tears spilled down Kirsti's face.

Her parents bowed their heads, stepping backwards as they did so, and turned. Kirsti caught the gaze of her mother and for a split second she saw the raw anguish and sorrow felt by the middle-aged woman. Quickly lowering her eyes, Kirsti stepped up to the coffin and placed her rose with the others. A lump formed in her throat again and her nose started to run. She fumbled for a tissue.

"This isn't goodbye, Owen," she whispered with a tight throat. She placed her hands over her heart. "You will always be in here." She stared at the face in the photo. *Why, Owen? Why?*

Unable to say anything else, she turned and walked away, the crowd parting to let her through.

"Folks, please make your way down to the front and say your goodbyes in an orderly fashion. Please don't linger as there are a lot of people behind you and another funeral is scheduled in half an hour."

The minister's words faded as Owen's favourite song filled all her senses and the crowd closed the gap behind her. She stepped out of the church and discovered more people lined up outside. So many people loved him, but it was not enough...

Kirsti took a deep breath and made her way down the steps and away from the sounds of sobbing. She couldn't bear it any longer. She needed to distance herself from it. Without looking at anyone, she walked to a small gazebo, beside a duck pond, and sat on a wooden bench.

She stared at the water, watching closely as the breeze gently washed it over the pebbles at the edge of the pond. "Why, Owen? Why didn't you come and talk to me? Why didn't you talk to Mum and Dad? Why did you have to kill yourself?"

II

Kirsti stepped out of the car and looked up at the white, two-storey house and sighed. It had been home for as long as she could remember. It was a place where she had always felt safe and loved, a place where she could retreat and find comfort and protection if she needed it.

When she was young, she believed the house was large. The rooms seemed huge and there were so many nooks and crannies to play or hide in. She loved the place. She remembered all the fun and laughter her family had shared here. She could almost see herself and Owen zooming down the driveway the day the training wheels had been removed from their bikes. They had screamed with fear and excitement. Afterwards, they had gone back to the top in fits of laughter, to do it again.

Her gaze moved to her parent's balcony. A ten-year-old Kirsti stood proudly with one hand on the railing. Dressed in one of her mother's evening gowns and donning a crown made from cardboard and foil, she issued orders to her loyal subjects below. The neighbours still teased her about that time in her life. It was a bit embarrassing to think about, but she had been so content and happy at the time that it really didn't matter what anyone said to her.

The kingfisher blue shutters had been added later. She and her mother liked them, but her father and the boys had never liked the colour. They said the colour was sissy, but they didn't attempt to change them. The immaculate landscaping looked plain at this time of year, but in spring the flower beds were alive with colour. And the aroma was magnificent. On a nice day, she would open her bedroom window and let the cool breeze bring the sweet smell of the garden into her room.

The house held so many happy memories, but now it was the source of bad memories too. Owen's car sat unused on the concrete driveway, waiting to be sold, the metal as cold as its owner. Her gaze shifted to the roller doors of the garage and all the happy thoughts evaporated instantly into darkness.

Skye O'Neal parked her sedan in the street and looked through the windscreen at her dearest friend, who stood on the council verge staring at her home. Pulled back from her pale face, Kirsti's mousy brown hair fell gently against her long neck. The black and white top she wore hugged her slim body and the black skirt stopped below the knee, allowing shapely legs to be seen. Normally, Kirsti would be carrying a small purse, slung casually over her shoulder, to match the high heeled shoes she wore, but not today.

"What's she doing?" asked Melody, who sat quietly in the passenger seat, also watching Kirsti.

Skye looked at Melody and shrugged. "I don't know, do I?" She stared at her own reflection in the rearview mirror and tried to fix her tear-stained makeup. "I don't know what's going on. The whole thing is horrible. Just horrible."

"She's remembering," said the third person in the car, Joanne, sitting in the back seat, "and grieving."

Skye stared at Joanne's red face in the mirror. Tears still welled in the other girl's eyes. There would be more to come no doubt. She gazed at her own face again and sighed. What was the point in trying to fix herself up? Only the funeral was over. Now they had to get through the reception.

"We should go to her." Joanne opened the car door and started to climb out. "She needs our support."

Skye watched Joanne walk towards Kirsti and another sigh escaped her lips. Joanne was the quiet one out of the four. You could set your watch by Joanne, she believed in being punctual. She wore a plain dress now, but she usually wore jeans and a t-shirt and wore her hair in a simple ponytail. She said she felt comfortable that way. Melody, on the other hand, wouldn't be seen dead in jeans. Skye cringed at the thought. She would have to be sure not to say something like that in front of Kirsti from now on. Actually, there were a lot of things she would have to be careful about saying, but she didn't want to think about that now, so she turned her thoughts back to the group of friends.

Melody was the outrageous one. Only black and purple would be seen on the black-haired vixen. And her clothing and makeup were so "out there" it made everyone turn to look at her and she loved every bit of attention she got.

For the third time, Skye looked at her own reflection in the rearview mirror. Green eyes, lots of freckles, puffy cheeks and long, red hair was what she saw. She shook her head. The four girls were quite a mix and match of personalities, but they had been friends forever and that wasn't about to change now.

"What are we meant to say?" asked Melody, still staring out the window at their two friends.

"I wish I knew," replied Skye. "Come on. We can't sit here all afternoon."

"I suppose."

The two girls got out of the car. Skye noticed more people had arrived and their cars were parked wherever they could find a spot in the street. Most of the neighbours would be in the Fowler's house too, so no one would be complaining. In fact, there had been more people at Owen's funeral than what usually turned up at the local footy games. It was amazing how many people knew the Fowler family and loved Owen.

Skye noticed the mass of blue above her. At least it hadn't rained. The weathermen had forecast rain, but they were wrong again. Didn't it always rain at funerals, wasn't it expected?

Yet another sigh escaped her. She knew she was putting

off the inevitable and turned her focus back to her friend. *Right, do it, Skye, and stop being a damn wimp.* She straightened her shoulders and purposefully walked towards Kirsti.

"Are you all right?" she asked. She would have kicked herself if she were able. What a stupid question to ask. What was she thinking? That was the problem. She wasn't thinking and from now on she would have to censor her words.

"We had so much fun together in this house." Tears welled in Kirsti's eyes.

Skye felt uncomfortable. She couldn't stand seeing her friend cry all the time. She hated seeing the anguish. "Come on, let's go inside and get a drink."

Kirsti didn't move. She lowered her head and Joanne quickly put her arm around the other girl's shoulder and gave her a gentle hug. "It's all right. Let it out. We don't mind," said Joanne.

Skye and Melody exchanged mortified looks. Melody messed around with the layers of her black taffeta dress, smoothing them out ... over and over again. Skye watched her for a while and then turned her focus onto the other guests. Everyone was sombre. All wore dark clothing. They all filed towards the Fowler house and disappeared through the open front door. Skye had never felt so powerless and speechless in her life. Everything felt so wrong! She had to make things normal again. She had to do what she did best, take control of the group of girls and get things happening.

"Come on, we can't stand out here all day," she said with a slight grin. "People will start talking about us."

"Yeah, we wouldn't want that," replied Melody. Her eyes sparkled. "I couldn't live with myself if that..." Melody's face froze and she quickly looked at Kirsti. "I'm sorry. I didn't mean anything by that. I..."

Skye groaned and shook her head. "She knows you..." but she didn't know what to say to fix things either, so she

15

took Kirsti's elbow and guided her towards the house instead. "We'll get a drink and find a quiet place to sit and talk. Does that sound good?"

To Skye's relief, Kirsti nodded and the four girls walked towards the house.

Kirsti stopped on the threshold. The house seemed darker than usual. Maybe it was her imagination, but something told her that the high level of sorrow in the house was the reason for the oppressive feeling that attacked her upon entering her home.

She felt her friends' presence behind her but found no comfort in the knowledge. No one knew what to say to her. They thought they had to be different around her now. Did they think she would break that easily? She had always seen herself as a strong person, adaptable to all situations. What did they see? Obviously, something else.

"What's wrong, Kirsti?" asked Joanne from behind her.

"Nothing. It's so dark in here, I needed to wait until my eyes adjusted," replied Kirsti. When had she started lying to her friends?

She strode into the hallway and turned right into the lounge room. The room was crowded with guests. Every seat had been taken. Most of the people stood around the room, against the walls and in the corners, staring at each other or at the floor. Some cried openly as they looked at the many family photos placed neatly around the room. All turned to look at her as she entered. She heard their murmurs of condolences as she walked passed them and she made the effort to nod a few times, but she couldn't pick out their words. She veered to the left into the dining room and found more people hovering. No one spoke. No one knew what to say or do.

"Kirsti, will you help me with the food please." Her

mother's voice filtered through the thoughts crammed tightly in Kirsti's mind.

Kirsti turned to her friends. "Go and sit in the garden. I'll be out soon."

Joanne extended one hand and touched her lightly on the arm. Kirsti looked at her friend's hand and felt nothing. She was void of all feeling. Would that always be the case now? Had her brother's death taken her emotions with it? Skye and Melody stared. She didn't like the way their eyebrows narrowed when they looked at her. It was as if they expected something from her. Kirsti didn't know what it was and she really didn't care either. She didn't have the energy to worry about it.

They nodded and without a word left the house through the sliding door. Kirsti watched them go for only a moment and then joined her mother in the kitchen.

Jenny Fowler darted from bench to bench on autopilot. Kirsti knew her mum wanted the distraction and said nothing about the amount of food piled high on plastic plates. Maybe the guests would eat it, but Kirsti couldn't eat a thing. The mere thought of anything in her mouth made her want to gag. Smelling the food was only marginally better.

"Where's Josh? I haven't seen him today," asked Jenny, her attention never leaving the tray of food in front of her.

Kirsti looked over her shoulder and shrugged. Her boyfriend had been elusive for the last ten days. And it had been ten days since Owen's death. Only a fool wouldn't make the connection and she was no fool. She didn't know if he had attended the funeral. If he did, he had kept well away from her. "I don't know where he is, Mum. Maybe he's with Tim. I haven't seen him since we left the..." She couldn't bring herself to say the word crematorium so she let the sentence fade into nothing.

Jenny paused for a moment before she busied herself once again. "Maybe."

Kirsti watched her mum, another lump formed in her

throat. "Mum?"

Jenny stopped what she was doing and turned to face Kirsti. Mother and daughter stared into each other's eyes without saying a word. Jenny grabbed Kirsti and pulled her against her body. Kirsti felt the breath squeezed out of her, but she didn't care. She closed her eyes and clung to her mother. For a split second, she felt safe and protected again ... and then the moment was broken.

"Jenny, let me help you. I'm an old hand at gatherings like this."

Kirsti was released and for a moment she felt giddy. She looked at her mum, but Jenny had turned her back on her and was busy moving plates of food from one spot to another.

"Scoot, Kirsti," said Aunt Celia. The elderly woman pushed Kirsti towards the door. "Go and play, child."

At twenty, Kirsti hardly thought she should allow her aunt to call her a child, but it didn't matter how loud or how long Kirsti argued the point, Aunt Celia would never stop thinking of her as a little girl. Today Kirsti couldn't be bothered confronting the old lady about it, no matter how much they used to love the banter.

"Give me the plates of sandwiches, Jenny, and I'll take them out to your guests. Do you have drinks ready? Shall I get someone to look after that for you?"

Kirsti knew her aunt would take control, taking the pressure off her mother. Aunt Celia was loud, but she always knew what to do and when to do it.

The people in the dining room had stopped looking lost and started to mingle. Everyone would soon settle down and the chatter could already be heard from the lounge room. Even laughter reached Kirsti. She cringed. What was there to laugh about? By the time these people left the house to go home, they would feel pity for the family. By the time they went to bed tonight, their grief would be over. But what about her family's grief? How long would that last? Forever?

Kirsti went to her room and closed the door.

Skye sat beneath the willow tree with Melody and Joanne in silence. They had nothing to say. Skye wasn't surprised. They were too caught up in their own thoughts and trying to think about what they would say to Kirsti when she finally joined them.

"What's taking her so long?" asked Joanne. "Maybe we should go and check on her."

"Nah," replied Skye, glancing at the house. "There are a lot of people, so I guess there's a lot of food to hand out."

"Yeah, she'll come out when she's ready," added Melody.

Skye looked at her two friends. Plainly Melody was feeling more at ease without Kirsti around. Skye didn't want to admit it, but she felt the same way. It was only Joanne who seemed ill at ease. The usually quiet girl was pale, her gaze shot around the yard and up to the house continually. Her mind must have been running at top speed.

"Joanne?"

Joanne turned to look at her. "Yes?"

"Are you okay? You seem edgy," asked Skye.

"Of course I'm edgy," replied Joanne. "Our best friend is in there dishing out food to dozen's of guests and we're sitting here soaking up the sun."

Where did that come from? Joanne must have been quite worked up to make a speech like that. "Settle down. Kirsti asked us to wait out here."

"Yeah, settle down, will ya. This is a bad day for all of us," said Melody.

"Well," Joanne's ponytail bobbed angrily as she spoke, "I think we should be in there helping our friend and her family."

"We'll go and help in a minute," said Skye. "I want to ask you something first."

"What?"

"You lost a relative last year, didn't you? An aunt, wasn't it?"

Joanne looked down at her hands, suddenly interested in the ring she was wearing. "It was my nan and we were close. Why?"

Skye looked at the house again. "You got over it pretty quick, didn't you?"

Skye jumped at the scowl on Joanne's face.

"Joanne!" said Melody.

"Look, Skye, grief is not something you 'get over'," replied Joanne, ignoring Melody. "It's not an illness, it's a ... a ... well, it's more of a process we go through. Everyone is different, but when my nan died I read a lot of books on grief and one of them said that it's quite normal to grieve for five years."

"*Five* years?" Skye was horrified. She shook her head. "That can't be right. You didn't grief for that long."

Joanne met her gaze. "How do you know?"

Skye felt her face redden. "I..."

Joanne climbed to her feet. Skye felt uncomfortable with the look Joanne gave her.

"I'm still grieving, Skye," said Joanne. "My nan was 93. She was old and sick and we were told to expect the worst. She had lived a long life, a happy life, but it still hurt like crazy when she died. I can't imagine how Kirsti feels though because her brother was only twenty. He had years and years of living to do."

The three girls stared at each other for a few moments then Joanne turned and started walking towards the house. "Now, are you going to sit there," she said over her shoulder, "or are you going to support a friend in need?"

Skye looked at Melody, who shrugged and stood. "She's right."

"Maybe so, but I don't like the way things have changed," replied Skye. "Joanne has never had so much to say for herself since we've known her and I no longer know how to act around Kirsti."

Kirsti's room had been pink and white for over a decade. Her father had offered to redecorate several times over the years, but Kirsti loved the room how it was and always told him it could wait a bit longer. Only last month she had asked her parents if they would change the colouring of her room for her twenty-first birthday.

Owen had looked at her as if she were crazy. "Sis, you'll be moving out of home soon, so why bother?"

Kirsti remembered looking at her parents and grinning. "I'm never moving out. I know where I'm better off. Here is rent free with all meals included and even a great laundry service. It's perfect."

Her parents had rolled their eyes and sighed, but she saw her dad elbow her mum with amusement.

"Not to mention the lack of chores you two have to do," said their mother. "I've been meaning to talk to you both about that."

"Oh, Mum!" The twins had said in unison.

The family had laughed.

"If she wants her room redone, then that's what she'll get," said her father, Stephen, a minute or so later.

Now, Kirsti sat on her bed and looked around the room as if seeing it for the first time. Changing the colour was no longer important. In fact, a lot of things seemed less important.

A group of people standing on the veranda, under her bedroom window, laughed. A voice floated up to her. "I've always loved Jenny's muffins. I should ask for the recipe."

"Not today, Susan," said another person, it sounded like the woman who lived in the house across the street.

"Oh no," replied Susan, "I'm not that crass."

Kirsti closed the window and immediately heard a

knock on the door.

"Kirsti, are you in there?" It was Joanne.

"Yes, come in," said Kirsti as she returned to her bed.

She wasn't surprised when the door opened and three faces stared at her. Her three best friends. Three people she had known since the first day of primary school. They had been through everything together and she wondered if they would continue to be there for each other in the future.

"What happened? You said you'd come out to the garden," said Skye, as she sat beside Kirsti on the bed.

Kirsti shook her head. "Nothing. I needed some time on my own."

"Do you want us to leave then?" asked Melody, who had taken up a spot beside the window and was peering down at the people on the front lawn.

Kirsti looked at Melody. She wore an extremely short dress made out of coarse material. It had a number of layers with the top layer being a thick net type stuff. The dress hugged the top half of her body, but the lower section puffed out at the waist in an awkward way. It looked uncomfortable to wear, but Melody wore these types of dresses all the time. Black fishnet stockings covered her legs and she wore a pair of clunky, platform boots with silver studs up her calves and thick black laces. She had toned down her makeup for the funeral so her eyes were only surrounded in black and purple instead of the normal outrageous colours she wore. Her jet-black hair streamed down her back.

Kirsti realised Melody was staring at her and blinked. "I'm sorry. No, I don't want you to leave."

"Can I put some music on then?" asked Melody as she moved to stand in front of Kirsti's CD player.

"Sure."

A song from one of Kirsti's least favourite CD's erupted into the room, the heavy bass grinding on Kirsti's nerves immediately. She kicked off her shoes and moved back across the bed so that her back was against the wall. Skye still sat motionless on the edge of the bed and Joanne sat sedately on the floor staring at nothing in particular. Only Melody seemed relaxed. In the middle of the room, she started moving to the music, lost in her own little world.

Nineteen-year-old Joanne Shepherd, the youngest of the group, sat on Kirsti's bedroom floor staring at the carpet for a long time. The awkward silence was awful. The music Melody had put on was awful. The way her friends were acting was awful. Everything about the day was awful.

Why did death stop people being themselves?

Joanne lived at home with her parents and three sisters—two older and one younger—not far from the Fowler house. She wouldn't say her family were close-knit. The Fowlers showed their love in everything they did, but Joanne couldn't remember her parents telling her they loved her, ever.

She sighed and looked quickly at her friends to make sure she hadn't drawn attention to herself.

At the same time, she knew there was still love beneath the surface. Her parents were not open with it, that's all. For years Joanne had stopped at the Fowler house on the way to school and witnessed the twins receive a hug before being told by Mrs Fowler that she loved them. That didn't happen at home, but she didn't question her parents love for her. She knew they did love her. The same way she knew that should she find herself in trouble she could go to them ... about anything.

Feeling loved wasn't the same as being loved. Secretly, Joanne envied the love Kirsti openly received from her mum. Joanne wanted that kind of love for herself and it was her nana who gave it to her. Nana gave away hugs and said "*I love you*" like they grew on trees. Joanne loved it and often visited the nursing home where Nana lived to receive as much loving as she could get. Because of those frequent visits, a deep bond developed between the pair. Joanne promised herself that, when she was a mother, she would be like Nana and Mrs Fowler.

Then Nana passed away.

Nana's death had hit hard. For the first time in her life, Joanne felt removed from everyone around her and it was at that time that she first realise that death was treated as a disease. She needed a hug and a shoulder to cry on, but she was given a wide berth.

Now the shoe was on the other foot and Joanne was experiencing death from another angle. She knew the small group of girls were not offering the support Kirsti needed, but the secret Joanne carried in her heart stopped her from fixing things.

She looked around Kirsti's pink bedroom, knowing everything in the room. She had spent many hours here and had slept over dozens of times. Her gaze paused on the photo of the twins and she caught her breath. Owen and Kirsti were almost identical to look at, except for their genders, of course. Their fine brown hair had always been a sore point for Kirsti, who could never do anything with it with success, but Owen had never cared about it for himself. Their blue eyes had always been piercing and bright. Their smiles infectious. Joanne had envied them in many ways and she had always loved every minute she spent in this house. In fact, it was Owen's eyes that had first attracted Joanne to him all those years ago. He had looked at her and seen her, and that had sent shivers down her spine. No one else had ever done that to her before ... or since.

Her unlikely friendship with Skye and Melody would never have survived if it hadn't been for the twins, and if it hadn't been for the way Joanne felt about Owen. Of course, she never told a soul how she felt about him, not even Owen. Especially not Owen. She doubted ... no, she knew he would never have laughed at her, and she knew Kirsti wouldn't have either, but she wasn't so sure about Skye and Melody. They would have fallen over with laughter, their sides painful, if they knew. No, Joanne had known for a long time that her friendship had always been centred on the twins.

Then, three months ago, Owen had broken up with his girlfriend. Joanne had been hopeful, to say the least, that her friendship with Owen would develop into something more. He treated her with respect and friendship, and she thought he looked at her differently these days, but he never acted on it. And now her secret dream of Owen realising what he had right there in front of him was dashed to pieces.

No one suspected how she felt when she was told the news. No one saw the tears she cried that night and every night since. No one could guess the words she wrote in the letter she placed on the coffin that morning. What she couldn't tell Owen when he was alive, she had said in a letter on his death. It was unfair.

Joanne turned to Kirsti. Her friend leaned back against the wall with her eyes closed. Was she tired? Asleep maybe? Was she enjoying the music? Joanne couldn't tell, but Kirsti opened her eyes and their gaze met.

Joanne felt her cheeks flame instantly. She had let her guard down and Kirsti would have seen everything plainly on her face, if she looked closely enough. But Joanne quickly pushed the thought away. Kirsti was consumed with her own grief. She had no idea what Joanne was feeling at that moment.

The song ended and another began. A ballad. Joanne immediately thought of Owen as he had played the song over and over again after the breakup.

"Turn it off, Melody." Kirsti leaned forward. Her face strained. Tears threatening to overwhelm her again. "I can't listen to that."

Melody stopped dancing and quickly pressed a button,

snapping the music off instantly. "Sorry."

Joanne sat quietly on the floor staring at the carpet. *Neither can I.*

III

Jenny Fowler closed the front door and sighed. It was over. The funeral. The reception. It was all over and she felt exhausted. She walked into the lounge and looked around at the dirty glasses, the plates with food scraps, the cards and flowers and continued walking. It could all wait. None of it was important anymore.

Owen was dead.

Stephen, her husband, sat at the dining room table cradling a mug of coffee in his hands. "I'm glad they've gone at last."

"Me too." She grabbed her own cup of tea and sat opposite him. "Receptions are strange things, aren't they? Everyone gathering for a death and all the family want is to forget."

Stephen reached over and placed a hand over hers. "Love, a reception is to celebrate a life. You want Owen remembered, don't you?"

Anger filled Jenny. She had noticed anger filled her more often these days. Previously, it would take a lot to get her fired up, but now the anger was always quick and complete. It was a strange feeling, yet a welcomed one. It reminded her that she was still alive. "Of course! What's that supposed to mean?"

"Jenny?" Stephen squeezed her hand, a look of shock spreading over his face. "I'm not suggesting anything."

"I know. I'm sorry." She pulled her hand free of his to lift the cup to her trembling lips. "I'm tired. I'm sad. And I don't believe in funeral receptions. Running around all afternoon looking after people while they act as if it's some sort of social event." She paused and thought about the many charity events she had organised over the years. She shook her head. "No, this wasn't a social event, yet I had to listen to them laugh and chat as if it were, when all I wanted to do was curl up in bed and cry."

"Curling up in bed isn't a good idea, but you should have said something," said Stephen. "I would have told everyone to go home."

Jenny stared at her husband, a tiny smile creasing her features. Yes, he would have done that for her. He would have had them out of the house in two minutes flat, if he'd known she didn't want them here. He was a good man and his family meant the world to him.

"I tell you what," he said after a few minutes of silence. "How about we take the kids out to dinner tonight? Just the four of us?"

Jenny looked around the house. "What about the mess?"

Stephen smiled. "If we're really lucky, maybe it will be gone by the time we get home. And if not, I'll help you in the morning."

Jenny sat quietly for a moment, and then shrugged. "I'm not that hungry."

"None of us will be, but I think we need to get away from the house for a short time. Besides, it will give us an opportunity to gauge how the kids are coping. What do you think?"

"Okay."

"Where are they anyway?"

"Kirsti's in her room with the girls and I haven't seen Tim for several hours." Her heart missed a beat and a coldness ran the length of her body. "Oh, Stephen, you don't think he—"

"Jenny, settle down!"

She left the table and rushed to the front windows. "Where is he?"

Stephen followed her into the lounge room and pulled

her into his arms. "He's fine. He said he needed to get away from the crowd and be on his own for a while."

"But what if—"

The sound of the phone interrupted. She pulled away from Stephen and picked up the receiver. "Hello?"

"Mrs Fowler? It's Josh."

That new feeling of anger washed over Jenny again. "Yes, Josh?"

"Is Kirsti there? Can I speak with her?"

"You didn't come to the funeral, Josh." It was a statement, because she already knew the answer.

"I'm so sorry, Mrs Fowler," said Josh. "That's what I want to explain to Kirsti."

"Well, I'm sorry." Jenny tried to keep the anger from her voice. "Kirsti will be spending the evening with her family and we are going out. You can phone her tomorrow."

Never before had Jenny hung up on Josh without saying goodbye. He was her daughter's boyfriend and even though Jenny had never liked him, she always treated him with respect. But the boy hadn't attempted to support Kirsti today, he hadn't bothered to attend Owen's funeral, and for that he didn't deserve her respect any longer.

Jenny looked at Stephen, challenging him to say something to her, but he nodded. "You did the right thing."

"I'll go and tell the girls it's time to leave," said Jenny. Although Kirsti's friends were almost part of the family, tonight she didn't want them here. Tonight, she wanted her family and her house to herself.

As Jenny drew closer to her daughter's bedroom she could hear the murmur of voices. She was glad Kirsti had friends to support her. It would make the next few weeks and months a lot easier.

She knocked and opened the door without waiting for an invitation to enter. The four girls were sprawled out on the floor, staring up at the ceiling.

"Sorry, girls, it's time to go home," said Jenny. "The Fowler family are going out for dinner tonight."

The girls rose to their feet and quickly searched for their shoes and handbags.

"Where are you going, Mrs F?"

Jenny smiled at Melody's nickname for her. "I really don't know. It's Mr F's shout tonight."

Melody and Skye laughed. "You're so cool, Mrs F," said Melody.

"I'm glad you think so," replied Jenny, not feeling the slightest bit cool.

Melody, boots in hand, squeezed past Jenny. "We'll see you tomorrow then, Kirsti," she said over her shoulder.

Jenny stepped into the room to save the embarrassment of Skye trying to squeeze past too, as she knew the doorway wasn't big enough for the both of them. As she walked past Jenny, Skye nodded but said nothing, which wasn't Skye at all.

Joanne stood beside Kirsti. Jenny could see she was unsure what to do. The young girl looked from Jenny to Kirsti and back again, finally deciding that it was appropriate to give them both a quick hug before following the other girls down the stairs and out the front door.

Jenny waited to hear the door click shut before she spoke. "Are you all right?"

Kirsti nodded. "Yes. Where's Tim? I haven't seen him since the..."

Jenny waited for the word and then realised Kirsti couldn't, or didn't want to, say it. "He needed some space and went out on his own."

Kirsti nodded again.

"Josh rang," said Jenny trying to gauge Kirsti's reaction.

"Did he? What did he want?"

Jenny told her what had been said, not leaving anything out, and Kirsti stood staring at the ground without commenting. Jenny wanted to give her opinion, but thought better of it.

At that moment, they heard a low rumble of a car pull into the drive. "Good. Tim's back," said Jenny as she walked to the window to look out. "Get ready, Kirsti. We'll leave in about half an hour."

Ma's Country Kitchen was renowned for their home-cooked meals, but tonight the place was almost empty. That was no surprise as Tuesday night was always quiet. It was a good night to sit in peace, with only the background music breaking the silence.

Stephen asked for a table near the window. He told the waitress that they wanted to watch the world go by, but Jenny didn't think it was necessary to sit by the window to see it happening. The Fowlers had been stuck in a time warp for the last ten days and she felt the world was quickly leaving them behind.

They ordered their meals and settled back to wait for its arrival. The background music played merrily to the silent family.

Jenny watched her two remaining children carefully. Neither held eye contact with anyone for any length of time and both preferred to stare at the napkin in front of them.

It had been a long, stressful day. Jenny didn't want to push them, but she felt something had to be said.

"Well," said Stephen, breaking the silence. "I'm glad that's over."

"It will never be over, Dad," said Kirsti, her eyes dark.

"Don't," said Tim. "Don't talk about it now. I've had enough for one day."

"Talk about what, Tim?" Kirsti's eyes narrowed as she swung around to look at her older brother. "Owen? Don't you want to talk about him anymore? Why not? Are you ashamed of what he did?"

"You're being bitchy right now," replied Tim, looking out the window.

"Stop it!" said Jenny. "Stop it right now."

Stephen squeezed her hand. "It's been a rotten day. We're all highly emotional right now and we should be careful not to say something we'll regret later."

Tim prodded the steak on his plate and rearranged the vegetables again. He couldn't stand being here. He didn't want to eat. He wanted to be on his own. Why didn't his parents understand that?

He stared at the steak and thought of Owen. Why? It was the only question he had asked his parents when they turned up at his dorm room to bring him home. They couldn't give him an answer, they said, because they didn't know themselves.

Since then, Tim had gone over everything he had been told about the suicide a million times, and none of it made sense. Not a scrap of it. Owen had problems, but didn't everyone? He had broken up with his girlfriend, but that was three months beforehand and everyone said he was doing fine. He was a trainee mechanic, and worked for their father, so he knew his job was secure so that couldn't have been the problem either. He had some learning difficulties, but that hadn't stopped him from finishing high school and he was passing the TAFE courses. Maybe his marks weren't brilliant, but a pass is a pass. Right?

What possible reason did he have to take his own life? The question baffled Tim because he couldn't find the answer.

"Tim?"

He looked up to find his mother staring at him. "What?" He instantly felt bad, because he didn't mean to be horrible to his family. He didn't want to make their pain worse, but he couldn't help it.

"Eat your dinner."

"I can't, Mum." He put the knife and fork down. "Not

tonight."

"But you have to eat."

"I will, Mum. Tomorrow. I promise."

His mother sighed and looked at her own half eaten meal.

"Maybe this wasn't such a good idea after all," said Stephen.

"It was, Dad," said Kirsti, her eyes round and large. "But none of us are hungry. It was good to get away from the house for a while though."

Tim watched the rest of his family eat in silence and attempted to eat some of his own meal.

It felt strange to feel awkward with her own family. Jenny placed more food in her mouth and chewed automatically, but there was no taste, no enjoyment. For the first time in her life, she felt speechless and confused. What can you say after something like they had experienced?

Then, without warning, she heard something that made her freeze. Her hands went clammy. Goosebumps rose on her arms and a frightening chill slithered down her spine.

The opening bar of Owen's favourite song was being played as the background music in the restaurant.

Jenny sat staring at her food for a second longer and then she moved into auto pilot. She placed her knife and fork gently on top of her plate, looked up and met the wide gaze of Kirsti and she immediately started talking.

"Your father is right," she announced. "He did the right thing bringing us here. We need to sit together as a family after the day we've had. We need to talk about what has happened."

The first words of the song could be heard. Jenny refused to listen to them and she refused to let the rest of her family focus on them.

"There was a lovely turn out," she went on. "I was surprised by the number of people at the church. I never knew..." she didn't want to follow that train of thought, "but it did my heart good to see the love Owen had from his friends."

"Everyone he knew at school turned up, Mum. Everyone," said Kirsti. "Even some of the teachers were there."

"I know. It was wonderful."

"All the boys in his TAFE classes were there too," said Stephen. "Some of them introduced themselves to me."

"They are probably hoping to take his job," said Tim sarcastically, his face grim and his eyes dark.

Jenny saw Stephen frown at their son. "It doesn't matter. Owen was loved and it did help me to know that about him."

The chorus. No, she wouldn't listen. She would only cry and she couldn't cry again. Not now. Not right here in the restaurant. Not in front of her vulnerable children.

"Someone told me the police investigated us for murder," said Tim.

Jenny groaned. Why did he have to do this now? "It's true. We were served a warrant on the night it happened and they searched the entire house for clues."

"Why would any of us do that to him?" asked Tim, pushing his plate away from him.

"It's standard procedure, son," replied Stephen. "They were doing their job. We had nothing to hide so it made no difference to us."

"And what did they find?" asked Tim.

"It sounds like you're suggesting there was something to find," said Kirsti. Her face red, her voice high pitched.

"Don't be a baby," replied Tim. "Why would I suggest that?"

"Enough," said Stephen. "They found nothing. They were hoping to find a suicide note."

"They didn't find one?" asked Tim.

"No."

"I've searched for one too," said Tim. "It would have given us a reason why."

The song finished. Jenny gulped in air and sat stiff in her chair. She had seen Tim searching Owen's room and searching the garage. She didn't have the heart to tell him she had already been through the same drawers, the same boxes, the same everything. They all had searched, but there was nothing to find.

Wednesday, 31st May

Kirsti didn't have to return to work until the following Monday, so the next morning she slept in much later than normal. It was good to sleep. Surprisingly, she slept soundly. She didn't dream. She never stirred. She slept the whole night through.

Like she always did.

She felt guilty. Did the fact that she slept well mean she hadn't loved her brother as much as she thought? Kirsti stared up at the ceiling and shook her head. No, that couldn't be true. They were twins. No stronger bond existed between two people. All the same, she didn't think it was normal.

In the kitchen, she found Tim preparing a bowl of cereal.

"Hey, lazybones," he said when she walked into the room. He had showered and dressed and looked ready to go out.

"Where you going?" she asked.

"None of your business, Sis," he replied. He carried the overflowing bowl into the dining room and that's when Kirsti saw his bags.

"Are you leaving?" she asked, shocked.

"Yep."

"But ... you can't leave."

"Why not? I'm twenty-two years old. I can do as I please," he replied.

"But what about Mum and Dad? What about me? What about...?" She couldn't say it.

"Owen? Is that what you were going to say?"

She nodded.

"Owen isn't here anymore. He didn't think about us when he decided to leave. Besides, I don't want to miss any more lectures than I have to. I'm finding it difficult enough as it is."

Kirsti lowered herself into a chair. "What did Mum and Dad say when you told them?"

Tim stared into his bowl and kept spooning the contents steadily into his mouth.

"You haven't told them, have you?" asked Kirsti.

"No."

Silence. They glared at each other.

"Look, Kirsti, I'll phone them when I get back to the dorm tonight. They got up early and went out. I don't know when they'll be back and I don't have time to wait around. I'll tell them over the phone."

Kirsti was furious. "You're a real bastard. You've been acting so weird ever since you got home. You've been calling me names and I don't know how to talk to you anymore."

"I call you names? What did you just do? Huh?" He dropped the spoon into the empty bowl. "Get out of my face, Kirsti. I'm not in the mood."

Kirsti pushed herself to her feet and retreated a few steps. Anger flowed through her body. "Yeah, that's right. Grab your things and run away. Go on. We don't need you here anyway."

The sound of the bowl smashing against the tiles echoed in Kirsti's mind for ages afterwards. She had never seen her brother act violently before, so when his arm swept across the table sending the bowl flying, Kirsti had screamed and ran back upstairs to her room.

Moments later, she heard the front door slam. She stood at her bedroom window and watched him load his things into the boot before getting into the car. He took one last look at the garage doors then reversed the car out of the driveway and speed off down the road.

"He what?"

Jenny watched Stephen's face contort in anger. Then his shoulders slumped and he turned and left the room.

Jenny's gaze returned to her daughter. "What did he say? Why would he leave like that?"

Kirsti looked about the room uneasily. "He didn't say much at all. He said he was missing too many lectures and he had to go back to uni. He said he'd phone you tonight."

Jenny could tell that more had passed between brother and sister, but she knew Kirsti would not share whatever it was. She paced the lounge room—back and forth, back and forth.

What was happening to her family? Why was everyone acting so abnormally? Why did she feel a sense of dread in the pit of her stomach? She thought she knew her children, but she suspected otherwise. She certainly hadn't known what Owen was thinking or feeling. She didn't know what to say or do any more.

"Kirsti, it's all right. Come and sit down," she said. The words felt and sounded foreign to her, but she wouldn't fail her daughter like she had failed her son.

"No, Mum," replied Kirsti. "I need to get out for a while. I'm going to walk over to Josh's."

Jenny groaned. *The boy didn't even come to your brother's funeral, Kirsti. Why are you even bothering with him?* But she said nothing. Some things were out of her control. Actually ... it turned out that a lot of things were out of control these days.

She looked at her daughter's face and saw a young, confused girl staring back at her. Jenny wanted to take her into her arms and comfort her, but something stopped her from doing that. It was the same thing that stopped her from asking her surviving children certain questions. She wasn't exactly sure what that something was, but she did know that it was growing steadily.

When Kirsti broke eye contact and left the room, Jenny did nothing to stop her.

Kirsti checked her mobile phone as she walked away from the house. The screen showed the date and time, which meant there were no missed calls and no text messages. Usually, she would have received quite a few of both in a single day from her friends. And from Josh. But since the suicide, there was hardly anything anymore.

Josh Edwards had been Kirsti's boyfriend since high school. They had known each other for years and had been friends for most of them. Then, in the last year of high school, Josh had asked her out. It had caused a lot of talk at the time. Josh was the most popular boy in the year and Kirsti was the envy of many of the girls.

Their relationship was not intense, not like the relationships Kirsti had heard other girls talking about. They saw each other every Friday and Saturday night, without fail, but the other nights of the week they both had the freedom to do things without the other. Josh spent a lot of time at the gym and Kirsti was part of a volleyball team, and in summer enjoyed her frequent visits to the swimming pool. They each had their own circle of friends too. They respected each other's lives and that fitted well with their lifestyles.

Then Owen died and Josh seemed to back away from Kirsti. She had left many messages on his mobile and he never returned her calls. She had called around at his house numerous times and he was never home. She had even stopped by the gym but couldn't find him anywhere.

She made allowances for him, but when he didn't turn

up at the funeral...

Kirsti swallowed the lump in her throat and tried to push the thoughts away. It wouldn't do her any good to turn up on his doorstep with wet eyes and tear stains down her cheeks. That wouldn't do at all.

She turned her face to the sun and soaked up the warm rays. It was a gorgeous autumn afternoon. Not too cold, but not too warm either. Soon, they would have to drag out their winter woollies, but for the time being, they could still enjoy the warmth of the sun.

She turned into Josh's street and continued her slow walk. If he wasn't home today, she wouldn't turn around and go home, she would keep walking. She needed fresh air. But then she saw Josh walk away from his car, carrying his gym bag, and enter the house. He was home. She smiled. She was desperate for a hug.

A few minutes later, she walked slowly up the steps to his front door and knocked. She waited. Josh didn't answer the door. She knocked again. Still no answer. Perhaps he had gotten straight into the shower. If so, he wouldn't hear her knocking. That had to be the case. She left the veranda and went to the side gate. She lifted the latch and let herself in. She walked around the corner of the house and saw the back door open. If he was in the shower, he'd be a few minutes yet so she opened the screen door and stepped into the house. He wouldn't mind her waiting inside for him. The interior was quite cool. Goosebumps prickled her skin. She walked down the hallway and into the lounge.

She halted in her tracks. Her gaze locked with Josh's as he sat in his favourite chair, right opposite the front door. Kirsti moved further into the lounge room so that she was standing between Josh and the front door. "Are you avoiding me?"

He shook his head and got out of the chair. "No. Of course not. I swear I didn't hear your first knock."

Kirsti glared at him. "Is that right?"

He nodded, his gaze left her face and roamed about the

room.

"Well, if you didn't hear my first knock, how do you know there was one? I didn't mention how many times I knocked." She stared at his face. His uneasiness was unmistakeable. The colour rising to his cheeks told her that he was lying. "I'm also eager to learn why you didn't respond to my second knock since you quite obviously heard that one too."

He wouldn't look her in the face. He opened his mouth to say something, but thought better of it and remained silent. Turning, he walked away from her, casually picking up discarded plates and cups. He'd recently had some people around and she hadn't been invited.

"What's going on, Josh?" she asked, her voice almost breaking with hurt. "Why didn't you come to Owen's funeral? He was your friend. He was my brother. You should have been there. Everyone else was."

Josh paused with his back to her, she saw his shoulders slump, and then he put the pile of dirty crockery down and turned to face her. "I ... I ... what do you want me to say?"

"I want the truth. Why didn't you come to the funeral?"

"You know how hard I've been working towards setting up my own gym?"

She nodded.

"I had a really important meeting with an investor yesterday," he replied, his face reddening again. "I couldn't stand the guy up, could I?"

"You could have phoned him and explained what had happened. You could have postponed the meeting until today, tomorrow, next week," said Kirsti, her voice growing louder. "He would have understood if he was half decent."

"I couldn't do that because I have another meeting, with another investor, on Monday and I had to speak to this man before I saw that one." He went quiet and stood there staring at her, knowing his reasons were weak and not logical.

What did he want her to say? It was all right. Would that

make him feel better? Well, it wasn't all right and, at this moment, she didn't care how he felt. His priorities were wrong and now she was angry.

"So that's your excuse for not attending the funeral," she said after a moment's silence. "Now tell me your excuse for not opening the door to me just then."

Josh sighed. Kirsti didn't think it was relief, she had known him long enough to know that the sigh was from frustration. She waited for him to sift through his responses.

"I just got in. I'm tired."

Is that the best you can do? "Neither of those things has worried you before, Josh."

"But that's not the reason I didn't open the door," he replied quickly.

"What is the reason then?"

He dropped down into his chair and looked at her, resigned to the fact that she wouldn't let him off easily. "Okay, I'll be truthful. I didn't open the door because I don't know what to say to you anymore."

I Kirsti pushed the hurt aside. This wasn't the time to place blame. She swallowed and sat on the three-seater lounge opposite Josh. "Be yourself, Josh. Talk about things like you normally would. Talk to me and listen to me. Be normal. That's all I want. Nothing has to change. Nothing has changed."

The words tumbled out of her mouth. Did Josh believe them? Did she? Everything had changed. The way she felt. The way she thought. The way the world acted. Everything.

They sat in silence for several minutes.

"So how did the meeting go?" she finally asked.

Josh smiled. His smile lit up the room, or so she had always thought. It was a bit dim today.

"The guy is from Japan. He's looking to finance businesses here. He listened carefully to my plan and he looked over the figures twice." Josh's eyes sparkled with excitement. "I'm sure he's really interested. He asked a heap of questions and he told me to give him a few days to think about it."

"That's great." Kirsti tried to smile, tried to show enthusiasm. "What about the other meeting you mentioned?"

"The Japanese guy is the finance and the next guy will be the equipment. He's Japanese too, by the way. I'm trying to work out some deal where I get the equipment in the gym and pay less for it because of advertising ... or something. I'm still working on the details."

"Sounds like it's coming together," said Kirsti.

They stared at each other for a moment and then Josh leaned forward in his chair and extended a hand. "Come over here."

Kirsti wanted to cry then. She didn't dare speak and give herself away so she took his hand and slid onto the chair beside him. His arm felt good around her shoulder, she put her head on his chest and nestled close.

II

Jenny stood at the lounge room window looking out at the street. Stephen had been called into work for an emergency. He promised he wouldn't be long and he'd come straight home afterwards. She had assured him that she would be fine, but it was different in the house now. It was too quiet. And she didn't like being left alone with her thoughts. It was too painful.

She looked at the phone ... again, and checked her watch. Tim should be back at the university by now. Why hadn't he phoned? Could he have been driving recklessly and had a car accident? Was he dead somewhere between here and the university and no one knew about it? Or had he told them he was returning to the university when he really had other plans? She needed him at home, where she could keep an eye on him.

She looked at the street again and thought about Kirsti. Josh wasn't right for her. He only thought of himself and yesterday it showed more than ever. Why couldn't Kirsti see that? Why hadn't she come home yet? Was she all right?

Jenny pushed the thoughts aside. She'd go insane if she didn't stop thinking about it. She turned away from the window and her gaze went from the dozens of cards placed haphazardly on any surface available, to the many vases of fresh flowers. They smelled wonderful. At the moment, the aroma of flowers was the only pleasant thing in her life.

"Owen? Where are you?" Jenny stared at the ceiling as if she were talking to her son in heaven. Tears welled in her eyes. She had shed so many that even she was surprised there could be more. "Why did you do this? Didn't you know how much I love you?"

She scooped up a photo album from the coffee table. Seating herself by the window, next to the phone, she opened the album to the first page. An anguished sob escaped her as she stared through her tears at her lost son. Why? She knew everyone was asking the same question. Why had a seemingly healthy, happy twenty-year-old ended his own life?

She had no clue.

As she turned the pages of the album, she saw her son's life unfolding. Every page was filled with a smiling face and she would always remember him in that way. Then there were the hugs. He was unlike other boys of his age, he was open with his feelings and quick to give a hug when he thought the receiver would benefit from it. She knew how he felt, but did he know how she felt? Did he know she loved him? She had assumed they all knew, but did they? Had she assumed too much? Had she made a mistake? Was it her fault her son was gone?

When was the last time she had told Owen she loved him?

Jenny looked up from the album, one hand over her

mouth. Tears spilled down her face and she didn't bother wiping them away. When had she told him? The memory was close to the surface because it fell into the group of memories that would never leave her. The days leading up to, and the days following, the death of her child would always be strong in her mind.

The day before Owen was found dead, he had gone to stay over a friend's house. In fact, he had spent a lot of time over his friend's place in the last three weeks of his life. Jenny had commented on it to him one evening when he was at home earlier than usual. She had warned him not to outstay his welcome. He quickly assured her that his friend was the one who asked him to stay over and his parents were fine about it. But she noticed that he started coming home to sleep after their chat and she had quickly forgotten her concern.

The day before his death, Owen had told his mother that he and a group of friends were going out and since it was going to be a late night, he would be staying at Terry's place. She had thought nothing of it as Owen and his friends often made these arrangements, but they always showed up for work the next day. They were reliable, level-headed boys. Owen had never given her anything to worry about.

Now, she realised he was distancing himself from his family.

She had been given a sign that something wasn't right, but she didn't know it at the time. If only she had, then her son might still be alive. As they say, hindsight is a wonderful thing. On the night of their outing, Owen had phoned home and talked to Jenny for a few minutes. Jenny remembered thinking how strange the phone call had been. They talked about the weather and what a lovely night it was. They talked about the death of the family dog of 18 years, who had died the week beforehand. They talked about the upcoming football final which Owen would have been a part of. They talked easily and they laughed, but there was no real point to the telephone call. Jenny hadn't been overly concerned and had brushed it aside as a young person thing that she didn't have a hope of understanding. During the conversation, Owen had said something that would remain with Jenny for the rest of her life. He had said, "I want you to know that I really do love you, Mum."

"What a strange thing to say," Jenny had replied. "I know you do. And you are my world. You know that, don't you? I love you too, Owen."

Jenny thought he was embarrassed at the turn of the conversation, so when he said nothing to that, she wasn't surprised or disappointed.

A moment later, he said, "Bye, Mum."

"Bye, darling. Have a lovely night and I'll see you tomorrow," Jenny had replied.

He didn't say anything and a second later the phone went dead.

That was the last conversation she had had with Owen. Later, she found out that there was no planned outing and he didn't stay with Terry. She didn't know where he had been when he called her, but he had spent the night in their garage ... dead.

The credits rolled up onto the TV screen and Kirsti pushed her legs off the lounge and sat up. "It wasn't a bad movie."

"How would you know," said Josh. "You slept most of the way through it."

"I did not," said Kirsti, but she knew it was true.

After their initial argument, when she first arrived, they had barely said a word. She felt sure Josh had suggested watching a DVD for that reason and she had been quick to agree. Watching a movie meant they didn't have to talk. But now it was over.

Josh left his spot on the lounge to fiddle with the DVD

and Kirsti sat watching him. The awkwardness between them was worse than a first date. A fly on the wall would think they hardly knew each other, when in fact they knew each other well.

Not keen to be caught up in the uncomfortable silence again, Kirsti stood. "Well, I know it's early, but I promised Skye I'd see her after work, so I have to be going now."

"Oh, do you have to?" Josh stood.

Kirsti looked into his eyes and felt hurt at the insincerity she saw there. "Yes. Phone me."

She opened the front door and turned to Josh, but he remained standing in front of the DVD player. *I guess there will be no kiss goodbye then.* She tried to keep her voice even and her face unreadable. "See ya then."

"Yeah, bye."

The door clicked shut behind her and she walked slowly down the path and onto the street. She wasn't ready to go home yet and she hadn't really made plans with Skye, so she walked slowly away from Josh's house. She sighed. Things would improve between them. He was excited about his business venture and he didn't know what to say to her about Owen's death. The two things didn't mesh together and he was feeling mixed emotions over it. He'd work it out soon. She hoped.

Then Kirsti felt her own face redden. She had told two lies in as many days. What's more, she had lied to people who meant something to her and she'd never done that before. What was happening there?

She decided to put things right by heading over to see Skye, like she had told Josh. It wouldn't cancel the lie out completely, but it would make it ... somewhat better.

Skye lived in shared accommodation not far from her workplace. The two were conveniently so close that Skye could easily walk to work, but she was too lazy and often drove. She shared with two other girls, who also worked full time. Kirsti didn't know them well, and after two years still remained distant with them. It was something that seemed strange, as she usually got on with everyone.

The three bedroom apartment was on a side street, off the busy main road. This meant they lived close to everything, which was handy. The three girls respected each others space. And from what Skye had told her, there were only two rules to abide by. No men were allowed to sleep over and all bills were split evenly three ways.

As Kirsti approached the apartment block she noticed Skye's car parked on the street, which was unusual. Perhaps she planned on going out. Kirsti didn't bother thinking about it too long. She turned onto the path that would take her to the entry.

The apartment block used to have a security entrance, but that was before the current owner purchased the block and made a heap of changes. A lot of people had moved out when the security was taken away, making way for less desirable tenants. Skye's apartment had been broken into twice in the last year.

She pushed the door open and walked to the elevator. Pushing the button, she turned to stare out the glass door just in time to see two women pointing at her, their heads close. Kirsti felt self-conscious and turned away. *I guess we're the talk of the town now.* She didn't like the thought one bit. The elevator chimed its arrival and she quickly stepped in and pushed the button for the fourth floor.

Kirsti knocked on the door and listened. The television was on, or was it the radio? She couldn't be sure. She heard someone say something and a moment later the door opened and one of Skye's flatmates was standing in front of her.

"Oh, it's you," the girl said and moved to one side to let her in. "We were expecting the pizza guy."

"Sorry," said Kirsti, stepping through the door and walking straight down the hallway towards Skye's room without saying another word. She knocked and waited, turning to look down the hallway to find the girl who opened the door still staring at her. Kirsti wanted to say something smart, but she held her tongue.

"Come in if you're cute," said Skye from within the room.

Kirsti pushed the door open and peered into the small, cramped bedroom. "I'm not cute, but can I come in anyway?"

Skye laughed. "You are cute. Come on in. Has the pizza guy been yet?"

"No." Kirsti closed the door and joined Skye on the two-seater lounge. "Why?"

"He's new and he's *really* cute." Skye laughed again. "We seem to have a constant craving for pizza all of a sudden."

They laughed together, but Kirsti didn't find it particularly amusing.

"How was work?" asked Kirsti a moment later.

"Oh, you know," replied Skye. "Boring as Hell."

Skye's face instantly turned red to match her long, wavy hair. An awkward silence followed.

"I saw Josh this afternoon," said Kirsti, trying to break the silence.

Skye refused to look at her. She never had liked Josh and vice versa, but they had always been civil to each other for her sake.

"Did you? What did he have to say for himself?"

Kirsti related what had happened and what was said. Skye sat quietly listening, her green eyes dark, her face blank.

Skye finally looked up at her when she had finished talking. "You should have dumped him on the spot."

Usually, Kirsti would have brushed the comment aside without a thought, but today she had trouble dealing with it. Josh had let her down. Now, Skye wasn't being supportive. Kirsti knew Josh had done wrong, but she couldn't deal with it right now, didn't Skye understand that. All Kirsti wanted from Skye was an ear to vent in and maybe a shoulder to cry on. She got neither.

"Skye, I'm having trouble coping with Owen's death," said Kirsti, unable to hold it in a moment longer.

Kirsti saw Skye's face cloud over even more. "You don't need to talk about it," she said. "It will only make things worse. You need distractions to keep your mind off it. Tell you what, I'll ensure you don't have time to think about it."

Already feeling low, Kirsti was stunned by Skye's words. Obviously, Skye didn't want her to talk about it, but Kirsti knew she needed to talk to someone. It was the only way to put things into perspective. And she wanted to do that with her best friend.

"Skye," said Kirsti, "I do need to talk and you're my best friend. I thought..."

"Yes, I'm your best friend," cut in Skye. "We have been through everything together and that's why I know what's best for you. True, you've suffered a great loss, but talking about it will only depress you further. Don't worry, I won't allow that to happen."

Kirsti felt the emotions bubbling over. Tears stung her eyes. "But, Skye ... I need to get things off my chest. I need to talk about what happened, what I saw ... when I found him."

"You found him?" Skye's face paled instantly. "Oh, Kirsti, I didn't know. I don't want to know. No, please, don't talk about it. I can't listen..."

You can't listen, thought Kirsti, *but you expect me to live with the images of my dead brother hanging from a beam in our garage? You think I don't have to talk about that? You think you know what's best for me, but you know nothing. Nothing!*

The two girls stared at each other. Kirsti felt a mixture of emotions—anger, hurt, sadness, defeat.

"Did I tell you about the pizza guy?" Skye seemed to have deleted the last few minutes from her mind. "He's so gorgeous. There's a house bet going at the moment, which one of us will get him to ask us out. I know he likes me, but he hasn't popped the question yet."

Kirsti didn't care about the pizza guy or the house bet. She didn't care about a lot of things anymore. She rose to her feet and moved to the door.

"Where are you going?" asked Skye. "Don't you want to stay for pizza?"

"No," replied Kirsti. "I told Mum I'd be home for dinner. Maybe another time."

"Yeah, sure."

"I'll be going now." Kirsti wanted to be out of the apartment, away from Skye. "I'm going to be busy over the next few days so I'll contact you on the weekend."

"Yeah, whatever," said Skye.

They moved down the hallway and there was a sudden knock at the door. Skye rushed the rest of the way and grabbed the door only a split second before one of her flatmates. "Beat ya," she said with a laugh.

"Bitch," the other girl said with a smile. "You'll keep."

Skye flung open the door, a huge smile on her lips. "Well, fancy that. A pizza."

"Someone from here ordered it," came the quick reply.

Kirsti paused at the door and exchanged a quick glance with the pizza boy. He looked to be about eighteen years old, but other than that, Kirsti didn't notice anything cute about him.

"I'll be going then," she said to Skye. "See ya."

"Yeah, see ya later," replied Skye without taking her gaze off the pizza guy.

Kirsti heard the flirting between the two as she walked away. She didn't bother waiting for the elevator. Instead, she slammed open the stairwell door and rushed down them as fast as she could. Out on the street, she ran down the road and when satisfied that she was out of sight of the apartment block, she sank to the pavement and burst into tears.

III

Later that night, Kirsti lay in her bed and stared at the only light source in the room—her window. She felt exhausted, but sleep escaped her. She left her bed and opened the blind so that she could see the stars. She stood at the window for a while looking up at the sky thinking about Owen.

They had been twins. Weren't twins supposed to instinctively know when the other was in trouble or in pain? Weren't twins meant to share a special bond that was closer than any other relationship between people? If these things were true, why was it then that she knew nothing of Owen's problems? Had she been so self-centred that she had not noticed? If Owen had hidden his problems from her in recent days, what else had he hidden from her?

The questions rolled around and around in her head. Guilt fluttered in her stomach. She should have known there was a problem. She should have done something to help him. She should have saved him. But she had done nothing.

She crept to her bedroom door and inched it open. She listened carefully but heard nothing so she stepped out onto the landing and turned in the direction of Owen's room. She took a few steps and a sound made her go rigid and stop. Her senses awoke and she heard all sorts of sounds. The house settling in the cold night air, a tree branch scraping against a downstairs window, the hum of the fridge in the kitchen, and ... her mother crying.

Kirsti stood still, unable to move. The sound of her mother sobbing into her pillow was heartbreaking. Then, she heard the murmur of her father's voice as he tried to comfort his wife. None of them slept. All of them suffered in their own way. Kirsti wished with all her heart that her mother would break down in front of her, instead of behind closed doors. If her mother cried in front of her, then Kirsti could break down and cry too. They could find com-

51

fort and solace in each other's arms. They could talk about that terrible night and the morning after, which in some ways, was much worse.

But her parents were careful not to break down in front of her, so she knew she had to be careful and not break down in front of them. By the sounds of her mother's sobs, Kirsti thought that maybe her parents couldn't handle any more stress and pain. She understood that. It was terrible to lose a sibling, but it must be even worse to lose a child. Kirsti would not make the same mistake she made with her brother, with her parents. From now on she would make herself more aware.

She took a step towards Owen's bedroom and then another step, hoping the floorboards didn't squeak. Finally, she stood at the door. She pushed it open and stepped into the room.

Inside, at last, she closed the door quietly behind her and turned to look around the shadows. She had searched the room, more than once, trying to find a suicide note or some other clue as to why her brother had hung himself but had found nothing. She had seen her parents searching the room too. However, they had been careful to put everything back exactly how they had found it. They didn't want to disturb anything and the room was exactly how Owen had left it, even down to the pile of dirty clothes on the floor.

Kirsti sat on the floor, beside Owen's dirty t-shirts. For a short time, her fingers touched the blue denim of his jeans and then she picked up one of his shirts. She held it in her hands for a long while before lifting it to her nose and drawing in a deep breath. Instantly, images of Owen filled her mind just as his scent filled her nostrils. Tears, again, filled her eyes. She could no longer hear her mother's sobbing, but now her own sobs filled the room. *Why, Owen?*

Still holding the shirt, she crawled to his bed and pulled herself up on top of it. Lying on her side, she held the shirt to her nose and let the images pour into her mind ... and then she truly let go and sobbed and sobbed.

Jenny pushed her face into the wet pillow in an effort to muffle the sound she was making. Daylight hours were bad, but lying in bed at night with nothing but her thoughts was torture. She forced herself to keep control during the day, but couldn't stop the flow of tears at night.

Stephen tried to comfort her, but whatever he did or said didn't help. She heard the words, but she could also hear the croak in his voice and knew he didn't believe the words himself. She didn't blame him for trying. In fact, she loved him all the more for it. But words didn't help. The tender way he held her didn't help. Nothing helped.

Not only did she think about Owen's pain, she thought about her failure. Her failure to keep her child safe. Her failure to recognise that something was worrying her son. Her failure to fix things when they went wrong for him. Her total failure as a mother.

Jenny's thoughts turned to Tim. His sudden departure, so soon after the funeral, didn't feel right. The fact that he promised to phone her, and didn't, only increased her anxiety. And then to top it off, his mobile phone was turned off and when she rang the dorm, several times during the evening, she was told repeatedly that he wasn't there. This worried her even more. Finally, the person on the other end assured her that he had seen Tim on the grounds, carrying his bags towards the dormitories and into his room, but he couldn't tell her where Tim had gone from there.

What was he doing? Why wouldn't he talk to her? She needed him to be here, where she could keep an eye on him. Where she could see him with her own eyes instead of having to rely on other people to tell her they had seen him—alive and well. Because it was only when she could actually see him that she knew, without doubt, that he was all right.

Then there was Kirsti. She had always been a bright, bubbly girl, but now she was hollow-faced and quiet. So quiet. It scared Jenny. Every time she wanted to broach the subject of what had happened to Owen and their family, the words stuck in her throat and no matter what she did, she couldn't say the words she felt needed to be said. What if her words made matters worse? What if her words put ideas into the young girl's head?

Her gut instincts had let her down, so she could no longer trust them. She felt as if she had lost control of her life. More sobs raked her body.

Stephen turned over and wrapped his arms around her. "We'll get through this, Jen."

She covered his hand with hers but was unable to speak. How could he be so sure? She wasn't sure that they would get through it. She wasn't sure she was strong enough. She had to keep her two surviving children safe. She had to do for them what she was unable to do for Owen. But she didn't know what to do, what to say. She didn't know how to keep them alive.

And Jenny realised then what the real cause of her constant pain and torture was. She had convinced herself—and felt with all of her heart—that one, or even both, of her remaining children would follow Owen into death.

Monday, 5ᵗʰ June

Six days after the funeral of her brother, Kirsti returned to work. She had spent those six days doing something she had never done in her life. She lied to everyone she knew about where she was going and who she was with. She couldn't stand the silences. She couldn't handle the blank stares. And she didn't know what else to do.

She told her parents she was meeting up with Josh during the day, but she walked the streets alone. Or she sat by the river and stared at the water for hours without moving.

She told her friends she was spending time with Josh in the evenings too. She spent those hours in her bedroom, trying to stay away from the stares of her mother. The stares were expectant and made her feel uneasy. On the few occasions when she sat in the lounge room and quietly watched TV, she felt her mother's stare boring into the side of her head as if she was trying to read her mind. Kirsti couldn't stand it and quickly retreated to her room.

At night, she would sneak out of her room, onto the darkened landing, and into Owen's room. It was the only way she felt close to her twin. And feeling close to him felt more important than anything else. She would sniff his clothes, hold his belongings and sleep in his bed. In the morning, before her parents rose from their bed, she would sneak back into her own room and close the door, but she never climbed into her own bed. She hated it there, choosing to sit by the window and watch the street below come to life.

Now, she was heading to work. Skye had told her over

the phone the night before that it would be good for her. She needed the distraction. Kirsti felt anger bubble up inside her at the comment, because how did Skye know what would be good for her. Her mother seemed to think that being at work, surrounded by people, would do her good too.

"You've always shined around people," her mum had said that morning over breakfast, "and you've been so ... so withdrawn this past week. Maybe being at work will be good for you."

At least she hadn't said that it would help. Her mother knew better than that. Kirsti didn't know how she would go, but she'd soon find out.

Fifteen minutes later, Kirsti stood at her desk. She looked around the small, enclosed area which consisted of her desk, a bench, a bookshelf and four chairs for waiting clients together with a small coffee table.

A temp had filled in for her while she was away. Everything had been left neat and tidy. A pad sat beside the keyboard. Hurried handwriting of a stranger informed her that a Mr McLeod would be phoning today for a quote. The temp had already organised the pricing to be done but hadn't had time to type it up. That would obviously be Kirsti's first job.

Kirsti felt the pressure hit home as she pulled the chair out from under the desk and sat. Booting up her computer, she ferreted in her bag for her mobile phone. Usually, she would place it within arm's-length in case someone tried to phone her, today she switched it to silent and left it in her bag.

She grabbed her mug and walked through the office to the coffee machine. It was her favourite part of the day because she got to chat with the people in the office and catch up on their news. Today, however, everyone seemed too busy to talk to her. Most of them greeted her cheerfully, but they quickly turned aside and continued with their work. Some left their chairs and walked in the opposite direction as she approached them. None stopped her for a chat.

In the tea room, Kirsti approached the coffee machine and pressed a couple of buttons and waited for her mug to fill with the mission brown liquid. It looked disgusting, but it didn't taste that bad. It could have been worse, she always said.

"Kirsti."

A female voice interrupted her thoughts. She turned and found Lisa Portland, her boss, standing in the doorway.

"I'm so sorry for your loss," said Lisa. Her heavily made-up face was serene and sincere.

Lisa walked towards her and Kirsti found herself wrapped in the woman's arms. Shock didn't allow her to relax so she stood rigid and speechless. Lisa stepped back from her, still holding Kirsti's shoulders.

"Are you okay?" said Lisa. "Are you sure you're ready to come back to work?"

Kirsti nodded.

"Good girl. That's the spirit." Lisa smiled at her and turned to walk away. "Oh, there's a meeting in ten minutes." And the woman was gone.

Kirsti picked up her mug and walked back through the office, this time avoiding the gaze of her fellow workers. In her own secluded area, she put the mug on the table and placed her hands over her cheeks. They felt hot. Really hot. Hot with anger. Angry ... like the rest of her body. Angry at herself for almost believing someone understood how she might be feeling, she was even angrier at her boss for saying the right things, at the right time, but not meaning them.

The phone rang.

Her voice sounded strained, even to herself, but she managed to say the necessary words that were expected of her as the receptionist for the company.

"Hello, my name is Anthony McLeod. I spoke to you on Friday," said the deep voice of a man.

"I wasn't in on Friday, but the—"

"I want to speak to the person I spoke to on Friday. Is she there?"

"No, I'm sorry. She was filling in for me, but she left me details—"

"Well, that's not good enough," said Mr McLeod, annoyance clear in his voice. "I suppose that means I have to repeat everything to you that I told her?"

Don't get angry. She tried to keep her voice level when she spoke. "That won't be necessary. I know exactly what you are after. The quote will be ready this morning. Would you like me to fax or email it to you?"

"Email, of course," said Mr McLeod. "This is of the utmost importance. I hope you realise that. I need the quote straight away, within half an hour."

"That shouldn't be a problem." Kirsti remembered the meeting with Lisa. "Oh, wait, I can't get it to you by then. I have a meeting—"

"A meeting?" said Mr McLeod as if he'd never heard of the word. "My quote is more important than a meeting. I need it. You have to get it to me. I can't stress how important this is."

Kirsti had heard enough. She took a deep breath, but it didn't help. "Mr McLeod, if receiving a damn quote is the most important thing in your life then you should think yourself lucky."

"Excuse me?" He sounded astounded. "How dare—"

"Your quote will be emailed this morning," Kirsti continued. "I have your details here. Have a lovely day."

She placed the phone back on its cradle and left her office to attend the meeting.

Kirsti thought the meeting would be a short affair, but everyone wanted to waste time debating things they had debated last month and the month before. Normally she would sit and listen, and feel glad of the time she didn't have to answer the phone. But today, the stupid comments being repeated over and over again got on her nerves. Who cared how much a client was charged for a photocopy of their report? What was the point of arguing with Lisa over her latest brainstorm of charging staff for cups of coffee ... and extra for biscuits? The change would be implemented no matter what they said, so why bother? And when the subject turned to toilet rolls and how they weren't being replaced in the ladies toilets when the roll was empty, Kirsti stopped listening.

She sat doodling on her pad. Life was more meaningless than she ever imagined. People put importance on stupid things that should mean nothing. Meanwhile, the really important things, like how people were really feeling, were pushed aside, ignored and overlooked.

Kirsti sat within the murmur of the room, ignoring everything that was happening. She doodled for a bit longer but quickly lost interest in that. She stared out the narrow window for a short time, but staring at a brick wall didn't do much for her either. And then she noticed the mirror on the wall behind Lisa.

At first, she saw bright colours swirling around and thought how pretty the effect was. Later, she found herself looking around the room for the source of the colour in the mirror. Strangely, she could find nothing. When she looked back at the mirror, she saw a cloudless blue sky. She knew it was sky because she could see long grass too.

Her gaze shot to the window again. A red-brick wall. She craned her neck and saw nothing but more bricks. She inched her chair backwards. Then, she left her chair and walked to the window and looked out. If she looked straight up she could see the sky, but there was no grass anywhere.

"Kirsti." Lisa's sharp voice forced its way into her senses. "What are you doing? Are you all right?"

Kirsti held her breath and froze to the spot, her head still out the window. She remained where she was for a split second and then pulled her head back into the room and turned around. "Oh, I'm sorry ... I ... I felt a bit sick ...

and ... and I didn't want to..." she waved her hand at the plush carpet, "well, you know, make a mess if I threw up."

Another lie. She was getting good at it. She was sure her face hardly changed expression.

But Lisa's did. She frowned and pulled a face of disgust. "Do you need to go to the bathroom?"

Kirsti shrugged. "Well, no ... yes, I suppose I should. Just in case."

She scooped up her writing pad and walked to the door, passing Lisa and the mirror, as she did so. Her eyes slid over Lisa and focused on the mirror beyond. All she saw was a sea of blank faces staring at her back, then her hand grasped the doorknob and a moment later she was out of the room.

Kirsti spent the rest of the meeting sitting in a toilet cubicle thinking about what she'd seen in the mirror or what she thought she had seen. Now she wasn't so sure. She had been under a lot of stress lately and the grief was more than she would have ever imagined possible. She was still sleeping well, so it had nothing to do with that. So what was it?

She fiddled with the toilet roll, pulling squares off and tearing them into tiny sections. The pile in her lap was quite large when she realised what she was doing. She scooped the pile into her hand, stood, opened the toilet lid and dropped the torn paper into the bowl before sitting down again.

First, she saw something in a mirror that couldn't possibly be there and now she was tearing paper into small pieces. Something definitely wasn't right, but what? What was wrong with her?

She heard movement in the office. The meeting must have ended. She didn't want to go back to her desk. She didn't want to speak to clients. She didn't want to avoid being avoided by her workmates. She didn't want to be here. Period.

She sighed.

The bathroom door banged open. Kirsti rose to her feet and looked around the cubicle urgently.

"Kirsti?" called Lisa from the other side of the door. "Are you all right?"

Kirsti groaned.

"Are you still puking?" asked Lisa.

"No," replied Kirsti, flushing the toilet and fumbling with the door latch. "No, I'm fine. Really."

"Good." Lisa stared into Kirsti's eyes.

Kirsti shifted uncomfortably.

"You need to keep your fluids up. You look a little pale. Grab some water before you head back to your desk."

Lisa twirled on her heel and left the bathroom. The door swung shut behind her. Kirsti slumped against the basins and groaned again. Then, her head jerked upwards and she spun around and looked in the mirror. A pang of disappointment snagged at her belly. Her white face stared back at her.

"Pull yourself together, Kirsti," she said to her reflection. "You're kind of acting like a looney tune."

Five minutes later, Kirsti returned to her desk with a glass of water, which she knew she wouldn't drink. She sat and looked at the pile of work in the In tray. It had grown since she walked in this morning, whilst the Out tray remained empty.

"Right," she said to herself. "I better do Mr McLeod's stupid quote and get that emailed before I do anything else."

II

Jenny stared at the phone, willing it to ring. Needing the caller to be Tim. But nothing happened, the phone remained silent.

Stephen and Kirsti had returned to work this morning,

but Jenny wasn't ready to face the world yet. Her mind was preoccupied with death and she knew she needed to find a way of curtailing that.

Later, she would do some research on the internet, but right now talking to Tim was her first priority. She had left numerous messages on his mobile and the house answering machine, but not a word. Jenny had a sick feeling in the pit of her stomach that wouldn't respond to reason. She imagined him hanging from the ceiling fan in his room. She couldn't push the image away. The only way to put an end to the images was to hear Tim's voice.

She picked up the phone again and dialled his mobile number. The computerised voice she heard confirmed, again, that the mobile was still switched off and then she heard his voice asking her to leave a message and he'd get back to her. She didn't bother leaving another message. What was happening? Where was her son? Why wouldn't he phone her? Didn't he know how worried she was?

After the final beep sounded and there was silence on the other end of the phone, she continued to press the receiver against her ear even though she knew there wasn't even the slightest hope that she'd hear his voice now. She thought for the longest time before replacing the receiver and standing up. She'd make a cup of tea. That would relax her, a bit. Before she managed to take three steps, she quickly turned and grabbed the phone book. Pushing her glasses up her nose, she searched for the number she needed and quickly dialled before she lost courage.

As the phone rang at the other end, Jenny felt her stomach turn over. She needed to know about her son, yet she was scared of what she would be told.

"Mr Brighton's office, Kate speaking," said a young, cheerful voice.

"Hello, my name is Jennifer Fowler," said Jenny.

"Good morning, Mrs Fowler," said Kate. "How can I help you?"

"My son, Timothy Fowler, attends the university," said

Jenny. "Recently, his brother..." Her voice broke and the words refused to pass her lips. She swallowed and forced herself to continue on. "His brother passed away—"

"Oh, that's terrible," said Kate in a sedate voice. "I'm so sorry."

"Thank you." Jenny paused, taking a deep breath. "He died by suicide and the funeral was last Tuesday. Tim returned to uni the next day and I haven't been able to speak to him since. I'm worried ... I need to know that he's all right, that nothing has happened to him."

"Mrs Fowler," said Kate. "I have no idea what you're going through, but I can sort of understand what you're saying. Would you like me to make some enquiries on your behalf and phone you back?"

Tears spilled down Jenny's face. "Yes. Yes, I would like that. I was going to ask Mr Brighton, but if you are willing to do that for me, I'd be so grateful."

"We don't have to bother Mr Brighton with this." Kate paused for a moment. "Not that you're a bother, of course. I didn't mean to make it sound like that."

"No, it's all right. I understand," replied Jenny.

"Is Tim living in the dorms or is he leasing a house nearby?"

"He has a room in the dorms." Jenny knew she should say which room, but her brain wouldn't supply the information she needed. "I ... I can't remember the number or floor, right now."

"It's all right, I can look it up. I have some errands to do in a minute," said Kate. "I'll return via the dorms and will do some investigating for you. How does that sound?"

"Wonderful," said Jenny, clasping the phone tightly to her ear. "Thank you."

Kate asked for Jenny's phone number and promised to phone her back within the hour.

Tim sat in the stuffy lecture room and tried to concentrate. The content of the lecture was boring and the lecturer didn't help by having a voice that droned on and on. Tim found it difficult to stay awake, let alone listen and make notes.

"Hey, Tim," said Karl, who sat across the aisle from him. "Did you find your mobile phone?"

"No," replied Tim, resting his chin on his hand in boredom. "I don't know where it is. I've lost it."

Karl shook his head. "Not having access to a mobile would kill me." He went bright red. "Oh, sorry. I didn't mean anything by that."

Tim shrugged. "It's cool."

Karl smiled. "Is it affecting your social life?"

Tim thought about that question for a while. His social life had been affected, but it wasn't because of the loss of his mobile phone. He was sure of that. "Sure is. I might have to buy a new one."

"Now ya talking," said Karl, as the lecture came to an end. "Did he give us homework? I wasn't listening."

"Wouldn't have a clue," replied Tim.

Outside, Karl continued to walk with Tim. "Tim, I haven't told anyone this, but my dad killed himself, so I know what you're going through. Go easy on yourself, mate. If you want to talk, you know where to find me."

Without waiting for a response, Karl turned and walked away. Tim stood quietly watching him, not sure what to think or feel. When he turned back in the direction he had been going, a short blond stood in his path. She had a good figure and looked to be about his age. Her head was tilted to one side and she gazed at him with knowing blue eyes, rimmed with long black lashes.

"I'm Kate," she said. "I'm Mr Brighton's assistant."

"Oh, hi," he said and took a step sideways to go around her.

She stepped sideways too. "Hang on, don't run away. I

need to talk to you."

Tim stared at the young woman. "Why? Have I done something wrong?"

She smiled and her eyes lit up. "No, it's nothing like that."

"I'm on my way to my next lecture," replied Tim, stepping around her and walking off. "I can't afford to be late."

She fell in step beside him. "I'm heading that way, so I'll walk with you."

Tim glanced at Kate from the side of his eye and kept walking.

"Timothy Fowler, isn't it?"

He nodded. "Tim. Most people call me Tim."

Kate smiled. "Tim, your mother rang the office this morning. She's worried about you and I promised I'd ring her back and let her know how you are."

"Oh." What did she expect him to say?

"So how are you?"

"Fine. I'm fine."

He felt her hand on his arm and he stopped walking. Their gaze met.

"Tim, your mother sounded really worried. I know about your brother and I think your mum needs to hear your voice." She squeezed his arm. "When I phone her, can I tell her that you'll phone her when your lectures for today have finished? I know she wants to hear from you quite badly."

He felt his face flush. Her eyes were the deepest blue. He could look at them forever, but he pulled his gaze away. "Yes. I'll phone her later this afternoon."

"Now, you're not going to make a liar out of me are you?" asked Kate, tilting her head to the side again.

Tim shook his head. "No. I promise I'll phone her."

She released his arm and continued to smile. "Thank you. She'll be so happy to hear from you. I'll let you go now."

Kate turned and walked towards the administration

building, clutching a wad of papers in one arm. Tim watched her for a few seconds then continued to his next lecture.

Jenny folded the washing and put each item into a separate pile, depending on who owned the piece of clothing. Ever since the phone call from Kate, she had been feeling a little lighter of mind. Kate had talked to Tim, which meant that he had been alive this morning. The young girl had told her that Tim had promised her that he would phone this afternoon. Kate had been so convincing that Jenny couldn't help but believe her. She looked at the phone again and continued folding the washing.

It was close to three hours later when the phone finally rang. Jenny reached for the receiver. "Hello."

"Hi, Mum." The sound of Tim's voice sounded like music in her ears. The effect on her heart was magical.

"Oh, Tim, thank you for phoning," said Jenny. She had decided that she wouldn't mention the lack of communication. It would only make him defensive and she didn't want to scarc him off. "How arc you coping?"

"I'm fine," replied Tim. "I'm phoning from the communal phone, because I've lost my mobile. Could you check my room later to see if I left it behind? If it's not there, I guess I'll have to buy another one."

Jenny breathed a sigh of relief. He hadn't been ignoring all her phone calls. "Of course, darling. Do you want me to phone you back and let you know..." she didn't want to sound as desperate as she felt, "...later maybe or tomorrow?"

"I'll phone you after lectures tomorrow," he replied. "How's Dad and Kirsti?"

"They both went back to work today. I don't know how they're doing with that."

"What about you, Mum?"

"Going back to work? Or how am I?"

"Both."

Jenny smiled. He did care after all. "I'm coping, I guess, but I'm not ready to return to work yet. I've got time owing me so I'm going to take a couple more weeks off. How are you finding uni?"

"Boring, but it's okay." There was a short pause while he spoke quickly to someone else. "Mum, someone is waiting to use the phone. I have to go."

"Okay, darling."

"Don't forget to look for my phone. And stop worrying about me. I'm fine."

"Okay. I love you."

"Love you too, Mum. Bye."

Jenny hung up and burst into tears.

III

It had been a long day. Kirsti sat behind her computer and stared at the screen without seeing what was in front of her.

She hated Lisa. The woman said all the right things but quickly wiped it out by expecting Kirsti to be "normal". She didn't push Kirsti to get the work done and Kirsti was thankful for that, but it was something about how Lisa spoke to her that got right up Kirsti's nose.

She hated her workmates. Apart from Lisa, no one else acknowledged Kirsti's loss and that upset her. Sure, she understood they probably didn't know what to say to her. They only had to say that and it would have been enough. But, no, they said nothing and because they said nothing, they stayed away from her which only made Kirsti feel worse.

She especially hated the clients. They rang and expected

everyone to drop everything as if they were the only clients the company had. If that was all, Kirsti might have got passed their shortcomings, but that wasn't all. The comments they made about how important their job was, angered Kirsti the most. One man had insisted nothing was more important. Kirsti had given him a mouthful and hung up in his ear.

She hated the world. Kirsti wasn't stupid. She knew no one was to blame for Owen's death, but she hated the world anyway. She hated it because "life goes on" and she didn't want to leave Owen behind. She also hated it because the state of the world had taken away some people's hope and it might be a key reason for why Owen had ended his life.

She hated everything.

Lisa strolled into her area. Kirsti noticed her boss looking at the overflowing *In* tray and she saw the frown on Lisa's face deepen, but the older woman didn't say anything about it.

"See, it wasn't too bad, was it?"

It was more a statement than a question and that made Kirsti resent the words even more. *How would you know?* "I didn't get as much done as I usually do. I found it difficult to stay focused."

"You'll get back into the swing of things tomorrow," said Lisa with that fake smile Kirsti detested.

"Maybe."

"Think positive, Kirsti. Push all else from your mind."

"I'll try." She hated herself more than anything else. She hated being weak, but she said aloud what Lisa expected to hear. "Tomorrow will be better."

Lisa grinned from ear to ear. "That a girl. I'll see you bright and early in the morning then."

Kirsti bit down hard on her lip to stop herself saying something she might regret later.

Kirsti sat in the car, holding onto the steering wheel until her knuckles turned white. She didn't feel anything except exhaustion. There were no tears, no thoughts, no anger.

She turned the key in the ignition and felt the quiet rumble beneath her which told her the engine had kicked over. Having a mechanic for a father had its advantages. She sat for a full minute more before pulling away from the kerb and driving towards home.

It was a fifteen-minute drive on a quiet day, but during peak traffic, it could take anything up to forty minutes to get home. Not in the mood for road rage on top of everything else she had put up with today, Kirsti decided to take the long way home.

The back roads were less crowded. She travelled along them listening to a CD, but not really taking any of the words in. A truck came up behind her. The shield on the front looked huge in the rearview mirror. It felt so close, almost as if it could run straight over the top of her. Kirsti pressed down on the accelerator a bit more, trying to put a bit of distance between her car and the truck. The truck sped up, quickly closing the gap. She pressed on the accelerator a little more. So did the driver of the truck. Her gaze stared at the road ahead of her. Why didn't the truck overtake her and forge ahead? Her stomach lurched with fear and then...

She looked into the rearview mirror and saw green grass and blue sky. A gentle breeze caressed the grass so that the green moved slowly beneath the blue. Kirsti stared at the scene in the mirror, mesmerised. Warmth and calmness filled her. Peace inched its way into her mind. Kirsti relaxed. It was a feeling she hadn't experienced since the morning she left home to go to work, almost three weeks beforehand. She had been relaxed and happy as she was getting ready for work, and then ... she had thrown open the garage door and had found Owen's body hanging dead and purple beside her car.

The boom of the truck's horn echoed.

Kirsti's eyes focused again on the mirror and she saw the edge of the truck pass from view. She looked back at the road and found her car on the wrong side of the road. She looked down at the pedals and couldn't remember what she had to do. She held onto the steering wheel but didn't know how to manoeuvre the car. The car continued along the road. The truck sounded its horn again. It had dropped back. The driver hung out the window. He yelled at her, but she didn't hear his words. A car came around the bend ahead. It was travelling fast. She was heading right at it. She was going to die. And there was nothing she could do about it.

The truck sounded its horn for the third time. The spell broke.

Kirsti's mind snapped back into action. She swerved the car off the road and onto the dirt, her right foot automatically finding the brake. She screeched to a stop, dust billowing up around her. The car heading in the other direction careened past. Kirsti caught the gaze of the truck driver as he passed and she felt the heat rising as he shook his head.

She sat rigid, in a cold sweat, her heart pounding in her ears. She had forgotten how to drive! But inwardly she knew it was more than that. She knew that she had forgotten how to function in those few seconds. If her mind hadn't started working again, she might be dead now. She realised she didn't care. Her life was unimportant. What she did care about was the fact that she may have taken the driver of the other car with her.

Tim sat on the wall with a bunch of other students. Lectures had finished for the day and they were discussing their plans for the evening. Tim had always been a participant in the evening activities, but of late he found the guys didn't seem to feel comfortable with him around.

However, Tim felt that he'd let the rift grow too wide and it was time to do something about it. When he saw the group gathered, he joined them. He had been greeted with unsure smiles and Tim tried to be as normal as possible.

Because what did he want more than anything? Normality. It was the reason he came back to uni in the first place.

"Let's go to the pub," said one of the guys.

"Nah, we did that last night," said another.

"What about buying some grog and going back to Atchison Street?" Atchison Street was a house where a bunch of them rented together.

"Better not," said the one who had suggested the pub, "our neighbours are starting to complain about the noise."

"Damn bastards. What are we going to do then?"

"Hi, Tim."

The female voice sounded so foreign beside the male. Tim looked up and found the blond from earlier in the day staring at him. What was her name? Kathy? No, that's right. It was Kate.

Tim was aware that his mates had gone quiet. All eyes were on Kate, waiting.

Her gaze went over them and settled on Tim again. "Can I talk to you for one minute?"

He looked at his friends and quickly stood. "Sure," he said, feeling slightly embarrassed, but not entirely sure why.

They walked away from the guys before Kate stopped and turned to face him. "I didn't think you'd appreciate it if I asked this question in front of your friends."

Tim stared at her blue eyes but said nothing.

"Did you phone your mum?"

He nodded. What was wrong with him? When had he become a mute? He felt the heat in his cheeks and hoped it wasn't visible.

Kate smiled. "I'm so glad. She sounded distraught when I talked to her. I hope she feels better now."

"I think so," said Tim. "I said I'd phone tomorrow after-noon too."

"Good." Her smile revealed even, white teeth. "That's so good."

Tim and Kate stared at each other for a moment. Tim was vaguely aware when his mates moved away from the low wall they had been sitting on.

"Well, I'll let you get back to your friends," said Kate. "I wanted to make sure you made the phone call."

"Thanks." He wasn't sure what he was thanking her for.

He found himself watching her walk away again, but quickly pulled himself together and ran to catch up with his friends.

"So what was decided," he asked.

"The pub and a game or two of darts."

IV

Due to her talk with Tim, Jenny felt better than she had done for several days, so she endeavoured to cook a nice meal for her working family. She had to admit that it felt good to do something worthwhile and looking after her family had always been worthwhile. It was only when the children started school that she turned to fund raising to fill in the time. Then, when she returned to work full time, she couldn't turn her back on the charities she had chosen to help. She no longer needed fund raising to occupy her mind, but they still needed her help so she continued her work. Now, she found herself wondering if that contribut-ed to Owen's death. Had she spent too much time on other things? Did he feel neglected? She would have to put more thought into it, but for now she would concentrate on making the house more like a home.

By the time Stephen walked through the front door, the house was filled with cooking smells. "Honey, that smells delicious," he said, taking the lid off one of the saucepans and peering inside. "What's that?"

"A new creation," she said, taking the saucepan lid from his grip and replacing it. "I hope you like it."

"I'm starving. I'd eat anything right now."

He kissed her.

"Anything?" she asked.

"Yep." His eyes sparkled.

"Even those dirty socks you stuffed in a corner of the closet last summer, which I found today? They are quite disgusting."

He frowned. "Maybe not those, but I'll eat anything you cook for me." His frown turned into a smile. His face was a mass of smile lines. He used to smile a lot. It was something he didn't do that often these days. "Where's Kirsti? Is she in her room again?"

"No, she isn't home yet," she replied.

"What?" The smile disappeared. "She should have been home ages ago. Where is she?"

"Why, what time is it?" asked Jenny, automatically looking at her watch. 6.10pm. The bottom instantly fell out of her motivation. She gasped. "My god, she's really late. I had no idea."

Guilt took over from there. She had already lost a son, and now she hadn't even noticed her daughter's lateness. She deserved all the pain she felt. She deserved the torture. A bad mother shouldn't expect anything less.

"Stephen?"

"It's all right. I'll go out and look for her."

He grabbed his car keys, but before they reached the front door, they heard Kirsti's car pull into the drive. She parked beside Owen's car. Jenny had noticed that she no longer insisted in having a spot in the garage.

Jenny felt Stephen pulling her away from the door.

"Now, listen to me, don't pounce on her as soon as she walks in. Give her a chance to tell us."

"What if—"

Stephen cut her off. "If she doesn't tell us, let it go. She's home now and she's safe. That's all that really matters. Give her some space."

Jenny nodded and they quickly headed back to the kitchen.

Kirsti climbed out of the car and made her way to the front door. Her body shook. She felt like she was going to throw up. Something was wrong with her and she needed to do something about it.

The house smelled nice. Her mum had been cooking. That was a good sign. Did it mean Tim had phoned? It had to mean that. Her dad sat at the table, nursing a cup of coffee, whilst her mum was busy in the kitchen.

"Hey, sweetie," said her dad. "How was your day?"

Shit!

"All right," she said, dumping her bag on a chair. "Not great, but I made it through the day. How about you?"

She wanted him to tell her he had hated every minute of it. She needed to know she wasn't alone.

"It was busy," replied her dad. "But they left me to my own devices for most of the day, which I appreciated."

Hope slipped further away.

"Mum, how was your day?" asked Kirsti.

Her mum turned around, a tea towel slung over her shoulder. "Tim rang. He lost his mobile, so he didn't get my messages. I checked his room and the mobile was on the floor beside his bed."

All hope was gone. Kirsti couldn't break her parent's bubble. She couldn't add to their worry and stress. At that moment, she knew she had to keep her secret safe and work it out on her own.

"What's the matter, sweetie," said her dad, leaving his seat and stepping around the table to face her. "What's up?"

"I ... I..." Kirsti looked at her father and decided she could share some of the truth, but she had to protect the secret at all costs. "I almost had an accident on the way home."

Her mum dropped the tea towel onto the bench and rushed to her. "Are you all right?"

"What happened?" asked her dad.

"I don't know." She fumbled for words to explain what had happened without giving away the real cause. "It's been a long day and I feel exhausted. I haven't been feeling well either, maybe my concentration wasn't what it should have been. After it happened, I sat in the car and waited for the traffic to quieten down a bit." She paused and then looked straight into her dad's eyes. "I'm okay. Nothing happened. No one was hurt. But can you drive me to work tomorrow?"

Her dad frowned. "Sure. I'll drive you there and will pick you up, don't worry about it."

Kirsti knew her father wanted to ask more questions and was glad when he didn't. She hugged him. "Thank you."

Dinner was a sombre affair. Sitting with her parents in the dining room, Kirsti felt awkward. She didn't like lying to them, but she had done, so many times in the last few weeks. Not only did she feel awkward in their presence, she thought they felt awkward in hers.

Owen had not only taken his own life when he died. He had taken everyone's confidence. He had left everyone feeling unsure and scared. And his family no longer knew what to say or do around each other. Her parents talked about mundane things, but she didn't listen.

Kirsti prodded her food and tried to eat as much as she could, for her mum's sake as well as her own. Food still tasted terrible, but after the events of the day, she knew she had to take better care of herself.

She thought about the mirror at work and then she thought of the rearview mirror in her car. In both, she had seen the same thing—grass and sky. Yet at both times, the areas surrounding the mirrors were void of these things. True, this afternoon she might have seen sky in normal circumstances, but there was a truck behind her and all she could see was the enormous grill of that truck. There was lots of bush on either side of the road, but no rolling grass. And the sky was overcast, not clear as she had seen in the mirror. Obviously something wasn't right and she decided that she must be unwell, and because of that she was hallucinating. It was the only explanation. She would start taking better care of herself and the hallucinations would soon stop. In the meantime, her dad had agreed to drive her to work.

"You're quiet, Kirsti."

It was her mother. Her face was pale and drawn. She had a look of searching and worry. A frown creased the section between her eyes. And her eyes looked tired behind those glasses she wore. Kirsti would have normally told her parents everything, but that was before they lost Owen. That was before all their lives took a dive for the worse.

"I'm not well," said Kirsti, "but I'm trying to eat, Mum. I think I need to eat a bit better and maybe go to bed earlier to build my strength up."

Her mum nodded. "We all need to do the same." She rose from the table and started clearing the dishes.

"It's all right, Mum. I'll wash up," said Kirsti. "Go and relax. I'll bring you a cup of tea when I've finished."

Her mum reached out and stroked her hair. "Thank you, darling."

Skye sat in her room watching the TV. Melody sat on the two-seater lounge beside her, crunching on potato chips.

"I'm feeling bad about not making more of an effort where Kirsti is concerned," said Skye. "She's our best friend and we haven't seen her since the funeral. Tomorrow, that will be a whole week."

"I know," said Melody. "I feel the same."

They continued to watch TV for a few minutes.

"I think we need to do something about it," added Skye. "Otherwise, we might lose her as a friend."

Melody paused, a chip in one hand, and turned to look at Skye. "That won't happen."

Skye shook her head and sighed. "How can you be so sure?"

"Look," said Melody, shifting uncomfortably in the chair, "we've all known each other since the first day of school. I don't know any other group of friends who can make that same claim. We're like sisters."

"Well, sisters would not abandon each other, and I feel like we've done that to Kirsti."

"Do something about it then," said Melody before tipping the nearly empty packet up to her lips.

"Okay, I will," said Skye. "We'll go to the movies on Friday night."

"That's a great idea."

"Yes," said Skye, satisfied that she was finally taking action. "I'll phone Kirsti and Joanne tomorrow morning and arrange it. But I think it's important that we help Kirsti as best we can. Don't mention what happened and don't allow her to talk about it. It will only depress her more."

"I agree," said Melody. "I don't know what to say anyway, so avoiding the issue seems like the best tactic."

"That's right," said Skye. "She'll get over it in no time with our help."

Tim sipped his beer and watched his mates make fools of themselves. Usually, he would be right in the middle of them being stupid too, but no matter how hard he tried, he couldn't do it tonight. He wasn't in the mood, which was becoming a regular thing these days. What was the point? Besides, they all looked stupid prancing about like ... dick-heads.

"How ya going there?" Karl pulled up a stool and sat beside him.

"Yeah, great," said Tim, not feeling as bright as he sounded.

"Tim, it's okay. You don't have to pretend with me," said Karl. "Suicide is a big deal. The people left behind don't have a clue, most of the time, what's going on. When Dad died, me and my little sister ended up in foster care for six months because Mum couldn't cope."

Tim didn't want to hear about it. He was coping in his own way.

"I hated Mum for that. But now that I'm older I can understand to some degree what she must have gone through. She got the biggest shock when I told her I forgave her," said Karl. "She cried like you wouldn't believe."

"Karl," said Tim, not sure what he wanted to say. "I appreciate what you're doing, but I really am fine. I'm finding my feet again, that's all."

Karl stared at him for the longest minute. And then he nodded. "Sure. I can see that you don't want to talk yet, but when you do ... let me know. I'll listen. But I won't judge."

Tim nodded and Karl joined the game.

Tim didn't want to talk about it. He didn't want other people talking about it. He wanted everything to be how it used to be. He wanted to laugh and have fun. He wanted his mates to feel at ease around him again. He placed the glass of beer on the bar behind him and stood.

It's up to me, he thought. I have to be the one to find what I used to have. Tomorrow, things will be different.

With a final glance at his crazy mates, and without a word to any of them, Tim turned and walked away.

V

Kirsti attempted to sleep in her own bed that night, but she couldn't sleep. She crept along the landing and crawled into Owen's bed and still couldn't sleep. It was the first night where sleep escaped her completely. She tossed and turned. She cried. And then she sat and stared at the wall.

Finally, she left Owen's room and went downstairs thinking a cup of hot chocolate might do the trick. The kitchen was dark and cold. Rain pelted against the side of the house. She stood at the sliding door, looking out. The neighbourhood slept. She thought she heard Owen's voice say her name in the wind, but soon pushed the thought away and returned to his bedroom.

Later, she placed the empty mug on the side table and pulled the blankets over herself. Squeezing her eyes shut, she willed herself to fall asleep. How was she to get better if she didn't get a good night of sleep?

Kirsti's body shook with cold. The sounds of night retreated and were replaced by a distant droning noise. She felt a presence standing beside the bed. A person looking down at her, bending over her, reaching out to touch her. She squeezed her eyes shut, pretending to be asleep. Maybe who ever it was would go away. Something as cold as ice burned her shoulder. She shrieked and sat upright.

Alone.

She shivered and reached for one of Owen's jumpers to pull on. But it wasn't there. She looked around and was surprised to see her own belongings, her own room. When had she come back here?

She got out of bed and walked to the door. Opening it, she stepped out onto the landing. Her teeth chattered, but she ignored that and walked to stand in Owen's doorway. The furniture was gone. A pile of boxes were piled up against the far wall. The curtains had been taken down. Nothing of Owen's remained.

"No, that can't be right," she said. Her voice sounded strange.

She turned to her parent's bedroom. The door stood ajar. She rushed over and pushed the door open. Again, nothing but boxes. Pushing Tim's bedroom door open, she saw the same thing yet again. What was happening?

Rain pelted on the roof and against the windows.

She moved to stand at the top of the stairs. "Mum, Dad? Where are you?"

No answer.

Kirsti grabbed the banister and quickly pulled her hand away. The wood was frozen solid. One stair at a time, she made her way to the bottom and stood beside the front door. It too stood ajar. In one quick action she pulled it open and stepped out onto the veranda. Heavy rain and mist blurred her vision. She quickly stepped back into the hallway and went into the lounge room instead.

All the nick nacks were gone, but the furniture was still there. Large lengths of plastic covered everything. Dust gathered in dirty piles and slid along crevices in the cold air to form muddy puddles on the floor. The dining room was empty. As were the kitchen cupboards.

Kirsti went to the sliding door. It was locked. She looked out and saw nothing but more rain and thick mist. Then she spotted a dim glow from a light in the garage. She turned and ran through the house back to the front door and out into the dark night.

The roller door was partially open. An orange glow shone from the gap.

She stepped off the veranda and the rain found her immediately. It slapped her with coldness. Goosebumps formed on her arms. She ignored them and continued down the few steps onto the path that would take her to the garage.

By the time she stood barefooted in front of the roller door, she was soaked right through. Her hair hung limp around her face. Her nightwear clung to her body. She shivered uncontrollably and took a deep breath before leaning down to grab the handle. She paused for only a second and then she threw the roller door up.

Kirsti immediately backed away from the garage. "No. No!"

Inside, three people hung dead from the rafters—her mum, her dad and Tim.

She screamed.

"Kirsti. Kirsti?"

Hands grabbed her. Shook her. She continued to scream.

"Kirsti, sweetie, it's all right. You're dreaming. You're safe."

Kirsti opened her eyes and looked into her father's concerned eyes. She burst into tears and he pulled her into his arms.

"Sweetheart, it's all right. You were having a nightmare."

"Where's Mum?" asked Kirsti, struggling to look over her father's shoulder.

"I'm right here. We're both right here for you," said her mum.

Kirsti listened to the rain outside. She listened to the beating heart of her dad. His arms around her felt warm and safe. "A dream," she said. "A bad dream."

She felt her mum's hand touch her hair. "You are fine."

Kirsti let go of her dad and discovered herself still in Owen's room. She looked at her parents and looked away quickly.

"Why are you sleeping in here," asked her dad, his voice gentle.

"I couldn't sleep," replied Kirsti. "I miss Owen."

A gasp escaped from her mum's mouth and she rushed forward to sit on the bed beside Kirsti. "We all miss him. We all miss him so much."

Kirsti felt her dad tug at her arm.

"Come on, come downstairs and we'll have a hot chocolate," he said. "I think we could all benefit from one."

"The garage?" asked Kirsti.

"The garage is locked. We've hidden the key," said her mum. "No one is going into the garage."

"You had a nightmare. That's all it was," said her dad.

"It seemed so real," said Kirsti. She rose from the bed and followed her parents out of the room. "It didn't make a whole lot of sense when I think about it now, but it seemed so real."

Tuesday, 6th June

Jenny stood at the bottom of the veranda steps and watched Stephen reverse the car out of the drive. She waited until it started to pull away before waving. Kirsti sat in the passenger's seat, her car parked behind Owen's.

She looked at Owen's car and walked over to place her palm on the metal. Owen loved his car and had spent many an hour doing it up. Jenny could see him bending over the engine, or lying under the exhaust as he fixed something that probably didn't need fixing in the first place.

Meanwhile, Stephen would be a few feet away, in the garage, working on restoring an old 1956 Ford Zephyr he had inherited from his bachelor uncle. The price Old Uncle Bill, as he was affectionately known, had paid to buy the car and have it imported was astounding. Years later, it remained, unused, undercover in the old man's shed. When Stephen saw it, he pleaded with his uncle to let him buy it, but Old Uncle Bill refused to let it go. After his death, a tow truck arrived at their house with the zephyr braced on the platform behind it. Stephen was amazed when he heard that it had been left to him in Old Uncle Bill's will.

Father and son loved their cars, old and new. Stephen, a mechanic, was quick to say yes when Owen asked if he could become an apprentice for the family business. Jenny didn't know anything about cars, but she had sat on the veranda and watched them fixing, washing and polishing their cars on many occasions.

Now, Owen's car sat neglected in the driveway and the

Zephyr sat neglected in the garage. Jenny knew that Owen's Falcon would have to be sold, one day, but that day wouldn't be any time soon. She wasn't ready to let any of her son's belongings go yet.

Jenny turned and purposefully walked back into the house. The sleepless nights were taking their toll and now she had a fresh worry. Kirsti was having nightmares and, even though she denied it, Jenny felt positive that her daughter was sleeping in Owen's bedroom every night. It was time to do some research.

The internet was a wonderful thing. Anything and everything could be found if you searched long enough. The researcher's only decision was if they trusted the source or not. Being middle-aged, Jenny knew her way around the internet and within half an hour she had scanned many pages about suicide.

She opened a new document and made a list of the warning signs.

Marked changes in personality.
Sudden change in sleeping or eating patterns.
Unexplained, significant drop in school or work responsibilities.
Verbal threats of suicide.
Loss of interest in usual activities.
Social withdrawal.
Lack of concern about appearance.
Lapses of attention and concentration.
Dangerous or illegal activities (running away, drug or alcohol abuse).
Recent rejection (from friends, clubs).
Giving away or throwing away prized possessions.
Explosive outbursts.
Reading stories or drawing pictures about death.
Possession of dangerous weapons.
Unexplained cheerfulness after prolonged depression.

Jenny stared at the list for a long time. At first, she shook her head, convinced Owen had displayed none of the warnings. But the longer she stared at the list, the more she could see the signs had been there.

Owen and his girlfriend had broken up three months before his death. He seemed fine about it, but now Jenny knew that wasn't the case at all. He was pretending. She remembered asking him about his weight about two weeks prior to his suicide. He had brushed the remark aside in a matter-of-fact manner and promised to take better care of himself. Now she wished that she had taken more of a pro-active step in making sure that he did. On the other hand, Owen had slept more than before too. Jenny wondered if he actually did sleep or was he removing himself from family activities on purpose. She would never know.

Owen had always taken pride in his appearance, yet in hindsight, Jenny remembered the frayed jeans, the stained t-shirts, the greasy hair and the fact that his face had broken out in more pimples in the last few months than he'd ever had in his life.

Then she remembered the day she had overheard him giving away some of his CD's to his mates. When she asked him why he had done it, she had believed him when he told her that he no longer enjoyed the music on those particular CD's. It was only after his death that she discovered that he had only kept one CD, the one in the player, which he played over and over again. When she had listened to it right through, she cried when she realised that all the songs were saying goodbye. She had heard them over and over again and had never suspected that's what he was actually doing.

And that wasn't all he had given away. All his DVD's were gone too, as were his Playstation games. One set of drawers in his room was completely empty and Jenny never knew until she had gone in his room, after his death, to look at his things. Had Owen thought he was doing her a favour by sorting out his own things? Being a considerate young man, she wouldn't have been surprised, but didn't he think that those things would have been treasured by his family ... treasured by his mother? What had he been thinking? Did he think no one cared?

But Owen had never had an explosive outburst. He was much too placid for that and she supposed he would have tried to keep any anger he might have felt to himself because that would have given him away.

He never once mentioned suicide to anyone either. That was the one question Jenny had asked all his friends and they all said the same thing, they were shocked at the news because they had no idea how he felt. Tears rolled down Jenny's face when she remembered the evening Owen's best friend, Terry, had come to the house to give his condolences. He looked devastated. He kept saying over and over again that he didn't know why it had happened. She remembered the anguish she had felt herself because she was unable to tell him.

None of them knew why this dreadful thing had occurred.

Jenny studied the list for a couple of hours. She found herself remembering little details that she could now see were clear warning signs and she became more upset as she realised that she had missed them all. To her, Owen had always been a healthy, happy young man. She didn't even know her own son was suffering. What kind of mother did that make her?

Jenny then compared the list with her surviving children and her heart rate immediately raced.

Tim and Kirsti were withdrawn and there was a definite change in both their personalities. Jenny wasn't sure about Tim, but Kirsti's sleep patterns had changed. Tim's outbursts may not fall into the category of "explosive", but they were angry and sudden. Kirsti didn't want to drive. She complained about going to work, which she had never done before, and she no longer saw her friends like she used to. And she had admitted, only yesterday, that her concentration wasn't what it used to be.

Jenny covered her face with her hands and pressed her temples. The pain in her head matched the pain in her stomach. Both her remaining children were displaying warning signs of suicide.

What was she supposed to do?

II

On Tuesday morning Tim awoke with a determination to make things go back to normal. Nothing would stand in his way. He would make sure of it.

He practised smiling while he shaved. He admitted the smile looked a bit wonky, but smiling at yourself in a mirror couldn't possibly be considered normal circumstances, so he told himself that he would probably do better out there in the real world.

The university had purchased a block of flats beside a hospital that used to be the nurses quarters. His room was small. It contained a single bed against one wall and a length of benches against the opposite wall. The benches were different heights and made out of different types of wood, so it was obvious they had been added at different times. He had a TV and DVD player on one bench. Another was piled high with odds and ends—books, CD's, deodorant, gel, posters he intended to stick to the walls one day, chocolate bars, and somewhere in there was a heap of photos and his camera. Under this mess stood a small bar fridge where he kept a few days worth of food and cold drink. The third bench was used as his writing desk. He sat at that desk for some time every evening, usually. He hadn't been near it since he got back from the funeral.

On the short wall between the bed and the benches was a glass door that went out onto a balcony. However, the balconies had been declared unsafe and the students had been forbidden to use them. Tim obeyed the rule, but he did place a clothes horse outside the door with his washing hanging from it every weekend.

Opposite the glass door to the balcony was the door to his room. Made of solid wood and fitted with a metal arm that never allowed the door to remain open unless something extra heavy was placed in front of it, the door slammed shut each and every time it closed. The sound reminded Tim of a firework exploding. All the rooms were exactly the same and all the doors banged closed day and night. At first, Tim hated the noise, especially at night when the sound would shock him awake, but now he hardly ever heard it.

Beside the front door stood a tall, narrow wardrobe for his few good clothes. The wardrobe also included four drawers for his undies and socks.

Situated halfway down the narrow, dimly lit corridor was a communal bathroom. Opposite the bathroom were two elevators. Down at the far end of the corridor was the communal kitchen. He had quickly learned not to place any food worth eating in the fridge because it was never there when he went back for it.

The block was eight stories high, not including the ground floor. The first four floors were for the girls and the top four floors were for the boys. Boys were not allowed on the girl's floors and vice versa. Some rules were meant to be broken, however, and that was one of them.

Tim left the elevator and paused. Apart from the office, where Tim had to go to pay for his room, the ground floor was a communal area for everyone—boys and girls. There was a large lounge with a big TV and DVD set up on the wall. Every Wednesday night the Games Committee organised a movie night, but not many people turned up for it. The movies were old hat. There was also a games room where they could play snooker, darts, indoor volleyball and chess or draughts. There used to be pinball machines in there too, but they were old fashioned and no one used them anymore. Besides, the noise drove everyone else out.

Tim checked the games room, but apart from two nerdy looking guys playing chess, it was empty. He poked his head in the lounge and found the chairs pushed back against the walls and a bunch of girls dressed in their skimpy exercise outfits. They were about to start a Pilates class by the look of it. Sometimes he and a few other guys would sit and watch them, but not today.

Where were the guys? He thought for a while and then decided that they must have had a big night and stayed over at Atchison Street. He'd done that a few times himself in the time he'd been here.

Tim left the grounds and quickly walked across the road. It was fairly early still and not many cars were about. On the opposite side of the road, he turned right and walked along the path. Less than a minute later, he turned into Atchison Street. Several houses down the street were rented by groups of students. Tim had been in all the houses at one stage or another. Today, he headed to the house, the fourth on the left from the corner, where his mates would be sleeping off hangovers.

The front door was open, which meant someone was awake. Tim didn't bother knocking, he walked through to the lounge room, passing several sleeping bodies as he did so. So this is what they looked like. He shook his head. It wasn't a pretty sight. No wonder most of them didn't have girlfriends. What decent girl would put up with this?

The lounge room was dark and smelled of stale beer and fart. Wrinkling his nose, he continued walking until he passed through the empty kitchen and was standing on the cement slab out the back. Karl and Jimbo sat with their backs pressed up against the wall of the house.

"Hey, Tim, what happened to you last night?" asked Jimbo. "You missed a great night."

Tim looked over his shoulder into the house. "Yeah, I can see that. I thought there was some ban on drinking at Atchison Street?"

"Yeah, well, there was, but we lifted it." Jimbo shrugged and then grinned. "But where were you?"

"I had some things to sort out," replied Tim with a quick glance at Karl, who was watching him carefully.

"Are they sorted now?" asked Jimbo.

"Yep," said Tim. "I've been out of circulation for too long."

They had no lectures until the afternoon, so Tim and his friends spend the morning lazing around drinking soft drink and coffee—not mixed together, of course. Tim made sure he was involved in every conversation they had and when the others acted like morons, he ensured he was right in there with the rest of them.

By lunchtime, he felt exhausted, but he refused to stop his pretence. At first, everyone looked at him a little strangely, but in the end, the guys relaxed and things almost seemed back to normal. Only Karl stared at him in a strange way the entire morning. He didn't say anything, but he didn't have to. Tim knew what he was thinking and he didn't like it, so he stayed away from Karl altogether.

At 1.30pm, when his first lecture commenced, Tim was secretly happy to be able to stop the pretending and sit quietly and listen to the drone of the lecturer.

At 3pm, Tim refused to believe he was making excuses to be away from his friends for longer than necessary. He had promised to phone his mum, so that's what he did.

"Hi, Mum."

"Tim," said his mum, "it's so good to hear your voice."

"I only spoke to you yesterday," replied Tim.

"I know," said his mum. "I'm sorry. I can't help worrying about you, that's all."

His mum had always worried about him, since the first day he had been here. But as the days turned into weeks and then months, she had backed off and there was a mutual understanding that she wouldn't phone too often as long as he phoned her once a week. It wasn't like he didn't enjoy their conversations, because he did, but he didn't want the guys thinking he was some kind of Mama's Boy.

Anyway, the agreement had worked well. Now, however, the agreement seemed to have gone out the window.

"I know, Mum, but you really don't have to worry," he said into the phone.

"Are you sure?"

Tim shook his head with frustration. "Yes, Mum, I'm sure."

"Tim...?"

Feeling irritated, he waited for her to say what was on her mind, but she remained silent. "What is it? Ask your question."

"Okay," he heard her take a deep breath. "Are you having suicidal thoughts?"

"What? Are you kidding?" Of all the questions he thought she might ask, that hadn't been one of them. He was floored by the question. How could she even think such a thing?

"Kidding? Why would I kid about something like that, Tim?" Her voice sounded extremely high. "I need to know. Are you having suicidal thoughts?"

"No. I'm not." Was his mother that worried about him? No wonder she had phoned administration and talked to the cute blond. "Is that what you've been thinking?"

"I don't know what to think."

He heard his mum gulp. Was she crying?

"Tim, I read on the internet about the warning signs and you fit into several of them."

Tim sighed. "Mum, I'm not suicidal. I do feel different. Depressed, maybe. A bit out of it. But I've never thought of suicide."

"Oh, I shouldn't have said anything," said his mum, almost like she was talking to herself. "I don't want to put notions in your head."

"Mum, settle down." For the first time since Owen's death he realised what his mother must have been going through. He felt an overwhelming urge to make her see that she was worrying for no reason. "I have seen what Owen's death has done to you and Dad. I have witnessed the anguish and grief of his friends. I have felt the loss and pain of losing a brother. Why on earth would I consider doing that to you again? Why? Do you think I'm that selfish? Do you honestly believe I could do that to you? I'm a lot of things, Mum, but I would never, ever do that to you. The thought never occurred to me for one second and never will."

"I'm sorry. I—"

"No, don't be sorry. You've done nothing wrong." He struggled to keep his voice even. "I know you love me and I know you worry about me all the time, but I will never cause you the same pain that..." Something stopped Tim completing the sentence. "I am *not* suicidal. That's one thing you don't have to worry about."

His mother burst into tears. He let her cry because he had run out of words to say. After a few moments the sounds of her sobs subsided and he held the phone to his ear without saying a word for the longest while.

"Tim?" his mum finally said.

"Yes."

"I found your phone," she said.

He knew she was trying to change the subject before they hung up.

"That's great," he replied. "I really didn't want to buy another one. Where was it?"

"On the floor beside your bed," she replied. "You must have dropped it when you were leaving."

"Probably." Nothing would surprise him. "There's a long weekend coming up, I'll come home then and get it."

"That will be wonderful. I'll cook your favourite meal," said his mum.

"Mum, I have to go. My next lecture starts in ten minutes."

"Okay, darling. I love you."

"I love you too, Mum."

Wednesday, 7th June and Thursday, 8th June

The next few days passed in a blur for Kirsti.

Her dad continued to drive her to work and he left the workshop early so that he could pick her up in the afternoon. The people at work continued to avoid her. She felt as if she had grown a second head and everyone was too scared to tell her. She became confused with her work and found herself making more mistakes. Lisa pretended to be understanding, but Kirsti knew each mistake made Lisa angrier and more distant. After the first day, it seemed like Lisa felt Kirsti had been supported long enough and started putting pressure on her as well. This made Kirsti make even more mistakes.

And the clients. Kirsti wanted to murder them all. But putting aside that small problem, Kirsti quickly realised that her memory was shot. A client would give her their name and by the time she had pushed the button to transfer the person … the name was gone from Kirsti's mind. She told herself that it happens to everyone, but Kirsti couldn't remember the simplest of instructions either. Her concentration and focus were completely gone and the only way she managed to get anything done was to write it down as a reminder.

She kept a pad beside the phone and wrote everything down. She took to emailing herself reminders on a regular basis. She left post-it notes on important things as reminders too.

The one thing that didn't happen in those few days was ... she didn't see anything in any mirror, anywhere.

On Thursday night, Kirsti approached her dad. "I think I feel ready to drive myself to work tomorrow."

"Are you sure?" he asked, looking up from the newspaper he was reading. "I can drive you if you want, and you can drive yourself starting from Monday."

"No, it's all right," she replied. "Besides, I'm meeting Skye and the girls after work for dinner and a movie."

Her dad stared at her over the top of his reading glasses. "Well, if you are sure."

"I am. And don't worry, I'm not going to drink anything alcoholic so I'll be safe to drive home."

"Okay, sweetie."

Friday, 9th June

On Friday, Kirsti drove straight into town after work. She parked her car outside *The Chinese Lantern*. The restaurant was small and cosy inside, and it was one of the girls' favourite places to dine. The owners knew them well and sometimes gave them an extra dish or a complimentary bottle of wine.

Inside, the Chinese lanterns were the only source of light. Even though it wasn't dark outside, it appeared so from inside the restaurant. The place was empty. Not even the staff wandered about. Kirsti made her way to the bar and sat on a stool, knowing Eddie would show his face eventually.

She checked her reflection in one of the mirrors while she waited. Her pale skin and dark eyes were a dead give away to how she really felt, but every time she said she was fine people seemed to accept her words.

"Miss Kirsti," said Eddie, coming up from the cellar. "It's good to see you. I'm sorry to hear about your brother. How are you and your family coping?"

Kirsti was shocked by Eddie's direct question and acknowledgement. It made her want to cry. Tears blurred her vision, but she quickly swallowed the lump in her throat and looked Eddie in the eye. "I'm barely coping, but I guess I'll get over it soon," she said. It was the first time she had admitted it to anyone. It was the first time she had said it aloud.

"Do you want a glass of wine? It's on the house," said Eddie.

"No thanks, orange juice please."

He poured the juice into a glass and placed it in front of her. "Kirsti, grief is not an illness. You cannot get over it. You will feel your brother's loss for a long time, but you will learn to live with it."

At last, someone who isn't afraid to talk about it. "Will I?"

"Yes, you will. In the meantime, be kind to yourself."

An older couple came through the door and Eddie excused himself. Kirsti watched as he seated them at a table by the window and gave them their menus. She sipped her juice and turned to look in the opposite direction. A small waterfall caught her attention.

"Do you like it?" asked Eddie, pouring drinks for his patrons.

"Yes, I do," replied Kirsti. "It's pretty."

"Unfortunately, some people say it messes with their waterworks," said Eddie with a wink. He placed the drinks on a tray and took them to the couple.

At that moment, the door opened again and a young family walked in; followed by Joanne. The family stood in the doorway waiting for Eddie to seat them. Joanne claimed the stool beside Kirsti.

"Hello. How are you feeling? It feels like I haven't seen you in the longest time," said Joanne.

"I'm fine."

Joanne pulled a face. "I realise that is the stock standard reply, but I really want to know how you are. The uncensored version."

"I really am fine, Joanne. A little messed up at times and I certainly want to cry a lot, but I'm fine. I'm coping."

Joanne stared at Kirsti for a moment. Was she trying to decide whether or not to believe her? "Okay. I suppose I'll have to accept that for now."

"Hi Eddie," said Skye as she pushed her way through the door and into the restaurant. "Where's that gorgeous son of yours?"

Skye made her way towards the bar. A moment later the door opened again and Melody raced in.

"Hi ladies," said Skye.

"I thought you were after the pizza guy," asked Joanne.

"No way," said Skye, allowing herself to look shocked. "Besides, one of my housemates is out with him right now. I hope she chokes on pizza."

Kirsti felt a rush of sadness wash over her. It was the simplest things that reminded her. She looked down at her juice and tried to recompose herself. It is just a word. It means nothing.

"Skye!" said Joanne, hitting her friend on the arm.

"What?" Skye looked from Joanne to Kirsti, and then shrugged. "Maybe we shouldn't talk anymore."

"Don't be stupid," said Kirsti. "Say what you would normally say, I will..." What? She will what? She didn't know what to say. "I miss Owen."

"I know you do," said Joanne.

Skye looked at Melody and the two girls moved closer to Kirsti. "We are your closest friends..." said Skye.

Please don't say what I think you're going to say. I don't need to hear that again.

"...and it's our job to get your mind off your problems."

Kirsti sighed.

"I don't think that's..." started Joanne.

"Don't be silly," interrupted Melody, looking at herself in the mirror and fixing her hair. "Of course it is. Starting right now. Is that a vodka and orange you're drinking, Kirsti?"

Kirsti shook her head. "I hate vodka. It depresses me. You know that. This is an orange juice."

"What?" gasped Skye. "We can't have that. Where's Eddie?" She looked around and found him standing at the other end of the bar. "Eddie, we would like to be seated now and please bring us a good bottle of plonk."

Skye and Melody bent over with laughter. Kirsti and Joanne stared at them in disbelief.

That's right. Brush it all under the carpet. I don't need your support. I can work this out on my own.

Dinner went reasonably well. Kirsti managed to find a new level of pretence that even she could believe. The four of them sat and talked for almost two hours. They even laughed, including Kirsti, on several occasions, although Kirsti felt dirty for doing so.

After dinner, with three of the four girls warm in their bellies from too much wine, they left the restaurant and walked to the cinema. Kirsti willingly handed over her portion of the money for a ticket, but she had no idea what they would be seeing. And she didn't care.

When they found a secluded spot away from the other people, they sat and Kirsti became engrossed in the screen. She discovered then that she was able to experience moments of relief from the pain. Whilst watching the movie, she was able to leave the world behind and become absorbed by the story.

She was unaware of everything around her. A feeling of total peace washed over her. Then, without warning, the final action scene started and within minutes the main character was being ushered up a set of rickety wooden stairs. A man blindfolded him, and it was at that moment that Kirsti went cold. Blindfolded, the man was pushed forward and a noose was placed around his neck.

Kirsti felt someone grab her arm. "Don't look, Kirsti. Come with me. We can leave now. Please, Kirsti."

But Kirsti sat rigid in her chair, her gaze glued to the scene in front of her. The noose was held in place, a person off screen said something and then the floor beneath the man's feet dropped away and the noose pulled tight making a terrible, loud cracking sound.

Kirsti rose to her feet, screaming. "My god, no. Owen!"

The hanging man jolted several times and then was still. "Owen!"

Joanne pushed Kirsti along the aisle and out of the theatre. Kirsti looked back at Skye and Melody and saw the shock on their faces. Once in the foyer, Joanne led Kirsti to a seat and they sat. Kirsti's body shook violently.

"Bloody stupid, that's what they are," said Joanne at her side. "They should have realised..."

Kirsti looked at her. "Joanne, I thought it was Owen." Tears welled in her eyes and spilled down her cheeks. "Why didn't he come to me? Why didn't he tell me he needed help? I would have helped him."

"I know," said Joanne. Tears spilled down her own cheeks. "I would have helped him too if I'd been given the chance."

Kirsti looked at Joanne. What did the other girl mean by that? She didn't have time to ask, for a second later Skye and Melody stood in front on them.

"Kirsti, I'm so sorry," said Skye. "I didn't know that ... I would never take you to see a movie with something like that in it. I didn't know."

"It doesn't matter. It gave me a scare. I admit that, but I'm over it now."

"You don't look over it," said Melody. "Perhaps one of us should drive you home."

"No," said Kirsti. "I'm all right. I haven't been drinking and I'm fine to drive home myself." She rose from the seat. "In fact, I think I'll head off right now. I'll see you tomorrow."

II

Josh reclined in his chair and put his feet up on the table. The meeting with the Japanese investor had gone better than he expected. He felt extremely proud of his efforts. Mr Shimizu seemed impressed too and that's what really counted.

Josh swung his feet off the table and left the small office. The gym was quiet today, but he wouldn't allow his own gym to be like this. There would be classes day and night to get the fanatics through the door. And then there would be the normal gym-crazy people who liked to work out until their muscles popped.

Mr Shimizu hadn't been so sure about the swimming pool and needed extra proof that an indoor pool would improve business tenfold. The fact that his gym would be the only one with a pool wasn't enough. Josh had to work on a presentation. That wasn't the problem.

The problem was that the Japanese valued family and Mr Shimizu had asked Josh about his family. Without thinking he had told the man about Kirsti and how they had known each other for years. When he said all these things, Josh didn't think much of it. He had built Kirsti up, but then Mr Shimizu had invited them both to a fundraiser dinner he was hosting at the end of the following week.

Of course, Josh had agreed without hesitation, but now he groaned. Would Kirsti be better by then? It had been three weeks so the worst was surely over by now. He grinned. He would phone Kirsti tonight and arrange to see her. It was about time that he broke the ice, it had to be done sometime. And it would never do to see her and then drop the news about the fundraiser in her lap. No, that would not do at all.

Saturday, 10th June

Joanne sat at home pondering what had happened the evening before. It had broken her heart to see Kirsti react as she did to the scenes on the big screen. And it had disgusted her the way Skye and Melody had treated Kirsti afterwards.

She considered talking to her mother about it but decided against it. Her mum would tell her what she already knew. She had to support Kirsti and the best way to do that was to offer a shoulder and an ear.

Yet Joanne had her own grief and the secret she carried stopped her from approaching Kirsti. The fact that her secret was never voiced before Owen's death made it impossible for her to say anything about it. And now the secret had built a barrier between them.

Don't mention it then.

Joanne threw herself onto the bed with a big sigh. "If only it were that easy," she said aloud. It feels wrong, dishonest, to keep the information to myself and then ask Kirsti to open up to me.

"What am I going to do?"

Tim spent the rest of the week doing what the guys did, which mainly consisted of hanging out at Atchison Street between lectures. He spent a couple of nights there, drunk and sleeping on the hard floor, but on other nights he retreated to the solitude of his own room. He always waited until most of his mates wouldn't even notice his disappearance and then snuck out the back door. Once he went home and then came back really early in the morning and lay on the carpet pretending he'd been there all night.

If anyone noticed, nothing was said. The same if they noticed a change in his personality, which he desperately tried to cover up, no one said a thing.

When they laughed, he laughed. When they drank, he drank. When they slept, he pretended to sleep. And he took it one step further when they were acting stupid, he over-compensated and acted worse. He liked the fact that they laughed—a lot—when he acted the fool, so he did it even more. It made him feel part of the group, which up until recently, he had never had to try to belong to.

On Saturday morning, he rose from the floor and stretched. He had slept for about three hours, which was better than other nights, so he figured he was doing well. Most of his mates were still asleep, some were snoring.

Tim walked along the hallway and pushed open the bathroom door. The front door stood wide open and he heard voices. He stopped for a moment and listened. He couldn't make out the words, but he knew one of the voices was female and that sparked his interest. Had one of the guys brought a girl to Atchison Street? Lucky bastard!

Letting the bathroom door swing shut again, Tim moved along the hall to the front door. The murmur grew louder, but he still couldn't make out the words. When he realised he couldn't get any closer without being seen, he turned and walked into the bedroom. Four sleeping bodies occupied the room. He stepped over them and made his way quickly to the window.

His mouth fell open.

Karl was sitting on the low brick wall, which was the front fence, talking to Kate. She wore shorts and a t-shirt, and joggers. It looked like she had been running before coming across Karl. Both their heads were bowed and he could see they talked easily together.

Kate looked at the house and Tim sank to his knees. In his mind, he knew she couldn't see him, but guilt swelled up from the pit of his stomach and consumed him. He felt like a voyeur staring silently through a window at something he shouldn't be seeing.

Kate's laughter filtered through the door. Tim rose and gingerly looked through the curtained window again. Karl was standing beside Kate now. They were still talking and they both smiled. Then, Kate threw her arms around Karl's neck, kissed his cheek and turned away. Tim felt a pang of envy.

Karl watched her run along the road, out of view of Tim. Then he sat on the wall again and lit a cigarette.

Tim made his way back to the hallway, went into the bathroom and locked the door behind him. So the blond had a boyfriend already. He should have known.

II

Jenny awoke with a start. She had dreamt about Owen. She had watched his movements on the night of his death and she saw him do it ... take his own life! In the dream her scream had been ear-piercingly loud, it was enough to wake her, but in reality, her throat only made a low, grunting noise. Her throat was quite sore and she was covered in sweat. It rolled off her.

She didn't try to leave the bed. She laid still, the images fresh in her mind. Had she been shown her son's last hours or had her mind merely provided something she so badly needed to know. She had never, not for a single minute, believed a decent human being would ever want to know the grizzly details of a loved one's death, but now she knew differently. Now she understood why people insisted on seeing their deceased relative, no matter what kind of condition the body was in. The brain couldn't accept death until it had seen the proof. And then it wouldn't accept the death until it had all the missing pieces of the puzzle.

The problem being that some puzzle pieces would never be found.

She sat up and throwing the covers back, she swung her feet to the floor.

"Are you all right, Jen?"

She felt Stephen's hand on her back.

"It was a bad dream. I'm fine." She rose to her feet. "Remember, we have an appointment at 9.30 this morning."

"What time is it?"

"Six o'clock," she replied. "Go back to sleep. I'll wake you up at eight with a cup of tea."

"That will be lovely."

Jenny pulled on her robe and went down to the kitchen. She hadn't slept well for several reasons. Firstly, Kirsti had gone out and, although she didn't get home late, Jenny couldn't help but worry about her. Secondly, she had been told by another student at the university that Tim hadn't been spending much time in his room. On the one hand, this could be ideal as Tim was obviously occupied. On the other hand, Jenny hadn't spoken to him since she had asked *the* question and wasn't sure if he was angry with her ... and avoiding her because of that anger. Lastly, today was going to be a big day, because she and Stephen would be picking up Owen's ashes and bringing them home. She already had butterflies in her stomach because of it.

She went about making a cup of tea purely on autopilot. She then went out the back and sat quietly at the outdoor setting on the small back veranda. She stared at the back garden for several minutes. The air about her was freezing, but Jenny welcomed the coldness biting into her skin.

Then, she put down the mug and picked up a pen. She opened her diary and wrote:

> I'm sitting here waiting. Waiting to walk out the front door in order to go and pick up my son's ashes. I never believed for a second, at any time in my life, that I would have to do such a terrible thing.
>
> The emotions within me are confused. I'm scared, I'm sad, I'm calm. Reality will probably hit me once I pick up the car keys and switch on the engine. For now, the only thing going through my tortured mind is that I'm going to bring my son home. Where he belongs.

A tear dripped onto the page. Jenny stared at it and then placed the diary and the pen on the table and allowed her gaze to wander back to the garden.

III

Kirsti sat on Owen's bed in a daze. She hadn't slept at all. Every time she closed her eyes, she saw the man in the movie swinging in the noose. After a while, the man became Owen and she became too scared to shut her eyes.

She heard her mum leave her room and go downstairs. Kirsti had become agitated then because she thought her mother might look in Owen's room and Kirsti didn't want to be seen like this.

She tip-toed to the door and listened to the sounds below. Knowing her mum was in the kitchen, Kirsti quickly returned to her own room. She sat on the bed. Her body felt weary, she could easily sleep for a short time. But no, she wouldn't allow it. She didn't want the nightmares or the images. She quickly got up from her bed and went to sit next to the window.

It was early, the neighbourhood slept. There was nothing to watch and she didn't feel like listening to music. She sat quietly.

At first, she didn't notice anything unusual. She wasn't sure what grabbed her attention, but she looked away from the window directly at the mirror over her dressing table.

Green grass and blue sky.

Kirsti gasped. She rose from where she was sitting and walked across the room. The image remained in the mirror. She pulled out the little padded chair with the iron back and fluffy pink cushion and sat.

She stared into the mirror.

This time there was a flowing river running through the grass. It wasn't wide. Kirsti imagined herself jumping across from one side to the other quite easily, so she reasoned it wasn't really a river. A creek perhaps. Or a stream. The water flowed slowly. There were no rocks or fish or tadpoles to be seen. There was nothing except the water, the grass and the sky. It looked so peaceful. So perfect.

A puffy white cloud rolled into view on the right. Kirsti watched it move slowly across the mirror. When it disappeared on the left-hand side of the scene, the image shimmered for a couple of seconds and vanished.

Kirsti cried.

IV

In the car, Jenny felt sick in the stomach and Stephen complained about a backache. They both touched their temples, trying to rub the tension into oblivion. And they both knew it was all from stress. No words passed between them once they left the area beyond their own street. What was there to say? Jenny knew how Stephen felt, and she knew he understood how she felt.

When they neared the memorial park, the pains in Jenny's stomach tripled. She felt physically sick. A feeling of dread came over her when Stephen parked the car and they climbed out and began walking towards the building.

Inside the small office, Stephen seemed calm, while Jenny shook with the emotions running through her body. The paperwork only took a few minutes, and then the woman said, "I'll go and get him."

Tears sprang to Jenny's eyes and she prayed the woman would return with a living Owen in tow. It didn't happen, of course. Instead, she re-entered the room with a white bag. Inside the bag was a motley-grey plastic container.

Jenny gulped.

Upon seeing the container, Jenny's resolve left her. She found it difficult to see the remaining form, let alone read aloud the number that identified the container as her son. It was a cold act that no parent should have to face. Once it was confirmed that they had the correct container, the woman placed the bag within Stephen's arms. None of them spoke a single word. Jenny and Stephen left the office.

As soon as they stepped out of the building the flood gates opened. They broke down. They stood on the steps of the crematorium and sobbed their hearts out. They didn't care who saw them or what was thought of them. Their thoughts went no further than the bag with the grey container inside. It would be a long time before either of them would be able to talk, let alone drive home. They managed to get to the car, Jenny sat in the passenger's seat and Stephen placed their son on her lap. The plaque from his coffin—Owen Stephen Fowler, Aged 20 years—shone up at her, blurred by the tears that wouldn't stop flowing.

They sat in the car for the longest time—silent and crying. Stephen, the man who had bravely carried Jenny through the last three weeks, finally broke. Everything came crashing down, and he lost all control. It broke Jenny's heart to see him like that, as much as it broke her heart to be holding her baby in a tiny, grey box.

Jenny didn't know how long they sat there. She did know they never spoke a word. They drove home and went into a cold, empty house and she felt that's how her heart had grown.

Home again. Owen was home again, but not in the way she wanted and needed.

For a while, she stood in the kitchen hugging the container close to her heart. Heartbroken. Stephen grabbed her shoulders and guided her to Owen's bedroom. They placed him on his bed, surrounded by the things that he hadn't thrown away.

Later, she sat with her diary, but no words could truly describe the anguish she felt, the anguish they both felt, so she put the diary away without writing a word. The pain was as raw and open as it could be. They cried on and off all day before the tears finally subsided and gave way to exhaustion. The emptiness that Jenny felt for three weeks had finally claimed its hold on Stephen. He told her that it felt like he was carrying a baby and that nothing on Earth could have separated him and Owen during that short trip to the car. He would have killed anyone who dared to try.

Jenny felt as if she could kill someone, anyone ... for no reason at all, other than she had lost her son to suicide and she hated the world because of it.

V

Kirsti watched her parents get into the car. They looked paler than usual and she noticed they didn't speak to each other like they normally would. Had they had an argument? That would be unusual too.

When they drove out of view, she rose from where she was sitting and left her room. Her stomach growled its annoyance at not receiving any nourishment as yet, but when she spooned the cereal into her mouth, it tasted foul and made her gag. After a few mouthfuls, she dumped the rest into the garbage and rinsed her bowl. She took a swig of juice from the carton and then went back upstairs to have a shower.

Before she managed to get into the bathroom, the phone rang.

"Hello."

"Kirsti? Is that you?" said a male voice she recognised instantly as Josh.

"Yes. How are you, Josh?"

"Good. Excellent, actually." He sounded excited.

Kirsti wondered why he had phoned.

"Look, Babe," said Josh. "We haven't seen much of each other since all this nastiness took place. How about I come and pick you up and we go horse riding?"

Horse riding? They hadn't done that in a long while, a couple of years. It used to be such fun. Maybe Josh had realised how he had practically dumped her after Owen's death and was ready to deal with it. If he was making an effort, she would too.

"Sure." She tried to sound positive. "That would be great."

It wasn't a complete fib; it would be great if she felt in the mood, if she felt normal.

"Great," replied Josh. "I'll pick you up in..." there was a pause, "...say ... half an hour. Is that all right?"

"Yes," said Kirsti. "That's plenty of time."

She was sitting on the front step when his car pulled up. He saw her but beeped the horn anyway. That annoyed Kirsti. It never had before, but things were different now and little things irritated her.

She opened the passenger side door and bent to get into the car. "Hi."

She felt his hand touch her hair. She jumped when she turned to find his face right up close to hers.

"How about a kiss?" he asked and puckered his lips.

Kirsti felt self-conscious and uncomfortable. She didn't know why. He was her boyfriend. They had kissed ... passionately ... many times. Hell, they had gone a lot further than just kissing too. But, right then, she felt like she didn't even know Josh and this was a first date.

She felt the colour touch her cheeks and quickly pecked him on the lips and turned away to fumble with her seat belt.

Josh laughed and the car moved away from the curb.

The riding school was a ten-minute drive away. Josh drove up the long, winding drive and parked under a huge tree. "I wonder if they still have that gelding I used to ride. The white one, with the lazy eye. What was its name?"

"Star," said Kirsti, getting out of the car.

Josh shook his head. "That's right, it always amused me because there wasn't a star to be found on that horse. It was a stupid name."

"For a stupid horse," said Kirsti. She looked at Josh. "Well, it was stupid."

"Yeah, yeah," he said with a laugh. "I know. But I liked riding him."

They walked towards the office as Mr Thompson came out and saw them. "Howdy, you two. How are things?"

"Great," said Josh before Kirsti had time to think about how she'd respond to the question. "We'd like two horses for the morning. Do you still have Star?"

"Yeah, he's still around, but we use him for the littlies these days," replied Mr Thompson. "I think you'll find him a bit docile."

Kirsti watched Josh's reaction. For a minute she thought he was going to ask to ride Star anyway, but Josh eventually shrugged.

"Oh, well, I'll have another one instead then," he said.

Mr Thompson smiled. "Okay, come on then. I'll take you to your beasts."

Skye let the phone ring for the longest time. Obviously, no one was home at the Fowler's. She replaced the receiver and shook her head.

Everything kept going wrong. She was trying to be supportive, but it wasn't working. Watching Kirsti drive away last night, in the dark with those large eyes, was more than Skye could stand. She had let her friend down ... again!

What was she doing wrong? Kirsti had clearly stated that she wanted them to be themselves, but Skye felt awkward around Kirsti now. It was something she had never felt before and it felt quite foreign. In her heart, she knew Kirsti was suffering a loss that she could never understand, but when she was around Kirsti her mind went to pieces and stopped working rationally.

Melody agreed with everything Skye said, and Skye didn't find that helpful. Joanne thought too much but didn't say anything and that annoyed Skye. It felt as if their safe little circle was falling apart. And to top it all off, Josh was useless as tits on a bull as Melody often declared.

Skye considered phoning her own mother for advice but quickly forgot that idea. She and her mother didn't get on. Never had really. They were too much alike. They would be fighting before Skye explained the situation and that would upset her more. *No,* she thought, *I have to try to be myself and stop acting like an idiot when Kirsti's around.* Skye picked up her mobile. *I've never felt out of my depth like this before.*

Skye expertly typed a text message to send to Kirsti, and then read it over several times before sending it.

> Soz, K. Can we meet for a drink l8r?
> Just u + me? Edgar's at 8. OK?

Once the phone verified sending the message, Skye dropped the phone into her lap and picked up the remote. She pressed the volume up button several times. The crazy voices of the morning cartoons echoing off her walls were much better than listening to her roommate and the pizza guy go for it in the next room.

So much for rule number one.

Kirsti read the message without emotion. It seemed every-one was trying to make an extra effort this morning. But in a lot of ways, for Kirsti, it was too little, too late.

She needed understanding a week ago. She needed someone to sit with her and listen to everything she want-ed to say, without comment or judgement. Now, she didn't care. Now, she had withdrawn from everyone and she felt terribly alone.

"Babe, come on," called Josh from up ahead.

His bay gelding pranced about uncontrollably. He never was much of a rider, although he thought himself to be brilliant.

"I got a message from Skye," said Kirsti, digging her heels into her mare to catch up. "She wants me to meet her later."

"Good." Josh checked his watch. "You need to get out more. I was going to suggest we go out for dinner, but lunch tomorrow would probably be better anyway."

She had never noticed how he assumed she was free. There was a lot about Josh she hadn't seen before. Maybe Skye and her mum were right about him after all.

"I'll come over to your place then at midday," she said.

Josh shrugged. "I'll race you to that tree and back." He leaned forward and forced the gelding into a gallop.

Kirsti groaned and followed suit. "If you beat me, it's your shout tomorrow."

After the ride, Josh took her to a milkbar for a salad sandwich and a cold drink. They sat in the gutter eating and talking easily about nothing—as they used to after school. Kirsti felt more relaxed than she had for a while. And she ate the entire sandwich, which pleased her too.

"Oh, that's right, how did that other meeting go the other day?" she asked once they finished eating.

Josh leaned back on his hands, his long legs stretched out in front of him. "Not bad. Excellent, in fact."

"That's really good." She sipped her drink. "Does that mean you've got an investor?"

"Not entirely," replied Josh. "The guy wants me to provide some more information."

"Oh, that's not a problem is it?"

Josh shook his head. "Nah, it's in the bag. But he wants us to go to some function he's holding in town next Friday night. I know it's short notice, but you can make it, can't you?"

Kirsti felt that stir of irritation again. "Yes, I suppose so."

"That's a girl," he said. "I want you to wear that black dress with the fancy bodice. You look great in that."

She knew it was meant to be a compliment, but it sounded more like an order to her. "I suppose I can. I hope it's a formal function if I'm going to wear a dress like that."

"Of course it is," said Josh. "We have to make a really good impression. Don't wear too much makeup. I don't want you looking whorish."

Kirsti turned to look at him. She couldn't believe he said that. But she couldn't be bothered arguing with him over it, so she let it drop.

They sat in silence for a few minutes before he got to his feet and offered her a hand. "Come on, Babe, I've got some stuff to do before the evening session at the gym. I better take you home."

Her parents would probably be home by now. She didn't want to explain to them why he didn't come inside and offer them his condolences, which she already knew he wouldn't do, so she said the first thing that came into her mind. "No, you go. I feel like walking home. It's not far and I could do with the fresh air."

He leaned over and kissed her. "Thanks, Babe."

Kirsti stood and stepped back from the kerb. She watched Josh get into the car and flash her a smile. Then the engine roared and he was gone.

Sometime later, Kirsti opened the front door of the house and felt the grief instantly grab hold of her. She remembered the way her parents were acting when they left earlier that day and found herself worrying about them. They hadn't had an argument, something else had happened.

She found her father sitting in the sun in the back garden. He had car parts spread out around him, but he wasn't looking at them. His focus was elsewhere.

"Dad, what's happened? Where's Mum?" Kirsti sat cross-legged on the grass opposite him, the car parts separating them.

He wouldn't look at her. She could see that he had trouble forcing words out of his mouth. Kirsti's heart sank and she stared at her dad expectantly.

"We ... we had," he paused and drew in a deep breath. Then his eyes were on her and Kirsti saw something she had never seen before in her father. Defeat. Agony.

"Dad?"

"Your mother and I had to collect Owen's..." he gulped and his gaze dropped to the ground in front of him. His fingers pulled at the short grass as he struggled to keep himself calm. Kirsti knew he was thinking of her. "Owen's ashes," he finished.

"Oh." Kirsti knew her dad didn't expect anything from her. She stared at the car parts and wondered why he had them out. She looked at the garage and wondered if he had been in there. He must have been in order to get the parts. Then she looked at the box sitting close to her dad's leg, one of his hands rested lightly on top of it. Owen's toolbox.

She stared at the toolbox. It was like it was something she had never seen before, but of course, she had. Compared to her father's, Owen's toolbox was small. But it held his own tools. He had always used his dad's tools, but these few were his own. Kirsti watched as her dad caressed the box with his fingertips and felt as if she were intruding.

"Where's Mum?"

"In bed," said her dad. "It wasn't a pleasant experience, Kirsti. I've never felt this terrible in my life."

Kirst stared at her father. She had wanted them to break down so that she could, but now that she watched her dad sitting slumped over, looking so defeated, she wished it hadn't happened. Now, she knew she had to stay strong for them.

"Should I check on her? Make her a cup of tea perhaps?" asked Kirsti. "Do you want one too, Dad?"

Her dad shook his head. "No. No, I don't want anything except..." He shrugged. Tears spilled down his face. "Give your mum some space right now, sweetie. She's really upset and, hopefully, she's asleep. She needs to sleep."

Kirsti got to her feet, but she couldn't leave yet, there was another question she needed to ask. "Dad?"

"Yes, sweetie."

"Where are the ashes?"

Their gaze met. Kirsti saw the warning in his eyes. *Don't do it to yourself,* they said. "On his bed."

They continued to stare at each other. This was the moment to say what she wanted to say, to share her feelings and fears ... and her secret, but she couldn't do it to him. She couldn't add to his pain. She didn't want to crush him further. Instead, she reached out and touched his shoulder and then turned and walked away.

Inside, she stood in the dining room for a while trying to decide what to do. Should she heed the warning in her father's eyes or should she head straight for Owen's bedroom? She wanted to see Owen so badly. She needed to be close to her twin. She ached for the peace that closeness had always brought her in the past.

Kirsti hesitated for only a second longer before walking through the lounge room, into the hallway, up the stairs and straight to Owen's door. She stood on the outside of the door, her hand on the handle, but she didn't open the door straight away. Her mind reached out to the room at the other end of the landing, her parent's room, but she heard no sound from there. Maybe her mum was asleep after all. Kirsti hoped she was.

Kirsti pushed the door open and stepped inside.

VI

Jenny knew it was a dream. She knew she was really lying in her bed, in her bedroom. But everything around her was so clear, so vivid, so real. It was exactly as it had been on that day. She smoothed the plain dress she was wearing with one hand and knew instantly which earrings she had on and what bag was clutched tightly in her other hand.

She knew that if she turned around, she would find Stephen in his best suit. He had always looked so handsome in that suit. Kirsti would be wearing a plain black pencil skirt with the lilac blouse she insisted made her look "grown-up". Tim would be looking uncomfortable in a pair of brown trousers and a white, short-sleeved shirt. She didn't turn around, of course, because she hadn't done so on that day and couldn't now.

The family were dressed as if they were attending a wedding, but they were actually waiting for something else. Something more important.

Jenny's gaze remained on the door in front of her. She smoothed her dress again. Her heart raced in her chest when the door opened and a middle-aged woman came out. The woman was only a few years older than her. She didn't smile. This wasn't the right time or place.

"My name is Patricia, Mrs Fowler," said the woman. "We spoke on the phone."

The women exchanged a look of mother to mother understanding, but Jenny remained silent, unable to talk, scared she'd lose her composure.

"Everything is ready," said Patricia. She looked over Jenny's shoulder at the rest of her family standing a few steps behind her. "Would you like to come in on your own first, or are you all coming in together?"

Jenny remained silent, her gaze on the door ajar just five steps away.

"Together," said Stephen. "We'll all..."

Jenny heard Stephen's voice break.

Patricia nodded and stepped to one side, pushing the door further open as she did so. "I have to warn you that he is cold. Please don't be shocked by that."

Jenny paused for a moment. She swallowed. She blinked a few times, willing herself to remain calm. And then she took the five steps that took her through the door and into the room.

Kirsti didn't look around the room as she entered. She kept her eyes averted and quickly turned to close the door quietly behind her. She stood facing the door for several minutes, waiting for her heartbeat to slow, her hand on the handle in case she found she had to make a quick escape.

Knowing calmness would not find her today, Kirsti turned slowly and let her gaze take in everything as if it were the first time she had set foot in the room.

Immediately beside the door stood an empty chest of drawers, with a CD player and extra large speakers on top. On the wall was an imitation musket that had belonged to his grandfather, which Owen had asked for when he heard it no longer had a place in his grandparent's home. Two low tables, which were really bedside tables, took up the space between the drawers and the corner of the room. On one was a pile of CDs, PlayStation games and DVDs. On the shelf underneath was the PlayStation console. On the other table sat the portable TV Owen had bought with money he had saved when he was eight. On the shelf below the TV was the DVD player, a few more DVDs and a couple of remote controls. On the wall above all this was a framed photo of his car. He loved his car.

Against the next wall, beneath the large window, stood a writing desk. Owen no longer used it for studying, but he hated discarding anything he'd owned all his life, so he insisted on leaving it where it was. Next to the desk was his bedside table. On this stood a lamp, a clock radio, a mug with some pens inside and an old money box from his younger days.

Kirsti quickly ignored the bed pressed up in the corner and spanning over half the length of the third wall. She turned her attention to the fourth wall. Old clippings from magazines of the actors and singers he once admired still stuck to the wall. A large wardrobe, with mirrored doors, obscured most of them, but Kirsti knew whose faces she would find if she moved the wardrobe away—Arnold Schwarzenegger, Jennifer Love-Hewitt and Johnny Depp were the favourites. In the corner stood a pile of boxes of all sizes and shapes, mostly empty as she had checked several times since Owen's death. He liked boxes and refused to throw them out. A line of shoes was neatly placed against the wall between the boxes and his bed.

Now it was time to look at what she had been avoiding since entering the bedroom. The bed. Neat and tidy. Certainly not Owen's doing. Kirsti noticed his pillow, and then the grey, rectangular box with a silver plaque on top. A single red rose lay beneath it.

Kirsti's throat restricted. She moved slowly towards the bed and read the inscription on the plaque. She swallowed and stared at the container, at the bed. She could almost see Owen lying there, but it wasn't the Owen she loved, it was the Owen she grieved. It was the Owen she had seen lying peacefully in the coffin the day before the funeral. She took a step backwards. She didn't want to remember that day. It was filled with bad memories.

She dropped to her knees and leaned her elbows on the bed. She couldn't sit there, not anymore, because it was Owen's bed. She knew that she wouldn't sleep in his bed again. It wouldn't be right. Not with Owen's ashes right there beside her.

Owen had reclaimed his room.

She closed her eyes and felt tears roll down her cheeks. Kneeling as if she were praying, she stayed in that position for a long time. Snippets of memories ran through her mind. Then she opened her eyes and reached out to touch the container.

"Owen?" she said, her voice a tiny whisper. "You should have come to me. I could have helped you. We could have found a solution to your problems. I know we could have."

She removed her hand from the container and her gaze blurred as she searched inside herself. "You should have left a note. Didn't you think we'd want to know why you did this? Didn't it occur to you that not knowing would torment us even more? It doesn't feel right that you'd not think of us at all. I know you were probably thinking of your own troubles, but it wasn't like you to dismiss other people's feelings." She looked around the room quickly. "I've looked everywhere, even in places I know you wouldn't have put it, but I can't find it. Why would you hide it? That doesn't make sense. Just like not leaving a note doesn't make sense."

Her face dropped onto her arms. "I wish I could help you. I wish I knew where you've gone. You can't be in Hell, surely not. You were the most selfless person I know. I need to know you're all right, Owen."

She sat quietly, bent over the side of the bed, for a long time. "I love you and I miss you so much."

The open casket lay on a silver trolley at the far end of the small room. Immediately beside Jenny were two long lounges set up in an L shape, with a large wooden coffee table in front of them. A vase of flowers sat in the middle of the coffee table. Two more stood on tall tables behind the casket.

Jenny took in everything in one sweeping glance. She knew why she looked away from the casket. She was prolonging the inevitable. The longer it took her to see who was inside, the longer she could pretend that it was not Owen. But then the thought struck her that it might not be Owen and if that were true, she didn't have to be suffering so badly. All she had to do was look.

She took a few more steps and then she felt Stephen take hold of her arm. He was holding her up, she realised. He walked with her the rest of the way. She heard the crying, the sobbing, the strangled screams, but she didn't know, then, that they had been hers. Now, the dreaming Jenny knew. She saw. She felt.

It was the spiked hair that broke her. She hadn't seen the face, but she knew her baby's hair. Wouldn't any mother know their child's hair? Then she saw his sweet face and all hope was gone.

Owen lay in the casket. His face was a strange colour, but Jenny could almost pretend he was asleep. His lips were slightly apart. It looked like he was nervously biting his bottom lip. His hands, one on top of the over, rested on the lower half of his stomach. The collar of his shirt had been pulled up to hide the evidence of the hanging.

"Why, Owen?" she cried. "Why did you do this to yourself?"

Stephen held her up. She wanted to fall into a ball and remain there forever, but Stephen's strong arm held her steady. She was vaguely aware of the sobbing of her living children beside them. But she could do nothing about that now. This moment in time was for Owen. Only for Owen.

Jenny reached out with her left hand and touched Owen's hand. The shock of the coldness froze her to the spot. She gasped and, even though tears were already rolling down her made-up face, the frozen touch burst the barriers.

Suddenly, the dreaming Jenny was looking down on herself and her family. It was like watching a movie and finding yourself to be the main actor.

She saw herself fall apart. She saw her family crumble. She saw them detach from each other and could see the rift open up and swallow them. The dreaming Jenny knew her family was in trouble, but there was nothing she could do, so she continued to watch the events that she could not remember during waking hours.

Her bag falling to the floor, Jenny collapsed over the casket. "Oh, Owen," she sobbed. "I need to know why. Please tell me why."

Stephen, tears wetting his face, grabbed at Jenny's shoulders and tried to pull her off the casket. "Jenny!"

Kirsti screamed. "Oh, Mum, please don't. Stop it. Make her stop, Dad. I can't stand it."

Tim refused to look at the casket or the scene before him.

The dreaming Jenny had no choice.

Jenny threw her head up and looked up at the ceiling. The look of pain on her face scared Dreaming Jenny. "Please, God. Take me instead. Put me in the coffin and give my son back his life." She kissed her son's cold face. Her fingers stroked his hair.

"I can't believe this is happening," said Kirsti, backing away from the coffin.

Dreaming Jenny knew her daughter meant the death, not the scene before her.

Patricia appeared. "Mrs Fowler," she said. One touch

from the woman and Jenny stepped away from the coffin.

Stephen grabbed her again and walked her over to the lounges. A tray with glasses of water rested on the coffee table.

"Let her sit for a while," said Patricia. "She'll settle down in a moment or two. It's a big shock seeing a child like this."

Patricia returned to the casket and guided Kirsti and Tim back to the lounges. "Sit and have a drink. I'll be back in a few minutes."

Dreaming Jenny watched herself and her family struggling with their grief. But Patricia was right. The shock was passing, the water helped calm their nerves. They were beginning to look more human again. If only slightly.

The few minutes passed, but Patricia didn't return.

Finally, Tim left his seat and walked back to the casket. "I'm sorry, Bro." Dreaming Jenny saw him whisper something else and wondered what it was.

Tim went to stand in front of his parents. "I'm going outside. I need a cigarette."

"I thought you gave up," said Stephen.

"I did, but I'm about to start up again," replied Tim. "I bought a packet on the drive home from uni."

Kirsti rushed out of her chair. "Wait. I want to come with you. I need some fresh air." She raced over to the coffin. She bowed her head as if she was praying and then she kissed Owen's forehead. She dabbed a tissue to her nose as she turned and returned to her older brother. She clasped his arm as they hurried out.

Jenny turned to Stephen. "I want to be alone with him."

Stephen frowned. "I don't know."

"Please."

They stared at each other. "Okay. I'll be right outside if you need me."

Jenny nodded.

Stephen squeezed her hand, and then he rose to his feet and walked over to the coffin. "Goodbye, mate. I love you and I hope you found the peace you were looking for."

As the door closed behind her husband, Jenny got to her feet and walked slowly to stand beside her son. For a moment, she stared at his face. She wanted to etch every curve into her memory. Then she placed her hand on top of his.

"I'm sorry for failing you, Owen. I'm sorry I didn't notice that something was wrong. I'm sorry I didn't fix it for you. I'm sorry you felt you couldn't come to me for help. I'm sorry for anything that I may have done which might have added to your pain."

She fell silent.

"I will always respect your decision and I will never be angry at you. I forgive you, Owen. I forgive you." And she did.

Jenny turned and walked away. She paused with her hand on the door handle, but she couldn't leave. Not yet.

She ran back to the coffin. "I'm not leaving you, my darling." She placed a hand over her heart. "You will live in here ... forever." She kissed him and left.

Dreaming Jenny reached out. She wanted another chance to touch her son. She wanted to kiss him again. She knew it was something she'd never again have the opportunity to do and would be satisfied with a stolen kiss in a dream.

The air started to shimmer around Owen. Dreaming Jenny panicked. *No, not yet. Please, let me look at him for a bit longer.*

The shimmering continued. It grew cold. The room disappeared, leaving the casket ... and Owen.

Dreaming Jenny found herself able to move. She walked closer to the casket. She looked down at her son's face. It was hazy. She couldn't quite make out his features. She reached out to touch him, one final time, and his eyes opened.

Jenny jumped back with a scream. A damp wall stopped her going any further. Where had that come from? A hand appeared over the edge of the coffin. My God! Jenny's breath came in short gasps. Owen's head appeared, then his torso. Red eyes glared at her. The hairs on her arms stood on end. She shrunk away from the advancing image of her son.

"No, it's not Owen." The words felt foreign in her mouth. "He wouldn't do this to me."

One leg left the coffin and found the floor, the other close behind. Now he stood before her and started to advance towards her.

It's a dream. Wake up! She had nowhere to run, nowhere to go. "Go away! Leave me alone. You are not Owen."

His arms were outstretched. His eyes glared. He made no sound apart from the shuffling of his decaying feet.

Jenny shrank away. She slid down the wall. She screamed.

VII

Kirsti heard a hoarse screech from her parent's bedroom. She rose from her position on the floor. As she turned to leave the room, the image in the mirror doors of the wardrobe caught her attention.

The grass spread out over the three panels of the mirror. Flowers, in a range of colours, grew throughout the tall grass and an old oak tree grew close to the water. Two parrots, red and gold, glided into view and landed in the tree. Kirsti leaned closer to the mirror. Was that a nest hidden amongst the branches? The water of the stream gently washed over rocks and continued on to an unknown destination. Butterflies and bees fluttered lazily around the flowers.

The scene was beautiful, peaceful. Kirsti felt the bottled up emotions ease away. The image was larger than life, she felt as if she could take two steps forward and step into the serenity it offered.

She took a step ... and a knock on the door made her jump. Kirsti spun around guiltily. "Who is it?"

"Dad. Can I come in?"

Kirsti looked back at the mirrors and sighed. She only saw herself. "Of course you can. I'm okay, Dad."

The door inched open. "You've been in there for a long time. I was worried."

Kirsti looked over her shoulder. The room was as it should be, except for the grey container which held the remains of her brother. "I was thinking. I'm fine, but Mum had a bad dream, I think. I heard her cry out."

It was her dad's turn to look over his shoulder. His frown deepened.

"I was about to check on her," said Kirsti.

Her dad turned and rushed into the bedroom he shared with his wife. Kirsti followed but remained in the doorway. The room was empty, but the ensuite door was closed.

"Jen, are you all right?" Her dad stood at the door. His face white.

"Yes. Why do you ask?" said her mum through the door.

"Kirsti heard you cry out," replied her dad. "She thought you might have had a nightmare."

"It was nothing."

Her dad didn't look convinced, and Kirsti didn't blame him. Her mum's voice sounded strange—tight, short.

"I'm going to have a shower to freshen up," she said a moment later.

Kirsti didn't know what to do. Everything had become so difficult lately. There was a permanent air of uncertainty. She saw her dad lean his forehead on the door frame. The familiar lump in her throat pained her again. How can one death in the family affect everyone so deeply? She would never have believed it was possible if it wasn't happening to her family right now.

He must have remembered she was there, for he straightened and turned to look at her. "I guess she's fine."

"I suppose. I'm going to watch a DVD."

He nodded and Kirsti quickly retreated to her own room.

Jenny stood under the water and let it wash over her exhausted body. Her mind pondered what had happened in the dream. Most of it had been exactly what had happened at the viewing. But the end bit ... that was something else.

Yes, it had been Owen's body, but Jenny rejected all notions that her son would do something like that. She knew, without doubt, that he wouldn't. It simply wasn't his nature. He would never harm anyone, especially his family. It was Owen's body, but it was *not* Owen.

So what was it?

It felt evil.

She turned off the water and stepped out of the shower. Drying herself, she didn't know what to think. When she had finished she used the towel to dry the mirror and she looked at her reflection. A darkness shadowed her eyes, her skin sallow and aged—she looked as terrible as she felt. How was she meant to pretend everything was all right when it was not?

Pulling her clothes on, she wrapped a clean towel around her hair and opened the bathroom door.

Stephen sat quietly on the bed waiting for her.

Their eyes met and Jenny froze. She had never witnessed such a severe look of anger from Stephen before. She felt uneasy.

In an instant, he was on his feet and in two long strides he had crossed the room and closed the bedroom door with a bang. Then he turned to her. "What's going on?"

"I don't know what you mean. What's wrong?"

He walked towards her, saying nothing. His gaze studied her, lingering on her neck and wrists.

She took a step backwards. She didn't feel threatened, but she didn't feel entirely safe either. It was a feeling she was unaccustomed to in her own home, confronted by her own husband.

Stephen stopped and looked around the room. He looked up at the ceiling fan. He rushed past her and looked in the ensuite, at the light fitting, in the bath.

Jenny felt panic overwhelm her. "What are you doing?"

He came back into the bedroom and grabbed her shoulders. "Are you thinking about harming yourself? Are you suicidal?"

The words shocked Jenny. She stared into his eyes and saw anguish and torment. Did he believe she would do such a thing after what they had been through with Owen? Guilt washed through her. She had thought the exact same thing about Tim. Now she understood his anger because she felt it herself.

"No!" Jenny pulled herself out of Stephen's grasp. "Of course not."

"What have you been doing in there all this time?"

She shook her head and sighed. "Having a shower. What's wrong with you?"

"For over an hour!"

He turned his back on her and she could see that he was trying to calm himself by taking deep breaths. When he turned around again, she noticed his face was white as a sheet.

"We've never lied to each other, Jen. Please, don't start now. I couldn't bear it," said Stephen, his tone calmer, pleading. "I'm worried about you. I'm worried about our children. I feel as if I've lost control."

Jenny sank onto the bed. The towel fell from her head and her hair dripped onto the bedding, but she didn't care. "I had a terrible dream and I guess I was trying to wash away the ... pain ... the hurt, I suppose." She paused. "I swear I wouldn't try to harm myself."

Stephen sat on the bed beside her and reached for her

hand. "I'm sorry. My mind is full of terrible things these days. You took so long that I was thinking about bashing the door down." He lifted her hand to his lips and kissed it. "The longer I sat here, the worse it got. Until in the end, I thought I'd find you ... dead."

They sat silently, neither of them knowing what to say or do. Each of them lost in their own torture. Jenny understood what her husband was trying to say. She also understood his reaction. Her mind was continually providing her with images she would rather not witness too. No wonder they felt so exhausted.

"Tell me about the dream," said Stephen, his voice soft and vulnerable.

Jenny told him. She told him everything, from beginning to end. She told him what she saw, how she felt, how pleased she was to have the chance to touch and kiss Owen's body again. And then she told him what had happened afterwards. Stephen remained silent while she spoke. It was only when she described Owens' actions that he shook his head over and over again.

"No. It wasn't him," he said when she had finished. "You know that, don't you?"

She looked at him. "Of course. He would never, ever do that. Never!"

Stephen lifted the hair away from her face and then they sat quietly holding hands for a long time.

"What's happening to our family, Jen?" asked Stephen eventually.

"I don't know."

Kirsti sat in her room listening to her parents shouting at each other. It didn't last long, but to Kirsti, it shouldn't be happening at all. The family was falling apart at the seams. Home was no longer the haven it had always been. She could no longer count on her parents, her brother—her family—to be there for her. In a lot of ways, she felt like an alien on another planet.

Two months ago life had been perfect. She had a family that her friends envied. They had been loving, caring, care-free and so easy to talk to. She had a boyfriend who gave her the space she required, to do her own things and to be her own person, but made her feel special when they were together. She had friends that she could count on, be her-self with. They had always been free to talk about anything with each other. Absolutely anything!

Now, her twin was dead and she had no idea why. Her parents were fighting and giving each other the silent treatment and she had no idea why. Her boyfriend hadn't once acknowledged Owen's death or asked her how she felt and she didn't know why. Her friends were acting weird and wouldn't allow her to talk about her grief and she did-n't know why.

Why? There were so many questions running around in her head and no answers. She felt as if she were going to explode.

It was quiet now. Her parents had stopped yelling and she hoped they were talking to each other. She wished she had someone to talk to. She felt alone for the first time in her life. It was a horrible feeling.

VIII

Edgar's was an unusual venue, but another favourite haunt of the four friends and the local youth because of it. It ca-tered for all types of evenings, right there in the one building. The entrance opened up to a grand foyer. Every time she entered the building, Kirsti was reminded of pho-tos she'd seen of the Titanic staircase. It felt magical to walk through the doors and take in the high ceilings and two massive chandeliers. The furniture looked antique, but Kirsti was uncertain of its authenticity. It didn't matter, it looked magnificent.

On the ground floor to the left of the foyer was the Blue Room, a cosy restaurant where couples dined by candle-light—although the candles were fake. Kirsti knew that for a fact. They were more like battery operated lanterns but in the mould of a candle. The food was moderately priced and delicious. It was always busy and arrival without a booking on Friday or Saturday nights would often see the patron leaving disappointed and with an empty stomach.

To the right of the foyer was a bar where people met for drinks. It was much like a pub inside, with snooker tables and dart boards. Males gathered there in droves.

There were three dance areas in the building. All were located on a different floor and all were paid entry, so people didn't usually swap and change between them too much in one night—unless they were extremely bored. The main foyer had three lifts dedicated to one floor only. Edgar claimed it kept trouble to a minimum and he was probably right.

The Pink Room was one of these rooms. A large area, filled with the warm, romantic sounds of soft ballads, it was a good place for the girls to hang out and talk with friends. There was even entertainment which consisted of older couples trying to dance to the slow tempo of the music. Occasionally there was a live show with women wearing feather head-dresses and skimpy costumes behind a solo singer imitating Bing Crosby or Frank Sinatra. That's when the old folks really let their hair down. Kirsti and her friends got a real laugh out of that. They looked so serious and silly, although the girls tried hard not to be rude about it.

The Purple Room was for the headbangers. Loud, metal type music ripped around the walls and echoed in the patron's mind. The room was enormous and nearly always dark. Large platforms of different sizes were suspended in the air and were connected by walkways. Conscious of his patron's safety, Edgar had enclosed all the platforms and walkways in sturdy mesh so no one could fall, jump or be pushed off them. Underneath all this was a huge dance floor. People danced where ever they were standing. It was usually chaotic, but it was a great place to get rid of frustration by jumping around like a crazy person. Kirsti found the headache she normally walked away with wasn't worth it. Melody loved it in there and that was the only reason Kirsti put up with it.

The Green Room was for the disco freaks. Several years prior, Edgar had announced that he intended to close the room down. The "disco era" had ended, it seemed the right thing to do, but the local teenagers told him to mix the 80's disco songs with modern dance music and it would be a hit. Edgar made a point of listening to his patrons, so that's exactly what he did, and it surpassed his dreams.

Kirsti walked into the foyer at 7.57pm and went straight up to the elevator that would take her to the Pink Room. Standing outside the pink door, she looked down at her dress feeling slightly nervous. *This isn't an interview*, she thought. *She's your friend. There's no need to be nervous.*

Taking a deep breath, Kirsti pushed the door open and went up to the counter to pay the entrance fee. A pink stamp of a flamingo, which matched the decorations in the room, was affixed to the back of her hand. It would allow her to leave and go downstairs to the restaurant if she wished, but that wasn't about to happen tonight.

Paid and stamped, Kirsti was free to enter the room. The music was soothing, the dance floor empty, as were most of the tables. Kirsti knew exactly where Skye would be sitting, if she was already here. The girls always claimed the same table, if possible. It was in the back corner, furthest from the dance floor and was the reason they got away with amusing themselves at the "oldies" expense.

Kirsti almost hoped the table would be empty and was surprised at herself when she felt a pang of disappointment when she saw Skye seated with her back to her.

"Hi," said Kirsti, as she came level with the table. "I hope you haven't been waiting long."

"Nah," replied Skye. "I've been here a couple of minutes, that's all."

Kirsti looked at the drink cradled in Skye's hand and wondered if she was telling the truth as the glass was almost empty.

Skye drained the rest of the drink. "What are you having? It's my shout."

"Scotch and dry, please," replied Kirsti. One drink wouldn't hurt.

Skye walked away and Kirsti made herself comfortable at the table. She was facing the dance floor. She'd be able to see anything interesting that might happen. Instantly, she knew the funny antics on the dance floor wouldn't amuse her tonight.

Before long, Skye had returned and was placing a drink in front of her. A quarter of her own drink was already gone.

"Are you driving tonight, Skye?"

Skye shook her head. "No, I'll catch a taxi home."

Kirsti nodded. It was already awkward between them. She had hoped it would be a while before that happened.

"I went riding with Josh today," she said, before taking a sip of her own drink.

"Did you? Is that where you were when I sent the message?"

Kirsti nodded. "It was fun. Not as good as the old days, but it was still good to be outdoors."

"Good," said Skye. "I phoned your house, but no one was home. I wondered where you'd gone."

"Mum and Dad went to collect Owen's ashes." As soon as the words left her mouth, Kirsti knew she shouldn't have mentioned it.

Skye squirmed in her seat. Colour rose to her cheeks. "Oh, that's not so good." There was a brief silence. "Did

Josh talk about the gym?"

Kirsti stirred the drink with her straw and watched the ice cubes float in circles. "Yes, it looks like he may have an investor."

"Good."

"What did you do with yourself today?" asked Kirsti, not wanting another silence between them.

"Oh, the usual Saturday stuff," replied Skye. "In other words, nothing much."

The girls used to spend Saturday at the shopping centre—shopping, having lunch, more shopping, laughing. Sometimes they would see a movie too. But that hadn't happened since Owen...

Kirsti pushed the thought away. That was then, this was now.

"Hey, did I tell you about the pizza guy?" Skye almost sounded like her usual self.

"No. What happened?"

"My flatmate got a date with him," said Skye, with a sigh. "I hate it. She so doesn't like him, but because she knew I did and because he asked her and not me, she's going out with him."

Kirsti tried to look upset for her friend, like a true friend would be.

"Last night he stayed over."

"Geez, that was quick," said Kirsti. "When was I over Monday afternoon, or was it Tuesday? It doesn't matter, here it is a couple of days later and she's already in bed with the guy. Anyway, what about the house rule?"

"Yeah, I know," said Skye. "I'm going to have to have a serious talk with her tomorrow. Besides, the noise they make when they do it. It's disgusting." Skye rolled her eyes. "They came out of her bedroom at midday today and she was all over him. I thought for a second she was going to climb on top of him right there in the kitchen. It really is revolting."

A few seconds of silence followed and then Skye added,

"He's so cute too."

Kirsti didn't agree, but her opinion didn't matter right now. "You'll find someone better."

"I better," said Skye. "I want to rub her nose in it."

"So ... do you get free pizza now?"

"No, we don't," replied Skye. "What a cheapskate! Do you want another drink?"

Kirsti looked at Skye's empty glass and then at her full one. "No, not yet."

"I'm so thirsty," said Skye and she left the table and returned to the bar.

The girls continued to talk for some time. It was never exactly comfortable, but Kirsti did feel less awkward after a while. However, she knew there was no point talking about Owen or her feelings because Skye was closed to those topics.

After she had finished her second drink, Kirsti excused herself and went to the ladies. By this time Skye was tipsy and had loosened up a fair bit. Maybe she would let Kirsti talk if she got drunk. Kirsti shook her head as she pushed the bathroom door open. It wasn't worth the risk.

Kirsti came out of the cubicle and stood in front of the mirror to wash her hands. It was a long mirror, spanning six hand basins. Kirsti looked in the mirror at the six empty cubicles behind her. She used the hand dryer and walked to the door. One hand on her handle she paused and then turned around to look in the mirror again.

The grass was there.

Her hand dropped away from the handle. She turned around and walked back to stand in the middle of the bathroom so that she could gaze at the entire mirror with ease.

The oak tree and stream were down the far end, as were the multi-coloured flowers and beautiful butterflies. To the right was a wooden cottage, surrounded by more flowers. Smoke came from the chimney. Beside the cottage was a shed or maybe a workshop. Kirsti wasn't sure which, but she did know a barn when she saw one. Inside, she could see a cow in one stall and a black horse in another. Beside one end of the barn, the end furthest from the cottage, was a pig pen and at the other end, between the cottage and the barn grew another oak tree. Hanging from the tree was a swing.

Kirsti stared at the cottage. If smoke came from the chimney, it had to mean that someone lived there. She wanted to see who. As soon as the thought entered her mind, the wooden door to the cottage swung open and a man came out.

He stood in the doorway for a second. For a moment, Kirsti thought he had looked directly at her. Her knees began to shake. She staggered backwards and leaned against the partition between two toilet cubicles and continued to stare at him. Maybe he didn't see her, because he stretched before scooping to pick up a metal bucket.

Kirsti gasped. She had had dreams where she knew the people in it, but they didn't look anything like they did in real life. Her friends had had dreams like that too. They had often talked about it and Kirsti had always been amazed at how the dreamer knew who the person really was. The person in the image didn't look familiar, but she knew in her heart that it was Owen. There was no doubt about it.

He walked like Owen, moved like Owen, but he didn't look like Owen.

He sauntered over to the barn and went into the stall with the cow. Kirsti couldn't see the stool he sat on, but she knew that's what he did next. He intended to milk the...

The bathroom door flew open and the image disappeared.

"No!" Kirsti panicked. She wanted the image to remain. She wanted to continue to watch Owen. How dare someone come in now and ruin it for her.

"Kirsti?" It was Skye.

"What are you doing?" asked Skye. "Are you all right?"

Kirsti's body felt strange. She continued to stand with

her back to the partition. She thought she might fall over if she tried to stand on her own. She nodded. She looked in the long mirror before her, wanting the scene to return. She wanted Skye to see it, to share it. Perhaps then she'd be able to talk about it. Most of all, she wanted to see Owen again.

"Kirsti?" Skye looked worried now. "What's wrong with you?"

"I ... I..." Kirsti wanted to tell Skye the truth. She wanted to tell her friend what she had seen, but she knew the other girl would never believe her. Who would? It was crazy to be seeing things in mirrors, even she knew that. "I felt dizzy. I haven't been eating much lately."

Skye looked at her through narrow eyes. "I heard you call out. You haven't taken anything have you?"

"Taken anything?" asked Kirsti. "What do you mean?"

Skye looked quickly around the bathroom and in the cubicle Kirsti stood beside. "You know what I mean. Ecstasy."

Anger forced her to move. "Ecstasy? Are you stupid?" Kirsti went to the hand basin and washed her hands again. "Those things fry your brain."

In truth, all four girls had tried the "love drug" once when they went to a nightclub. Kirsti remembered Joanne's reaction and wasn't surprised when the girl refused to do it again. She and Skye had continued to use them for about two months. A lot of their friends used it on the weekend, but when one girl died on the dance floor, in their last year at high school, the girls never took them again. Kirsti was never completely sure about Melody though. The girl seemed a bit ... unusual ... at times, but Melody didn't need drugs to come across like that. Her entire family were a little weird.

Kirsti didn't like the effects it had on her and had already decided to stop using them. Her memory was affected by them and she grew paranoid, which made her feel uncomfortable. And when she was coming down, she felt so miserable she sometimes wanted to...

She spun around and looked at Skye. "You don't suppose...?" She was thinking aloud.

"What?" Skye looked a little frazzled.

Kirsti shrugged and dried her hands. "I was thinking ...
you don't suppose Owen was taking ecstasy, do you?"

Skye went white as a sheet. "Well ... it's possible. They
are easy to get."

"Remember how depressed they made you feel," said
Kirsti. "Maybe that's why. Maybe it was a side effect from
taking drugs and that's why he—"

"Don't say it."

Kirsti wanted to say, Don't say what? That maybe the
drugs made him kill himself? Instead, she looked at the
mirror one more time and left the bathroom. "I need a
drink."

Jenny sat quietly at the computer. She had checked her
emails and found nothing new there. The websites that had
once entertained her no longer held her interest. Eventually, she found herself clicking on random links that took her
to page after page of information that meant nothing to
her. Knowing she was trying to waste time, she finally
leaned back in the chair and let out a big, sorrowful sigh.

Kirsti was with Skye. The two girls had been best friends
for fifteen years. If anyone was able to reach Kirsti and
make her laugh, it was Skye. *Besides*, Jenny told herself, it
would be good for Kirsti to talk openly to a friend about
what had happened and what she had seen. She needs to
get it off her chest. Jenny was fully aware that talking to
someone outside the family would be good for her daughter because some things were not easily said in front of a
grieving family.

Stephen was watching a DVD. Although the last time
she had looked, he was sleeping soundly with the movie

babbling in the background. She thought about waking him and sending him to bed, but she knew he would insist on watching the rest of the movie beforehand so she let him sleep instead.

Jenny returned to clinking on links and gazing indifferently at the results. Half an hour later, she shut down the computer and decided to do some housework instead.

Unlike Stephen, she didn't want to sleep. She was scared of what the next nightmare might bring. Instead, she folded washing and took piles of clothes to their owner's bedrooms. Finally, she held up a lone sock and stared at it for the longest time. It belonged to Owen.

His room smelled dusty when she opened the door. She would have to do something about that tomorrow. For now, she quickly went to the window and opened it a bit to let the cool night air enter the room.

Avoiding looking at the bed, Jenny moved about the room quietly. She held back the overwhelming urge to talk to the grey container. Her brain told her that the ashes were only the remains of Owen's earthly body, but her heart was so desperate to talk to her son, that she didn't care. It upset her to think that all she had left was a heavy box, when what she really wanted was her son.

"Owen," she finally said aloud. "Can you hear me?"

She looked up at the ceiling as if she expected an escalator to appear and Owen to descend. "Please lead me to the letter, if you wrote one. Show me where to look and I'll find it."

Nothing happened. In reality, she didn't expect it too either.

She stood at the empty chest of drawers and opened the top drawer. She didn't expect to see anything in there, so she wasn't disappointed. She put her hand inside the drawer and felt with her fingers along the underside of the top of the chest of drawers. Nothing. She pulled the drawer out and looked for something that might be stuck to the drawer. Nothing. She checked all the drawers and then she pulled the chest of drawers away from the wall and checked behind it. Nothing.

"Why am I doing this?" she said aloud. "If you wrote a letter, you wouldn't hide it. Would you?" She thought for a moment and then shook her head. "What would be the point?"

She didn't know anymore. She was unsure about so many things these days. She never used to be. It was another new, and horrible, feeling that she guessed she'd have to get used to.

She returned to sit on the edge of the bed. For the first time since entering the room, she looked, really looked, at the grey container. Owen. It had been a stressful day. Collecting the ashes had affected her and Stephen in ways she didn't think possible. What were they supposed to do now? Clean out his room? Store his belongings ... or worse still, give them to charity?

No. She wasn't ready to do any of that yet. She wasn't ready to make a decision of that multitude ... not yet. Maybe next month. Jenny shook her head. Maybe next year would be closer to the mark.

Owen's room would stay as it was right now. Except ... she would clean it. A mother cleaned her son's room; even when he was able to do it himself. Isn't that what mothers did? Of course, it was. Tomorrow, she would clean, dust and vacuum Owen's room. And she would come in ever day and open the curtains and window in the mornings and she would close them again at dusk every afternoon.

Owen would like that.

Skye watched Kirsti over her drink. Her friend had started taking the occasional sip from her drink and now she was drinking far too much alcohol. What had happened in the bathroom before she had arrived on the scene? Skye found herself asking that question a lot. Kirsti had acted quite strange when Skye first approached her, but after a moment or two, she had returned to normal. Well, normal for all of them was a bit off centre, but she didn't act high or anything. None of them had touched drugs in ages.

When they got back to their table, Kirsti took Skye's seat. It wasn't a big deal, but they always sat in the same chairs, so that gave Skye something else to ponder too.

But then the drinking started. Heavy drinking. And that was unlike Kirsti. What was she doing?

"Where's your car?" asked Skye a moment later.

"Outside."

"You don't intend to drive home, do you?" asked Skye, a tad nervous at what Kirsti might say.

"No, of course not." Kirsti looked annoyed. "I'm not stupid."

"I know," said Skye. "Don't get mad. I was just wondering."

"I'll leave the car here overnight and will pick it up tomorrow, after lunch," said Kirsti.

"Who are you having lunch with?"

"Josh." Kirsti smiled.

It was good to see Kirsti smile, but Skye knew it was fake. The alcohol was affecting Kirsti. Skye didn't like that. Normally, it didn't matter, but tonight was different. Strange. Scary even. Skye wanted the old Kirsti back; the girl who naturally smiled and laughed. Skye knew she had started the night drinking heavily herself, but seeing the way Kirsti was acting now had quickly sobered her.

Skye didn't know what else to say, so she sat quietly watching her friend. Now it was Skye's turn to drink juice.

Then, she saw something that didn't surprise her at all, but it did worry her a lot. She saw Josh come in with another girl on his arm—it looked like one of the instructors from the gym. Skye knew without a doubt that Josh had cheated on Kirsti, many times, but it was a waste of time trying to warn her friend. Kirsti wouldn't have a bar of it.

Skye had always wanted proof and this would have been it. Except Kirsti was in no shape to deal with another blow. Skye couldn't allow that to happen. In fact, she would ensure it didn't.

"Kirsti," said Skye, when she saw Josh and the girl walk around to the secluded area out of sight of where they were seated. "How about we go and see if there's a table in the restaurant? I'm starving."

Kirsti drained the rest of her drink and shook her head. "No, there's never empties on a Saturday night. You know that."

"Well, forget the restaurant then. Let's walk down to Mackers or something. I'm bored with this place."

Letting an ice cube glide into her mouth, Kirsti shrugged. "Whatever. I don't care."

"Come on then," said Skye. She checked her watch. "It's eleven o'clock. It's later than I thought. Let's go now."

The girls stood and left their table. They almost made it to the door when Josh's fancy piece came prancing around the corner in her high heels and her boobs bouncing around in the low cut dress she was wearing. She almost ran over the top of Kirsti.

"Oh, sorry," said the girl.

"Crystal," said Kirsti. "Fancy seeing you here. You look great in that dress."

"Thanks," said Crystal, her face reddening.

There was an awkward silence.

"We're just leaving," said Skye. "Enjoy your evening."

"Yeah, thanks." Crystal turned and scurried away.

"I wonder if she's on a date," said Kirsti. "I've never seen her with anyone."

Skye was worried that Kirsti might follow Crystal and question her. Normally she wouldn't, but in her current state, anything was possible. "Come on. Let's get out of here."

"No, I want to see her date. She looked nervous," said Kirsti. "Do you think she looked nervous?"

Skye grabbed Kirsti's arm and dragged her towards the door. "A little. Come on. If she's on a date, she won't want us hanging about."

She stabbed the elevator button and hoped the door would open straight away. It did. Breathing a sigh of relief, Skye pulled Kirsti into the elevator. "Food, here we come."

As the doors closed, they saw Crystal come out of the ladies and look around nervously.

Money spoke in volumes. Josh Edwards had discovered that fact soon after leaving the orphanage. In some ways, the orphanage had taught him more than life itself. In a place where nothing was truly your own and even the clothes on your back were taken away and redistributed when you outgrew them, a young boy learned to value the few things that remained.

He had been four when his mother died of cancer and his arrival at the orphanage coincided with that. He had no memory of either event and he had no idea what his mother looked like as there were no photos within the locked cabinet beside his old, squeaky bed. That small cabinet was his world—and his world only. It contained the few items that Josh could proudly call his own—a range of swapping cards he had collected or won over the years, a bag of used marbles he hadn't touched since he was ten, a couple of matchbox cars he found beside a dumpster years ago, birthday and Christmas cards from friends at school, the Valentine's card Kirsti had given to him in year eight, several packets of photos along with an old camera and a few other things he had purchased with money he had saved from his after school job. All the boys in the orphanage had a similar cabinet and all the boys felt protective of their cabinet and the treasures within. Forced entry into another person's world was deeply frowned upon. Those who tried it would get a beating from all the boys in the dormitory. No exceptions.

Not long before his eighteenth birthday, the orphanage told him it was time to leave and make a life of his own. It was a scary thought, but the administrator found him a small apartment to live in and got him his first job. He was grateful for that. When he left the orphanage gates for the last time, he felt sad and excited at the same time, but he refused to look over his shoulder for one last look. Only a weak person would do that. He walked with his head held high, carrying a small suitcase with a few clothes inside and his belongings from the cabinet. In his pocket was a parting gift of fifty dollars *to tide you over until you get your first pay.*

Three months later, his father turned up. At first, Josh was numb. His life had consisted of thoughts of a mother he didn't know and trying to survive in an all boy environment. He always understood that he must have a father too, but he assumed the man was dead. Why else was he in an orphanage? Being an orphan meant you had no family! But it seemed he had a healthy father and heaps of other relatives too, including an older brother. The initial numbness quickly turned to anger and nothing his so-called father could say to him would enable Josh to forgive him. It was on that day, when he saw his father for the first and last time, that Josh decided to show those people who called themselves "relatives" what they had thrown away. He would be successful and rich. He didn't need them.

That had been the turning point, his motivation. He quickly found a better job and moved into better accommodation. Within two years, only one week after his twentieth birthday, he put a deposit on his own home. And now at twenty-two, he was striving for his own business.

Yes, money spoke in volumes and Josh would never forget it. He sat at the small table in Edgar's and grinned. Reserving this table had been a good idea as it was secluded from the other patrons. Edgar was always open to doing him a favour, especially when money came into it.

Edgar wasn't the only one who appreciated Josh's money either. Josh discovered that with money, he had girls hovering around him too. Most girls melted in his hands, which pleased him.

He had met Kirsti at school. She was different from most of the other girls. Josh knew, without a doubt, that Kirsti genuinely cared for him—money or no money— whereas the other girls were only after one thing. And that happened to be different to the one thing he was after from them, but they didn't seem to care. Kirsti had always been the girl he invited to accompany him when he needed a nice girl on his arm. There was no nicer girl than Kirsti and anyone in town would agree with that statement. It had been a natural transition from being good friends at school to a long term relationship that worked for both of them.

However, who wanted a nice girl on his arm all the time? Sometimes a guy wanted a naughty girl to please him. And Crystal was Naughty!

Crystal had been a regular bedmate for months now, but she had been complaining about feeling used and abused and wanted him to take her out occasionally. This was their first real date. The Pink Room was Crystal's choice. Personally, he would have preferred a quick meal in the restaurant and then home to bed for dessert.

When he saw her in that hot, tight-fitting black dress she was wearing tonight, he decided that he'd play along with her. Because dessert was always worth waiting for and if he played his cards right, he'd still be having dessert in the morning. His smile deepened at the thought.

He looked around. What was taking her so long? "Girls and the bathroom," he said aloud. "That's one thing I will never figure out. What do they do in there?"

A moment later, Crystal came rushing towards him, her face flushed with anxiety.

"What's up, Babe?" Josh stood and looked towards the ladies. "Did some jerk put the hard word on my girl?"

Crystal shook her head. "No, nothing like that. I saw Kirsti."

Shit! Crystal knew about Kirsti, of course, but Kirsti knew nothing of Josh's games with other women and he wasn't interested in letting her find out. He had always planned to marry Kirsti, and he didn't want his fooling around to become a problem. Josh tried to hide the shock of Crystal words. "What? In here?"

"Yes, right over there," said Crystal, breathless. "A few seconds ago."

"Oh." *Stay cool, Josh.*

"I think she was leaving," said Crystal.

Josh felt himself relax a tad. "Be a good girl, and go and check." He winked at her. "I'll order your favourite drink for when you return."

He patted Crystal's bum as she walked away. *I love dessert.*

Sunday, 11ᵗʰ June

The next morning Kirsti woke feeling dehydrated. She felt like someone had stomped on her head. Multiple times.

It was the first night she had slept in her own room too. Being intoxicated helped, of course, but she knew she wouldn't take up drinking in order to sleep in her own room again. Besides, now that Owen's ashes were on his bed, Kirsti didn't feel right sleeping in his room. It felt inappropriate in some strange kind of way.

Kirsti felt uncomfortable in the house. Her parents were acting abnormally. Kirsti understood why, of course. What she couldn't understand was why they were arguing. Granted, she had only overheard them argue once, but when she got home last night her dad was asleep on the lounge and her mum had gone to bed. That can't be a good sign.

Kirsti lay in bed thinking about last night. She thought of Skye and the awkwardness of the evening. She thought of Crystal and how strange she had acted. At first, Kirsti thought Crystal was embarrassed about a date, but later she realised that she didn't want to talk to Kirsti because of the suicide. Maybe Crystal thought ill of people who took their own lives. Maybe Crystal should stay away from Kirsti then.

Kirsti pushed the anger aside and turned her thoughts to what she had seen in the mirror. She loved that she was seeing more now. And the fact that Owen was there was even better. Where was the place anyway? Was Owen trying to show her that he was okay and she didn't need to worry about him? Kirsti wasn't sure what to believe, but she knew the images gave her some level of comfort.

Then she realised something else. The larger the mirror, the more of the world in the mirror she saw. She would go back to Edgar's tonight, on her own. It was the only way to see Owen again. She shook her head. No, Edgar's never opened on Sunday ... or Monday. That meant she'd have to wait until Tuesday night before she got to see Owen again.

Kirsti groaned and got out of bed.

In the kitchen, she poured herself an orange juice and made some toast. Perhaps she'd be able to swallow toast easier than cereal. Maybe it was the milk that upset her tummy. She didn't believe this was the case, but she spread Vegemite on the toast anyway and took it outside to eat.

Sitting on the step of the veranda, Kirsti noticed the side door to the garage was open. Leaving the plate on the step, she walked hesitantly towards the open door. On that other morning, it had been much earlier and she had approached the garage via the roller door. This morning was warm and she could hear the radio playing. That had to mean everything was all right. Didn't it?

Kirsti stepped through the door. Her heart racing furiously in her chest. Her hands were clammy and beads of sweat gathered in the crevice of her shoulder blades. What if...?

Kirsti turned a corner and saw the boxes placed neatly on the shelves. Her mother sat on the floor. Silent, Kirsti watched her mum idly pulling things out of the box.

"Mum?"

Her mum jumped, her face pale and drawn. "Oh, Kirsti. You scared me."

"Sorry." Kirsti knelt on the dusty floor beside her mother. "What are you doing?"

"Looking through the baby box," said her mum, without looking at her. "I haven't done this in ages."

Kirsti looked at the tuft of hair in her mum's hand. "Whose is that?"

"Owen's." Her mother's hand delved into the box again, bringing out another clump of hair. "This is yours."

Kirsti smiled. "You've kept those all this time?"

"Of course," said her mum. "You'll do the same one day. Some things can never be replaced. I've been thinking about moving these things into the house, so they don't get ruined."

Kirsti nodded. "What's that in your lap?"

Her mum picked up the object. "My father gave this to Owen when he was born. It's something Dad treasured and he wanted it passed down through the family. I'll have to ask him what he wants to be done with it now."

"It could be given to me. I'd pass it down to my first son and the tradition can carry on."

"I'll see what Dad says."

Kirsti felt like an intruder so she got to her feet and took a couple of steps backwards. "Well, Mum, sorry to interrupt. I'll go and finish my breakfast, and then I'm going to go for a walk. I'm meeting Josh for lunch later, so don't prepare anything for me."

"Okay, love," said her mum. "I'll expect you for dinner then. Yes?"

"Yes." Kirsti paused when she reached the door. "I love you, Mum."

Tears shone in her mum's eyes. "I love you too, darling."

Jenny wiped the tears away and continued looking at the things she had kept from her children's childhood. She grinned when she held the hospital bracelets they had each worn when they were born. Three clumps of hair had been neatly placed in plastic and stashed inside a book. She even had the teats from their first bottles. Stephen had laughed when she told him she was going to keep them, but he didn't try to stop her.

The clothes they wore when they left hospital had also been packed away, along with the first item each child had grasped on their own. For Tim, that item was a car, even though he wasn't wrapped in cars like his dad or Owen were. For Kirsti and Owen, the item was a teething ring—a pink owl for Kirsti and a blue ring for Owen.

Jenny leaned back against the boxes and sighed. She wished she and Stephen had been able to buy a video recorder when they first got married or when the children came along. But they couldn't afford one. At the time, it didn't seem that important either, but now that one of her children was no longer with them, she felt as if she was missing out on something that might have brought her comfort.

Stephen's brother had promised to provide them with a DVD with all the Christmases and birthdays they had spent together. Jenny wasn't sure if she would be able to watch those happy times yet, but she knew that sometime in the future she would want to. She knew the first time would be the hardest. The first time for everything was always the hardest.

A chilly breeze washed over her. Jenny rubbed her arms and looked through the small window near the door. The sun was still shining. It didn't look like a change was on its way.

She put everything back into the box and sealed it. Getting the box down was one thing, putting it back was something else completely. It was too heavy to lift that high, so she decided to leave it for Stephen to do later.

She turned to leave and the cold breeze swept past her again. This time she noticed a stray photo lifted by the breeze and taken through the door into the actual garage. It was one of Owen's baby photos. She couldn't leave it. There would never be additional photos of Owen to add to their collection. She couldn't, wouldn't, allow even one photo to disappear. She quickly walked into the garage and stood beside Stephen's Zephyr and looked for the photo.

149

It was near the wheel. She bent to pick it up, but the breeze got to it first. The photo disappeared under the car. Jenny went down on her knees and peered under the vehicle. She spotted the photo on the other side. Moving quickly around the car, she bent to retrieve it again. This time her fingers closed on it before the chill enveloped her.

Owen's face smiled up at her. Cold air wrapped itself around her. Jenny straightened and realised she was standing beneath the spot where Owen had died. She looked up at the beam. Tears welled in her eyes. The coldness bit into her skin, making her shiver. She stood for a moment and then she felt the presence around her. Fear prickled the hairs on her arms and neck. Fear made her forget the cold. She took several steps backwards.

"No, I know you are not Owen. He wouldn't do this," said Jenny, her voice barely a whisper. "What do you want with me?"

As if in answer, she felt weird all of a sudden. The breath was squeezed out of her. She felt certain that she was going to die. Right here. Right now. Right where her son had died. And there was nothing she could do about it.

"Mum?" It was Kirsti.

Don't let her come in here. Please don't let her find me dead too. It will destroy her.

"Mum?"

The coldness disappeared. Jenny gasped for breath.

"Mum? Where are you?"

"I'm all right. I was..." she coughed, "I was getting a photo that the wind got hold off and took away from me."

"What wind?"

Jenny stood riveted to the spot, clasping the photo, not wanting her daughter to see her shaking and scared. "It came and went so suddenly. Go for your walk, I'm packing up to go inside any minute now."

"Okay, see you this afternoon."

Jenny listened to her daughter walk away and then scurried back to the boxes. She wedged the photo safely into the box and quickly left the garage and staggered back to the house. She avoided the computer room because she knew Stephen was in there doing something. She went upstairs, through her bedroom and into the ensuite. Locking the door behind her, she stared at herself in the mirror.

"What is happening to me?" Jenny murmured to the pale face and dark eyes she saw in the mirror. She hardly recognised her own reflection. She would not give in to the evil presence. She would find a way to defend herself and her family.

II

Josh looked surprised when Kirsti knocked on his door.

"Babe, I said I'd pick you up at midday." His eyes flicked around the room and Kirsti heard the annoyance in his voice when he spoke.

Kirsti shrugged. "I was ready so I walked. What's the problem?"

He held the door against his body and peered out at her.

"Aren't you going to let me in?" she asked when he still didn't move to one side.

He looked over his shoulder. "The place is a mess. You shouldn't surprise me like this."

Kirsti pushed on the door, but he refused to budge. "Josh, stop messing around and let me in. You've never given a toss about how the place looked before."

He seemed jumpy, but he still didn't let her in.

"Josh!"

"All right," he said, stepping to one side. "I just woke up. You shouldn't—"

"—surprise you. Yeah, you've said that already." Kirsti stepped into the house. It smelt like waffles and cream. She turned to look at Josh but didn't say anything. She was already feeling annoyed with him and didn't want to agitate the situation further.

The back door slammed. Kirsti jumped and looked down the hall that led to the back door.

"It's the wind," said Josh, grabbing her arm and dragging her further into the lounge room.

"Wind?" said Kirsti. "Everyone is obsessed with the wind today. There's not a breath of wind out there."

Josh shrugged and pulled on a t-shirt. Kirsti used to love looking at his body and would tease him about leaving the shirt off, but she found she wasn't the least bit interested now.

"So what have you been up too?" asked Josh. He seemed distracted and kept picking things up and throwing them in a cupboard.

"I went to Edgar's last night," she replied. "It was quiet."

"See anyone you know?"

"Yeah, actually I did," replied Kirsti. "Crystal from the gym. I think she was on a hot date."

Josh turned to look at her. "How do you know?"

"When a girl dresses like she was dressed, she has to have been," said Kirsti. "She was in for the kill. She looked quite sluttish, really."

Josh's face reddened.

What's wrong with him? thought Kirsti.

"She seems quite reserved at work," he said and then his eyes widened and he rushed over to her. "Come and have a look at ... at this thing in the kitchen."

Kirsti allowed him to pull her into the other room, but when they got there he seemed to forget what he wanted to show her.

"What?" she asked.

Josh looked over her shoulder and then visibly relaxed. "Oh, it doesn't matter. Where do you want to go for lunch?"

Edgar's, but it's not open. "I don't care."

"I know this restaurant down by the river that's quite nice. They do great lunches on a Sunday," said Josh.

"Sounds good."

The restaurant was nice. It was busy but quiet. The food was tasty, even though the quantity wasn't really enough— for the hungry. Luckily, it was perfect for Kirsti as she still couldn't eat much.

They sat opposite each other and Josh talked about the gym for some time. Kirsti only half listened. Then he reached across the table and took her hand. Kirsti felt uncomfortable. *What's he doing?*

"Babe, remember the Japanese guy?"

"The investor you found for the gym?" asked Kirsti.

Josh nodded. "Yeah, that's him." He grinned. "Well, he's asked us to attend a gala night next Friday night. It's for charity but he wants me there so he can take another look at my proposal, because he's leaving the country on Saturday."

"Oh, is that good or bad," asked Kirsti.

Josh frowned. "It's bloody marvellous."

"Didn't you already tell me about this?"

Josh straightened. "Did I? Hey, I think I did. I've got a lot on my mind, Babe."

Kirsti felt the anger swirl in her stomach. *He's had a lot on his mind? What about me?* A retort was on the tip of her tongue, but she bit it back. Now wasn't the time or place. She grabbed her bag and rose from her chair. "I'm going to the ladies."

Josh rolled his eyes and Kirsti walked away mumbling to herself. *Arrogant bastard.* "Excuse me," she said to a waitress, "can you tell me where the ladies is?"

The waitress smiled and pointed to a set of large doors. "Go through those and follow the corridor to the left. At the end, you'll see the sign."

"Thank you."

Kirsti walked through the large doors and that's as far as she got. The corridor was laden with square mirrors joined together. They spanned the entire length of the corridor. For Kirsti, it was heaven. Because in those mirrors was a scene Kirsti had longed for. The entire scene was there— the stream, the oak trees, the cottage, the barn, the swing. And Owen. He was right there. She stood watching him as he tied the horse to the pig pen and vigorously brushed its silky coat.

Kirsti was mesmerised by the sight. Where was he? He looked happy and content.

Owen put the brush aside and grabbed a saddle. Moments later he swung himself up onto the black horse and trotted past the barn into a large paddock. He rode like the wind. His hair fluttered behind him. The muscles of the horse vibrating strength and energy.

Kirsti couldn't take her eyes off him.

Then she felt a presence behind her. For a split second, she felt a chill but it soon vanished. She stood frozen, staring at Owen, but her mind focused more on the presence. For some reason, she couldn't turn around. But, even so, she felt calm inside.

Cold breath touched her ear. The hairs on her arms stood on end. Fear tinged the edge of her conscience, but something else washed over her. She couldn't put a word to it.

"You can go there too, you know." The voice wasn't male or female. It was somewhere in between, neutral.

That something grew inside Kirsti. She wished she could name it. "How?"

"You have the key," said the presence.

"Do I?"

"Yes."

The cold breath stopped and Kirsti had control of her limbs again. She turned around, wanted to ask the person more, but she was alone. The man, for that's how she thought of the presence, was gone. The corridor was empty apart from her, but the scene in the mirrors remained. Owen rode the black horse. The breeze gently made the swing sway. The birds and butterflies fluttered over flowers. The stream washed over the pebbles and rocks.

Her gaze returned to Owen. The horse stood still. Kirsti and Owen stared at each other. He smiled and held out his hand to her. Kirsti lifted her hand and stepped forward. She wanted to place her hand in his, but couldn't. She wanted to be carefree and content like he was. Life would be better in that world because it certainly wasn't in this one.

You can go there too, you know. The words, spoken by the presence, repeated in her mind. Yes, she could, because she had the key and she knew where to find it now.

Josh stared at the doors Kirsti had gone through and groaned. He never would understand the fascination girls had with toilets. He looked at the doors again. "What's taking her so long?"

His focus drifted around the restaurant. The girl behind the bar was looking at him. Who could blame her? He smiled and let his gaze linger for a second longer than necessary before checking out the rest of the people seated around him. Everyone looked content with their meal and the company they were in. He wondered how many were playing games. Then he thought back to a few hours ago and smiled. When Kirsti knocked on the front door he had been in the middle of enjoying Crystal. Talk about bad timing.

Crystal didn't look happy when he told her to get dressed and get out the back door ... and to do it quickly. The girl was great in the bedroom, but she didn't have much else to offer. She certainly didn't make wife material ... not like the faithful Kirsti. He guessed he'd have to find another plaything to amuse himself with sooner rather than later. The brunette behind the bar was cute and built for pleasure. He looked at her again and this time chanced a wink. Girls were suckers for a wink. They thought it meant they looked sexy. Maybe they did, but it was the sex he was interested in.

Josh was getting tired of the way things were panning out. Kirsti was no longer any fun to be around. In fact, he now considered her to be a liability and he was a firm believer that liabilities should be gotten rid of ... fast. The problem was that if he dumped her now, how would that look? He didn't want his reputation suffering over such a minor thing. He figured that it was in his best interest for people to think he was being supportive now and then dump her later. But how long should he wait to make the move? A month? He shook his head, his thoughts racing wildly around his head, knowing he had to get himself back on track as soon as possible. First, he had the investor to impress ... and then he could dump the baggage and start looking for another "nice" girl to take Kirsti's place. In the meantime, he could still have his playthings. That had never stopped him before.

He looked at the brunette. "Yes, Josh, it's time to buy a drink."

III

Tim sat in his room, his legs pulled up on the bed and his chin resting on his arms. The person outside his door knocked again, but Tim stared at the silent images on the TV and said nothing.

"He's not there." The boy on the other side of the door yelled to someone further along the corridor. "He's probably over at Atchison Street."

Tim heard a muffled answer, but not the actual words.

"I'm telling ya he's not in there."

He heard the retreating steps, but still, he didn't move. The afternoon movie progressed, but Tim wasn't following it. He was finding it difficult to concentrate on anything these days. His mind wouldn't allow it.

The lectures, whilst always boring, had not been particularly difficult ... until now. Keeping up with his friends had always been easy, he certainly had never had to think about what he was doing and how he was going to act before ... until now.

Now, everything had changed. He felt increasingly angry. His tolerance was so low that he was scared he would crack open and swallow the world if he continued to pretend. And Tim admitted that the last four or five days were the hardest days he had ever endured, not counting those first days after hearing about his brother's death.

He thought it would be easy to pretend everything was all right. He thought he could do it and no one would ever notice. But he'd been wrong on both counts. It was bloody hard and everyone noticed what a jerk he'd become. He didn't know why he was acting this way. He tried hard to stop it from happening, but there was nothing he could do.

He was a time bomb just waiting to go off.

Last night he had staggered home from Atchison Street, drunk, but he had realised that not even the booze made him feel any better. He stumbled through the door and had collapsed on the bed. He couldn't fall asleep so he had turned the TV on and he had sat and watched whatever came on the screen.

That was hours ago and he still sat and watched. He didn't see much, because it felt like his body had shut down; stopped working, given up ... or in. He had decided that he no longer wished to play the pretend game ... and he no longer cared about university.

"You're a silly thing," said Joanne's mum. "You should have said something sooner, instead of bottling all that up inside."

Joanne sat with her mum, sipping a cup of coffee. It was a relief to get her troubles off her chest and sharing them with her mum was even better, because Joanne would now have the benefit of an older person's wisdom.

"I didn't know what to do, Mum."

Her mum reached across the table and squeezed her hand. "That's when you should always come to me. Day or night. We can talk things through. I will listen to anything you have to say. You know that. We can work out options together."

Joanne nodded. She did know that. She had always known it. "Thank you, Mum. I do know that. So what do I do?"

Her mum drank some coffee and looked out the window of the café. "You have to talk to her. You have to give her the opportunity to talk. By the sounds of it, she isn't able to do that with your other friends."

"No." Joanne agreed wholeheartedly with that point. "I don't know what to say to her, Mum. I don't want to upset her even more."

Her mum leaned over the table. "Joanne, no matter what you say it will make her cry. That can't be helped." She paused and Joanne could see her mother remembering the loss of her own mum only twelve months prior. "It's when people say nothing that it hurts the most," her mum continued. "Say you don't know what to say. Say you're sorry. Say anything, but say something. Let her cry. Cry with her. She'll appreciate that more than anything else. Don't say nothing."

"Let her cry?" Joanne felt shocked by her mother's words.

"Yes, of course," replied her mum. "Crying is good for the soul. It helps relieve the tension. It's cleansing. And it's an important part of the grief process."

Joanne stared into her mug of coffee.

"Joanne, Kirsti needs to talk about what's happened to her more than anything else. Yes, she'll cry, but that doesn't matter. She'll feel better afterwards for two reasons—someone listened to her and because she'll feel relieved. She'll repeat herself over and over again, but don't worry about that either. Let her do it. In fact, encourage her to." Her mum squeezed her hand again. "You're a good listener. Just listen to what she has to say ... even if she says the same things a hundred times over."

Joanne nodded. Yes, she was a good listener. She could easily let Kirsti talk. Up until now, she hadn't allowed the situation to occur because she was scared about upsetting her friend, but her mother made sense. As usual.

"I love Kirsti like a sister," announced Joanne. "I want so much to help her."

"Love is a doing word, not a feeling," said her mum. "When a person has lost someone dear to them, doing little things for them is the biggest, most precious, gift you could give them."

"Thank you, Mum."

"You're welcome, my darling."

IV

Jenny walked into the opportunity shop and paused.

"May I help you?" The elderly shop keeper smiled.

"Yes, maybe you can." Jenny moved to peer in a glass cabinet against the wall. "I'm looking for a cross."

"As in a piece of jewellery?"

"Yes."

The old woman turned and walked towards the cash register. "We have some in the cabinet over here. Are you looking for anything in particular?"

Jenny bent over the glass. "Well, I don't know..." She saw a wooden rosary and quickly pointed to it. "That looks interesting. May I have a look?"

The woman smiled. "Of course." She removed it from the cabinet and handed it to Jenny.

The entire rosary was made of plain wood. She'd never seen anything like it before. She laid the cross in the palm of her hand and stared at it. "Yes, this will do nicely. Thank you."

"Do you want to know how much it is first?"

Jenny shook her head. "No." She delved into her shoulder bag and removed her pause. As she opened it, she looked into the cabinet again and saw another cross on a silver chain. "Oh, may I look at that one too?"

The woman handed it over. The silver cross was inlaid with a couple of tiny diamond chips. Jenny didn't believe they were real diamonds and she didn't care. The price tag indicated they were cubic zirconia. However, the chain and the cross were sterling silver and quite pretty.

"I'll take that one too."

"Too?" enquired the shop keeper with a lifting of an eyebrow. "You want them both?"

"Yes."

A few minutes later, Jenny left the shop and headed straight back to the car. At home, she went into her bedroom and retrieved a small bottle of jewellery cleaner. Within minutes, the silver cross was shining new and pretty, and Jenny placed it around her neck. "Please protect me."

Then she turned her attention to the rosary. Removing the small wooden cross from the rest of the beads, she dropped the rosary into a drawer. Holding the wooden cross in her hand she left her bedroom and went downstairs.

Kirsti returned to the table to find Josh gone. She quickly sat and adjusted her skirt. Then she looked around and found Josh leaning against the bar talking to the waitress. They were laughing and she saw him pass her something. It didn't look like money, but what else could it be? A moment later, he looked over at Kirsti and quickly straightened up. He said something else to the waitress before casually turning and returning to sit at the table with Kirsti.

"I thought you nicked off out the back door," he said, taking a gulp of his beer. "I was getting worried."

You didn't look worried to me, thought Kirsti. "I'm sorry I took so long."

Josh didn't press her for more information and she didn't offer.

She didn't have a drink and felt strange about asking for one, so she sat playing with the edge of her napkin. She sat quietly for a bit longer, trying to work through the feelings running around inside her, while Josh looked around the restaurant.

Suddenly, a calmness overwhelmed her. She sat up straighter and indicated that the waiter should come to the table. "I'll have a scotch and dry, thanks."

Josh sat opposite her, staring. She no longer cared about Josh and his minuscule problems. She didn't care about his gym and whatever else he was up to ... and, she had decided, he was up to something.

Something had changed within her. She no longer felt the anxiety she had been carrying for almost a month.

She had made a decision and she felt happy. It felt good to be happy again.

Jenny paused at the bottom of the stairs and took a deep

breath. She had never held anything back from Stephen before and she didn't actually know why she was going to start today. Remembering his reaction in the bathroom the day before, she knew in her heart that this was something she had to deal with herself.

She pushed the wooden cross into her jeans pocket and, taking another deep breath, she walked down the hallway and straight into the computer room.

"Stephen, you've been in here for hours. What are you doing?"

He leaned back on the swivel chair and stretched. "Has it been that long? I didn't realise. I've been reading other parent's stories about their experience with suicide."

Their gaze met. Jenny didn't know what to think of that.

"I know it sounds morbid, but it is comforting to know we are not the only ones to have gone through this pain," he added. "There are people out there who know what we're going through."

Jenny felt the all too familiar lump form in her throat. "It feels like no one understands, even though we've had all those people offer condolences over the weeks."

Stephen nodded. "Yes, but our friends don't understand. How can they? They haven't lost a child to suicide. They want to support us, but they don't know how." He looked at the computer screen again. "There are so many suicides each year. It's devastating." He paused and swallowed. Jenny knew he was having trouble putting the words together. "I never knew," he continued. "I never thought about suicide. It was just a word and it certainly never occurred to me that it could happen in my family."

Tears welled in his eyes. Jenny placed a hand on his shoulder. "Keep reading, if it helps," she said. "I have some things I want to do anyway. When I'm finished I'll make a cuppa and come in and join you. Is that all right?"

"Of course, Jen."

She bent and kissed him on the lips, then turned and left the room. She didn't pause again. She walked through the house and out into the back yard. She knew exactly what needed to be done.

As she approached the side door to the garage, her left hand rose to the silver cross around her neck. *Please protect me*, she thought, repeating the words in her mind that she had spoken earlier to herself in the bedroom.

The box she had been looking in remained on the floor where she had left it. Jenny stepped around it and looked through the narrow door that would take her into the garage. She touched the silver cross again before stepping through the gap and walking straight to the ladder, and dragging it to where Owen's life had ended.

She didn't pause to think about what she was doing. She had already spent plenty of time doing just that before putting her plans into motion. Once the ladder was in place, she strode purposefully over to Stephen's workbench and went through the drawers until she found a tube of glue. Getting the lid off took longer than she anticipated, but once done she quickly dabbed some of the glue onto the wooden cross she had retrieved from her pocket.

Returning to the ladder, she climbed a few rungs and pressed the cross onto the beam ... exactly on the spot where Owen had been found.

"Rest in peace, darling," she whispered, but she didn't linger and she didn't allow the tears to come. There would be time for that later. She had the rest of her life to cry. Right now, she had to quickly put everything back where it belonged and get out of there before the presence came back.

A couple of minutes later, Jenny stepped out of the garage and into the back yard. She had done what she wanted to do. She didn't know if it would work or not, but she felt pleased with herself. Smiling, she returned to the house to make that cup of tea she had promised Stephen.

Monday, 12th June

Monday morning found Tim still sitting in his room. He had attempted to sleep. He had managed to nap for a couple of hours. But he didn't show himself to the other people living on his floor. And he didn't eat.

He listened to the sounds of doors banging shut as the students headed off to lectures, or wherever they were going. He listened to the laughter and the chatter as they walked past his room. He remained quiet and his gaze remained focused on the morning cartoons flickering across the TV screen.

He had no intention of going anywhere.

Kirsti felt relaxed at her desk. She wasn't entirely focused on what she was doing, but the feeling of being overwhelmed had disappeared completely. It made it easier to concentrate. She continued to write notes to herself, but the notes were less work- related and more to do with the decision she had made the day before. She did her work systematically without too many errors. Best of all, however, was the fact that the phone sat quietly on its cradle. That put her in a good mood.

When Kirsti arrived back at her desk after going off to make her cup of tea at mid-morning, she found Lisa hovering around her desk.

"Oh, good, there you are," said Lisa, with a big smile.

Kirsti placed the mug on the coaster and sat. "Did you want me to do something?"

Lisa nodded. "Yes, I hear you've been invited to the function Mr Shimizu is holding."

"Mr Shimizu?" Kirsti thought about the name for a while. "I don't believe I know him."

"Yes, you do," said Lisa, a frown appearing on her face. "A friend of mine who is catering for the function said your name is on the list."

"Is it? Maybe it's someone else with the same name," Kirsti suggested.

"You're boyfriend's name is Josh, right?"

Kirsti nodded.

"Then it's you. This Friday night. It's a charity gala." Lisa's voice had raised a pitch or two.

"Oh, the gala," said Kirsti. "Sorry, I didn't know the man's name, but I am going to that. Why?"

"I'm told he's looking for a local solicitor to handle the legal side of some business opportunities he's looking in to." Lisa pushed a pile of cards into Kirsti's hand. "Make sure you make a good impression and don't leave without ensuring one of those is in his pocket." She grinned. "There are a couple of extras in case there are any other influential people there."

Kirsti stared at the pile of cards and frowned. She already knew she wouldn't make an effort to give out any of them. What she did in her personal time was up to her. "Yeah, sure. I'll get rid of these for you." *I'll throw them in the bin, Bitch.*

"Mr Shimizu's account will make a huge difference to the direction of this company, Kirsti. I'm counting on you." Lisa smiled and then returned to the main office.

You're counting on the wrong person then.

Jenny waved goodbye to Stephen and went back inside. The place was tidy, but not particularly clean. Today she would do something about that. She dragged the vacuum cleaner out of the cupboard and set about doing some housework.

She pushed herself to work diligently, not allowing herself to slacken off. She'd had plenty of time to sit and mope; now she had to start thinking about piecing back together the fragments of her life.

By mid-morning, she had worked up a sweat and was feeling good about her efforts. The downstairs was finished, now to tackle the upstairs rooms. The first door she came to at the top of the stairs was Owen's. She could leave the room to last, and for a moment she thought about it, but in the end, she forced herself to stick to her normal routine, so she pushed the door open and immediately set to work.

Jenny's progress slowed in Owen's room. She found herself stopping what she was doing and looking through his things, again. It felt wrong, like she was encroaching on his privacy, but then she reminded herself that he had left this stuff, and them, behind. It was her right and her comfort to look at his belongings, to cherish them. She believed Owen would understand.

She got on her knees and lifted the edge of the quilt. Pushing the vacuum cleaner's nozzle into the dusty darkness beneath the bed, Jenny's mind wandered to the nightmares she had been experiencing. She knew they were making her feel uneasy during waking hours and that was the reason her skin crawled when she thought of the garage, but she also knew she had to conquer this new fear. Her mind felt jam-packed with fear and worry and she couldn't afford to let this additional thing become a major problem. Maybe she needed outside help—confirmation that there was nothing in the garage except dusty boxes and bad memories.

The suction of the vacuum cleaner changed, slowed. She

pulled the nozzle out from under the bed and discovered a CD stuck to the end of it. Quickly switching off the machine, she sat staring at the writing on the top side of the CD—*Da Boyz*. Jenny gently allowed her finger to trace the lettering of her son's handwriting. Time seemed to stand still for a moment before she reached over to his bedside table and placed the CD into the player.

The first sound she heard was laughter—Owen's laughter. She smiled and sank back onto her heels. Following a few minutes of laughter and voices that intertwined until they made no sense, Owen and his friends settled down and Jenny was finally able to make out what was being said.

"Come on, Man," said Terry. "Stop being a dork and do it right."

"Stop shoving me, Matt," said DJ.

More laughter.

"Guys, do you want to do this or not?" asked Owen.

"Yes!" came a chorus of voices all at once.

"Right then, are you ready?" A pause. "After three. One. Two. Three."

Owen started singing. He hesitated for only a second when he realised his friends remained silent, but then he continued on by himself. He sang the words of a song, which had obviously been made up by the group. It was quite crude, but Jenny savoured every syllable. She felt dizzy listening to the laughter in his tone, the happiness of his friends as they started to rib him for his efforts. Owen was no singer, not by any means, and not even Jenny could pretend otherwise, but right now he sounded like an angel and she vaguely realised tears of joy rolled down her face.

She had longed to hear his voice and now she had something she could treasure forever.

Owen stopped singing and a torrent of voices followed. Jenny didn't know what was happening, but she continued to listen, hoping to isolate the one voice that meant everything in the world to her. Then it went quiet, the mood changed. Jenny felt a heaviness come over her. Something was happening and she wished she was watching a DVD rather than listening to a CD.

"Man, this is good," said DJ.

"Yeah," said Terry.

"Didn't you leave me one?" asked Owen. He sounded annoyed.

"No, there were only three in the packet," said Matt.

Jenny heard a noise that sounded like the rustle of a plastic bag.

"Bullshit," said Owen. "I bought them, I know there were four. Stop stuffing me around and give me a pill."

A pill? Jenny gasped. This couldn't be good.

Owen's friends thought otherwise.

"Ah, this is fantastic. Ecstasy is a bomb!"

Jenny's mouth went dry. The smile faded from her face.

"Give me a pill!" Owen was angry now.

His friends laughed, but they must have complied with Owen's wishes because he was laughing too. "About time. Now the world will be better."

The sound from the CD player changed and Jenny knew someone in the group of boys had pressed the stop button, shutting her out of their world. Staring into space, she began to tremble. Her son, the boy who always smiled and laughed and was full of life, was taking ecstasy. If that wasn't bad enough, Owen's last words echoed in her mind—*now the world will be better*. It was the only clue she had found that said Owen was disillusioned with life. How deep did those feelings go? Obviously deep enough for him to end his life.

Downstairs, the phone rang.

Jenny leaned back against Owen's bed, panting and sweating. Ignoring the ringing phone, she brushed the tears from her wet face and acknowledged the fact that she had no idea her son didn't like the world he lived in. Right now, the world didn't feel worth the effort for her either.

Tim hung up and retrieved the change from the pay phone. Relieved that no one was home, he dawdled along the street and into the park before dropping lazily onto a battered wooden seat. At least he could honestly say to his mum that he had attempted to phone her and he wouldn't be bull crapping.

He had missed his morning lecture. And he planned on skipping the afternoon lecture as well. He was tired of pretending. He was fed up with the nonsense that came out of people's mouths. He was ... he punched the seat beside him and then stared at two small children playing innocently on the playground equipment, not far from him. Their mother glared at Tim, got to her feet and called her children back to her. A moment later, they were heading away from the park ... away from him. He didn't care. He wanted to be alone. He preferred it that way.

His hand throbbed. It felt good. It was the only real thing he'd felt for some time now. He punched the seat again. It hurt. Another punch. Now there was blood. He pounded the seat yet again.

"Tim?"

He looked up and found the blond staring at him. "What do you want?"

She cocked her head to one side. "I saw you sitting there."

She looked at his hand and he was grateful that she didn't mention what he had been doing.

"I was doing some errands for the university," she quickly added. "May I sit down?"

Tim looked at the long bench and nodded. "Suppose. I don't own it."

"Thanks."

Tim smelled her move in closer to him and sit down. The sweet aroma filled his senses and he relaxed a bit. His fist ached now. The pain was the complete opposite to the sweetness of the girl beside him.

"You didn't go to your lectures today." It was a clear statement. She didn't look at him.

"No, I don't intend to go tomorrow either."

"Why?" she asked.

"Because I don't want to."

"I understand that, but for what reason. Tell me."

Tim turned and met her gaze. "Because," he said, his voice rising in pitch, "there's no point, is there? There's no point to anything we do. We're all going to die. It's just a question of when."

He jumped when Kate touched his hand. She pulled it towards her and looked at his knuckles. "That's going to bruise," she said, taking some tissues from her bag and dabbing away the blood. Then she looked up into his eyes. "We *are* all going to die. That's one guarantee we all have. I know you've been through a lot, but isn't life worth ... something."

"My brother didn't think so." Tim was surprised by the lump in his throat.

"Obviously not," said Kate. "But what about you? What do you think?"

Tim stared into her big, blue eyes and wanted her to put her arms around him ... and hug him. "Does it matter?"

"Yes, it does," she said, releasing his hand. "It matters to me. It matters to your mum. It should matter to you too."

"It used to matter, that's why I came to university," replied Tim. "That's why I wanted to do something I would enjoy doing for the rest of my life. I wanted to ensure my future wife ... and kids ... had a good life. A full life."

"And what's changed?"

"My brother killed himself." Tim couldn't stop the pain from showing in his voice. He heard it plainly and he knew Kate did too.

"That's my point," replied Kate. "Your brother chose to end his time here. He didn't end your life too. He wouldn't expect you to stop living. In fact, he would want for you what he couldn't find for himself."

"How do you know? You didn't even know my brother."

"That's true," said Kate with a nod. "I didn't know him, but if you were suicidal would you want the rest of your family to stop living their lives too? I don't think you'd want that for a minute. In fact, I doubt you would even be thinking about how your death would really affect those you would leave behind. Your brother was consumed with his own problems. He wouldn't have realised that his actions would devastate the lives of those around him." She paused. "Life can be good and, yes, it can be bad, but it's up to us to make the best we can of it."

"I'm not suicidal." He didn't know what else to say, but his words were true.

"I'm glad to hear that," said Kate. She stood and looked down at him. "I have to get back to the office before I'm missed. You should go home ... and I don't mean back to your room, I mean go home to your family."

Tim shook his head. He didn't know many things at the moment, but he did know that he wasn't suicidal and he didn't want to be at home. That was the reason for his phone call. He intended to tell his mum that he had decided to stay on at the university over the long weekend so that he could catch up with his work.

"Don't become a hermit then," said Kate. "See you around." With that, she turned and walked away.

Once again, he watched her go, fascinated with the way her hips swayed. He groaned. "That's another guy's girl you're eyeing off, Tim. She's out of bounds."

He punched the seat again for good measure.

II

Jenny found the number she had been looking for. Now

she had to make the phone call, but what would she say? She didn't want to sound crazy, but she needed help and had to tell the person what was happening in order to get that help.

She groaned then picked up the phone to dial the number.

"Hello, Reverend McPherson speaking."

"Hello, Reverend. My name is Jennifer Fowler. I was wondering if you have time for a chat."

"Er, yes," replied the reverend. "I gather you don't want to chat about the weather?"

Heat rose to Jenny's face. "No. No. Of course not. I have a problem that you might be able to help me with."

"Ah, I see. I don't recognise your name. Do you come to my church? Are you in my parish?" he asked.

Jenny faltered. Parish? How was she supposed to know and what difference did it make? "I don't know what you mean."

"Hmm. Where do you live?"

"Woodbine Lane," replied Jenny. She was quickly losing confidence.

"Yes, that's my parish." There was a pause. "What's the problem?"

Jenny cleared her throat. She felt self-conscious. "Well, you see, a month or so ago my son ... my son..." she swallowed quickly, "my son took his own life."

"Oh, that's not good. I'm sorry to hear that."

Jenny noted the change in the reverend's voice, but she wasn't sure if the change was for better or worse.

"It happened here in the house, well in the garage actually, and I've been feeling a..." What could she say? Her heartbeat raced.

"You've been feeling what?" asked Reverend McPherson.

"Well, I don't really know how to explain it."

"Try your best. Is it grief you're talking about? Do you need—"

"No, I'm not talking about grief. It's something else. More like a presence," Jenny interrupted.

"A ghost?"

He said the word so casually. Jenny's mind whirled. It sounded stupid. The man must think she was insane. "No. I don't think so. It's an evil sort of presence. I'm scared. I don't know what to do. Can you come over and do an..." what was it called, "...an exorcism?" There she had said it.

There was a long silence. She wished she could see his face. See what he was doing. Maybe then she would have an idea what he must be thinking.

"Mrs Fowler, you have suffered a loss. The grief after suicide is great. There's all the unanswered questions, the guilt, the shame..."

"Shame?"

"There's a stigma associated with suicide," said Reverend McPherson. "People whisper and assume. It's a terrible thing. You are probably in shock and I imagine the stress must be too much to cope with. I'm not surprised that you're imagining things."

"Imagining things?" What was he suggesting?

"You need to keep yourself busy and join a support group," the reverend continued.

"Please, I do keep busy, but the presence..." asked Jenny. "What can you do about that? Can't you come over and pray for us or something?"

Another long silence.

"I suppose I could," said the Reverend. "How about on Thursday at two?"

"No, that's three days away," said Jenny, disappointed and desperate. "Can't you come over today? Now or this afternoon? The sooner the better really. I need help."

"All right, all right. It's raining now, so I'll come over in the morning at about ten. Okay?"

Jenny looked out the window. A few spots of rain left spots on the concrete. She sighed. "Yes, tomorrow then. At ten. That will be fine."

Kirsti sat at her desk all afternoon working diligently. Every now and again, she looked at the pile of business cards Lisa had given her, but she didn't dwell on how they made her feel. She was learning that it wasn't worth the effort.

By the time 4.45pm came, Kirsti had finished everything on her desk. The *In* tray was empty. The Out tray was full. She didn't bother taking the work through to the main office. Someone else could do that ... tomorrow.

Kirsti returned her gaze to her computer screen. First, she went into the email program and deleted the folder she used to place private emails. Then she ran through the address list and deleted her friend's names. Second, she opened the My Documents folder and deleted everything in there. She did the same thing in the My Pictures folder; not that she had anything private in there, they were images she liked to use on her desktop. Finally, she went into the Internet options and cleaned out the cache, the temporary files and the history.

"Right," she said to herself. She checked her watch—4.55pm.

All the programmes she generally used had been shut down. All except one ... the word processor. She read through the letter on the screen and made some minor adjustments, then printed it out. She read through it one last time and smiled. Perfect! She signed it.

"Now, I'm done."

She shut down the computer, picked up the letter and the business cards and walked through the main office without glancing at anyone, but with her head held high. She noticed Lisa's office door was open, which meant she wasn't in there. *Good.*

Kirsti walked straight into Lisa's office, went around the desk and placed her resignation and the pile of business cards where they wouldn't be overlooked. Turning, she re-traced her steps, collected her bag, her mug and a small pot plant she had been given by an appreciative client and left the building.

She paused in the car, key in the ignition. She stared at the office she had worked in for two years. "Goodbye and good riddance."

Joanne finished up at the veterinary surgery at 5.30pm on Monday afternoon. She loved her job because she adored animals and enjoyed helping them get better—most of the time anyway. Sometimes pets had to be put down due to chronic illnesses or injuries and that was something Joanne had never enjoyed. But today she needed to do something else, which was much more important. She had to see Kirsti and offer her friend what she should have offered a month before.

"You're in a hurry to get out of here today, Joanne," said her boss, Geoff. "Have you got a hot date or something?"

Joanne grinned. "No, nothing like that. I have to help a friend."

"I see. Well, I'll finish up here. You go and enjoy your evening."

"Thank you." Joanne made her way to the door in case he changed his mind.

She lived close to her workplace, so she rarely drove the short distance between the two, preferring to get the fresh air and exercise on a regular basis. She turned onto the path and walked briskly away from the clinic until she could no longer see the sign out the front. Then she sat on a brick wall and pulled out her mobile phone. Geoff was a good boss, as long as you did your job. He didn't approve of mobiles ringing left, right and centre during work hours unless it was a real emergency.

She checked her missed calls. There had only been two. One was her mum and the other was a private number, so she had no idea who that might have been. Then she quickly checked for text messages. None. Just went to show how popular she was in this world.

Joanne didn't make a habit of dwelling on such things, so she quickly pushed that notion from her mind and pressed the button that would bring up her address book. She had a good memory but had never been good with phone numbers. She arrowed down through the names until she saw Kirsti's name and pressed the green connect button. The phone rang only a few times.

"Hello."

"Hi Kirsti, this is Joanne."

"Hi. How are things?"

"Good. How are things with you?" asked Joanne.

"Better. Much better," replied Kirsti. "I was going to phone you later this evening."

"Were you?"

"Yeah. I wanted to know if you wanted to come over tomorrow night," said Kirsti.

"Well, fancy that. I was going to ask if I could come over tonight," replied Joanne.

There was only a slight pause. "You can't tonight, but tomorrow would be excellent."

Joanne nodded and then realised Kirsti couldn't see her. "Yes, all right then. Tomorrow night."

"I just got home from work," said Kirsti. "I'm going inside, so I'll ask Mum if it's okay for you to have dinner with us."

"There's no need," said Joanne. "I really don't want to put your mum out."

"Hang on."

Joanne could hear Kirsti's parents talking in the background. They said hello to their daughter and then Kirsti spoke to them. "I had a good day. I'll tell you about it later. I've got Joanne on the phone. Can she have dinner with us tomorrow night?"

Kirsti's mum didn't even hesitate. "Of course. We haven't seen Joanne since ... well, for a while now."

Joanne smiled. Kirsti's parents had always made her feel warmly welcome.

"Did you hear that, Joanne? Mum said you can come over for dinner," said Kirsti.

"I heard," said Joanne with a smile. "What time?"

"Come straight over after work," said Kirsti. Then she paused. "Hang on. I'll drive by the surgery to pick you up on the way home."

"Are you sure?"

"Positive. I'll see you then."

They spoke for a minute or so longer before hanging up. Joanne dropped the phone into her bag and left her perch on the wall to continue her walk home.

"Thanks for letting Joanne come over for dinner, Mum." Kirsti hugged her mum and then went to the fridge to grab a cold drink.

"That's fine. I've always had a soft spot for Joanne. I often hoped she and Owen would end up together," replied her mum.

"You didn't like his girlfriend, did you? And you don't like Josh," replied Kirsti, matter-of-factly.

"Oh, don't say it like I'm some sort of control freak," said her mum, her eyes big.

Kirsti noticed her dad laughing at the table.

"No, it's all right," said Kirsti. "I didn't like her much either. She was..." Kirsti thought for a moment, but couldn't find the right word. "I don't know ... weird and unfriendly. One day you can tell me why you didn't like Josh."

Kirsti saw her parents look at each other.

"Have you broken up with him?" asked her dad.

Kirsti shook her head. "No, but it's only a matter of time. I've seen a different side of him and he's starting to annoy me a fair bit."

"Maybe it's everything that you've ... we've ... been through," said her mum.

Kirsti smiled. Her parents had always disliked Josh and here they were trying to offer reasons why she could see the things they had always seen. "You're right. It is because of what's happened, but not in the way you think." She put the cold drink back in the fridge. "I'm going to some gala night with him on Friday. I'll see how that pans out."

"Oh, is that the gala being hosted by Mr Shimizu?" asked her mum, her face paling.

"Yes, why?"

"That's a charity night," replied her mum. "I promised to help out and haven't done a thing."

"Well, there's still a few days to go, Jen," said her dad. "Why don't you call Brenda and see if she needs a hand."

"I think I might do that."

Kirsti stared at her parents as they chatted about the charity gala. Usually, her mum would have been right in there with the preparations. She was well known, in the area, for her charity work. When she started getting involved in that again, it would mean she was heading in the right direction. Kirsti hoped to hear that her mum did make that phone call.

"Mum, I'm going to get changed. Will dinner be long?"

"No, darling. I'll be dishing it up in about fifteen minutes."

That night, Kirsti sat in the lounge room and watched TV with her parents. She wondered why she had felt so uneasy around them. Maybe it was all her. Maybe they were finding themselves again. Maybe the decision was allowing her to relax a bit more. Whatever the reason, she wanted to spend the evening sitting quietly in the lounge with her parents. It was important.

They watched TV until about 8.30pm and then her dad

suggested they watch a DVD. "There's absolutely nothing worth watching on TV tonight."

He was right. Kirsti sat quietly watching an advertisement for the local Yuletide Festivities coming up in July. Usually, her family didn't bother with the celebrations as they preferred to wait for the real thing in December. However, tonight was slightly different. The decision made it so and Kirsti couldn't stop the memories from surfacing.

Christmas. What would Christmas be like from now on? How could they celebrate a happy time of year ... when they didn't feel happy? Owen had loved Christmas. Kirsti didn't think his family would ever enjoy it again.

"What do you want to watch?" asked her dad a moment later, unable to decide for himself.

"Scrooge, the musical," replied Kirsti, instinctively.

Her parents looked at her and frowned. "Christmas is months away. Why do you want to watch that?" asked her dad.

"It's Yuletide next month and Owen loved that movie. We all did. When we thought we were too old to watch it every Christmas, we used to sneak it upstairs and watch it anyway. He would have wanted me to watch it this year too." Kirsti felt uncomfortable with her parents looking at her in that strange way. "I would like to watch it with you tonight and then that's it, I won't be watching it again."

"Why?" asked her mum.

Kirsti lowered her gaze. "I'll watch it tonight in memory of Owen. After that, it's time to keep that movie as a treasured memory. It would never be the same without Owen right there beside me, stealing my chips while I was singing along with the songs in the musical."

"I never knew you both liked it that much," said her mum.

"It was hiding the fact that we were watching it that made it so special, Mum."

Her dad shrugged. "Okay. Scrooge it is."

"I'll get the chips," said Kirsti.

Tuesday, 13th June

Kirsti dressed with particular care and left for work at the same time as usual the next morning. She drove in the direction she always took, but instead of turning off the main road and heading towards the solicitor's office, she continued driving into the next town.

She wondered what Lisa thought and said when she saw the resignation sitting on her desk. It had been short, curt, to the point and effective immediately. It had told her not to bother phoning to ask questions as she would not speak with her under any circumstances. And it had told her that as a boss, she would make an excellent brick. Kirsti smiled at her own sense of humour, but she also knew she had been a tad rude. Lisa deserved it, so Kirsti felt justified in her words. Besides, she had done it deliberately so that Lisa would get so angry that she refused to phone the house. She didn't want her parents finding out what she had done yet.

Kirsti had not really thought too far ahead. She knew today would be filled with chores and that might spill over to Wednesday if she didn't get everything finished. But after that, she wasn't sure what she'd do. She surmised she would think about that when the time came.

She drove to the shopping centre. It was a large, four storey high complex. Its parking area was already filling up rapidly. She found a spot and quickly made her way into the building. The complex was abuzz with people. Noise echoed off every surface drowning out the piped music playing in the background. Kirsti stood for a few seconds and watched the hive of activity.

It was time to go shopping.

By 10am on Tuesday morning, Jenny felt nervous. She had paced the lounge room floor for almost an hour. Exhausted, yet unable to sit and relax, she peered through the curtains again. Where was the reverend? Would he laugh at her? She continued to pace.

When she heard the knock on the door, she jumped. She had not noticed his car pull up or seen him walk up to the veranda. By the time she opened the door to see a man with a black and white collar standing on the other side of the screen door, she was tense.

"Hello, Mrs Fowler?" he asked.

"Yes. You must be Reverend McPherson," replied Jenny, unlocking the security screen. "Come in."

The reverend smiled at her before stepping over the threshold. "It's a lovely morning."

Jenny looked out at the street. It looked average to her, but she didn't say anything about that aloud. "It is. Come through to the lounge room. Would you like a cup of tea or coffee? Or perhaps a cold drink?"

"No," said Reverend McPherson, holding up one hand. "I'm fine. Thanks. You have one if you feel the need."

"No, that's all right," replied Jenny. "Let's get on with it."

Reverend McPherson looked at her for a moment and then sat on the lounge. "What seems to be happening that is making you so worried?"

Ah, now that was the question she had dreaded since making the phone call the day before. She didn't think she'd get away with anything ... but the truth. So that's what she told him. She told him about the fear and oppression she felt when she was in or around the garage. She told him about the nightmares she was experiencing and the fact that she didn't want to go to sleep as a result. She told him everything she was feeling and thinking.

"I realise this might be a delicate subject, Mrs Fowler," said Reverend McPherson. "But was there any physical abuse in the family, towards you or your son, which may have caused this tragic outcome?"

Jenny felt cold inside. "What?"

Reverend McPherson was watching her carefully. He nodded. "It does happen. A lot. Is your husband abusive towards you?"

"No!" said Jenny, shaking her head and sinking down on to one of the single chairs. "Why are you asking a question like that? I've told you what the problem is."

"I'm sorry, I must ask. I hope you understand. I notice you have some bruises on your arm. Did your husband do that to you?"

Jenny looked at her arm and saw two small, yellowing bruises. She didn't know where they had come from or why the reverend was focused on them. Why wasn't he listening to her?

"No. Stephen would never do something like that."

"In my experience, wives often try to cover up physical abuse in the family and will say anything to get help without implicating their husbands."

Jenny was horrified. She expected him to think her a bit crazy. She could have dealt with that. But not this. "I swear, none of what I've said has anything to do with abuse," she said, wanting to cry because she could see her problems getting worse instead of better. "I phoned you because I've felt an oppression in the garage ever since my son passed away."

"Grief unsettles the mind. It brings out the worst in us," said the reverend. "Some people, who have never hurt another living being in their entire lives, can suddenly find themselves angry and resentful. If your husband did this to you, you can tell me. I can help you."

"Why aren't you listening to what I'm saying? No one has done anything to me. In fact, Stephen thinks I'm suicidal," replied Jenny.

Reverend McPherson sat up straighter. Jenny knew she had said the wrong thing; she had made matters worse.

"Well, yes, I can see that maybe I have been looking at this all wrong," said the reverend.

Jenny sighed with relief. "You have? Thank heavens for that. If you can say a prayer and perform an—"

Reverend McPherson nodded. "Yes, suicide devastates a family. There have been many reported cases of another member of the same family trying to follow the first victim. Mostly, they are unsuccessful, but sometimes they do succeed. I call this the domino effect."

Jenny listened to the words but didn't understand what he was saying. All she really wanted was a prayer and an exorcism. Why did he have to try and counsel her? Why couldn't he do whatever was needed to get rid of the evilness she felt in the garage? She looked up and found him looking expectantly at her.

"I'm sorry. I don't understand what you're saying," she said.

"It's not uncommon for the surviving members of a family affected by suicide to attempt suicide themselves," he said.

Jenny dropped her face into her hands. This wasn't what she had expected.

"Mrs Fowler, I can give you phone numbers for helplines and support groups. I can urge you to come to the church this Sunday and become a regular part of our congregation. Once you find God, you will feel whole again. You don't need to try to follow your son." Reverend McPherson paused for only a moment. "Your son did a selfish thing, but God will forgive him and accept him if he repents."

Anger welled in Jenny. "First, you accuse my husband of physical abuse. Second, you accuse me of attempting suicide. And now, you condemn my son. How dare you!" Jenny rose to her feet and pointed to the front door. "Get out! Get out of my house. I asked you for help against something evil, and you are evil itself. Get out of my house."

Reverend McPherson rose to his feet and stared at Jenny. "I came here to help, but I see you are not ready to accept that help as yet. I will leave my card. You are welcome at the church at any time. New members are always welcome."

He's trying to convert me, not help me, thought Jenny. "For the record, my husband is a gentle, loving man and has never raised a hand to me or any of his family. Secondly, I would never attempt suicide. I've seen what it does to the people left behind and I would never, NEVER, do that to my family. And as for my son. You know *nothing* about him, yet you feel you have the right to pass judgement. You don't have that right. Now get out of this house or I'll phone the police."

Reverend McPherson's smile evaporated. He pressed his card into her sweaty hand and, without another word, he walked out the door.

Jenny rushed up to the door behind him, slammed it shut and bolted it. Then she sank to her knees and burst into tears.

II

Kirsti pulled up outside the veterinary clinic early. Turning the engine off, she checked her watch again and then settled back to wait for Joanne. It wasn't long before her friend appeared.

"You're early," said Joanne. "How'd you get here so fast?"

Kirsti shrugged. "There wasn't much work and Lisa let me go early."

Joanne stared at her. "Really? I didn't think she had a nice bone in her body."

Kirsti didn't respond.

"It's good to find out I was wrong," said Joanne as she climbed into the car. "How was your day?"

"Good." Kirsti couldn't look at her friend. "How was yours?"

Joanne nodded. "Not bad."

Kirsti started the engine and pulled away from the kerb. "I'm glad you are spending the evening with me, we should have done this sooner."

Joanne nodded. "Yes, we should have."

The girls sat quietly for the rest of the short trip back to Kirsti's house.

"Well, here we are," announced Kirsti, feeling awkward.

They got out of the car. Kirsti looked at the parcels neatly tucked behind the seats and decided to leave them until later. How would she explain where they had come from? She would wait until Joanne had gone home and her parents had gone to bed before coming back to retrieve them.

Joanne followed Kirsti into the house. All the lights were on. It wouldn't be dark for at least half an hour yet, so it felt strange for the house to be lit up like it was, but she didn't say anything.

The house was chilly and silent, which was also strange. This home had always felt so warm and comfortable. Everyone was always so bright and cheery. But not today.

"Hello, Joanne," said Mrs Fowler with a half smile.

Before Joanne could open her mouth to reply, Kirsti's mum had pulled her into her arms and was squeezing her in a warm hug. Some things never change! "How are you feeling, Mrs Fowler?"

"Oh, not so good, but I think you know why that is," replied Mrs Fowler.

"Yes, of course."

"I'm sorry. Dinner won't be anything fancy," said Mrs Fowler. "I've had a bad day and didn't feel like cooking."

"I don't have to stay," said Joanne immediately. "I can go home and come back for a visit on another day if you want me to. I don't mind."

Mrs Fowler smiled. "I know you don't, but it's not necessary." She looked at the two girls. "Go and relax for a while. I'll call you when it's ready."

"Okay, Mum. Come upstairs, Joanne. We can have a chat," said Kirsti.

Joanne followed Kirsti up the staircase. She paused outside Owen's room, knowing she had no right to ask for anything, but not able to stop herself. "Kirsti, can I go into Owen's room?"

Joanne felt her cheeks burn under Kirsti's stare.

"His ashes are in there. Are you sure you want to go in?"

Joanne nodded. She wanted to be close to Owen. "Yes," she whispered.

Kirsti pushed the door open.

A cold breeze washed over them and Joanne could see the curtain moving as the late afternoon air stirred outside and came through the window. Stepping into the room, she drew in a deep breath hoping to detect Owen's scent, but all she could smell was a faint hint of polish. Her gaze found the container holding the ashes and she held her breath.

Conscious of Kirsti beside her, Joanne turned to face her friend, but Kirsti was staring at the mirror. "I'm sorry, Kirsti."

"For what?" asked Kirsti without looking away from the mirror.

"For not doing and saying the right things," replied Joanne. "For not coming over and crying with you. For not allowing you to talk about how you feel, what you saw. I'm sorry for not being a better friend, but I'm here now and

I'm a good listener."

Kirsti's gaze left the mirror and moved to Joanne's face. Joanne felt something happen between them, but she couldn't put into words what it was. She couldn't even say with any certainty if the connection was good or bad.

"Can we sit in here for a while and talk?"

Kirsti faltered.

Joanne saw the uneasiness on her friend's face and in her movements. "What are you thinking, Kirsti?"

Kirsti squirmed inside. She needed someone to ask her that a month ago, even a week ago. She didn't need or want the question now. It was too late.

"Nothing. I'm not thinking about anything," she replied quickly. "I try not to think too much."

Joanne moved towards the bed, her gaze on the container. She reached out and touched it. Kirsti felt a twinge of familiarity for a split second. She turned and looked at the mirror. She wanted to see Owen again. She needed to see him. But he wasn't there.

"Did you know that Owen came and had lunch with me the week before he died?" asked Joanne.

Kirsti stared at Joanne. "No, I didn't know that." She paused before continuing. "Why?"

Joanne lowered her eyes. "I'm not sure why. He phoned me and asked if it were all right. Of course, I said it was and we sat in that small park at the end of the street. He didn't say much, but that was all right. I was content being..."

Joanne looked at Kirsti, her face bright red.

"Anyway," she continued, "he said he should have asked me to the formal instead of Clarissa. He said things might have been different then. I didn't know what he meant, but I like to think that maybe he..."

She stopped talking and Kirsti saw pain on her friend's face.

"I miss him," said Joanne.

The words were simple, but the meaning behind them was strong. Kirsti and Joanne held each other's gaze for the longest moment and then a lump formed in Kirsti's throat as a tear rolled down Joanne's face.

"Joanne..." Kirsti stepped towards her friend, but before she could continue they heard her mother's voice calling out to them that dinner was ready.

Jenny watched the two girls approach the table. They were different. Much different to what they used to be like, before Owen's death, but also different to when they had walked through the front door that day. What had passed between them in such a short space of time?

There was once a time, not long ago, that she would have asked them. Been direct with them. But that time was gone. She wasn't confident enough to do that these days. What was she scared of? What did she think they would say to her? She so badly wanted to know, but fear forced her to hold her tongue.

"We should do this more often, Joanne," said Stephen. "How's your mother? We haven't seen her in a while."

"She's well," replied Joanne. "She got that promotion and started the new position today. I don't know how she went."

"Well, be sure to tell her that we said congratulations," said Stephen. "She's waited a long time for this."

Joanne nodded. "That's a beautiful cross, Mrs Fowler. It's new, isn't it? I haven't seen it before."

Jenny felt her face colour and her hand automatically reached up to touch the cross. "Yes, I bought it recently from an op shop," she said, her gaze shifting quickly to

Stephen.

He stared at the cross, a fork full of mashed potato forgotten in his hand. "You've never worn a cross before."

Jenny's cheeks continued to burn. "I know. I saw it and liked it." Her gaze went around the table, pausing for only slightly longer on her daughter. "I feel ... different. I need to believe in something."

But it wasn't Kirsti ... or Stephen ... that gave a reaction. Joanne leaned forward and nodded. Jenny knew she understood and instantly felt like taking the girl in her arms again and giving her another big hug.

"I understand what you mean," said Joanne. "I've never known if I believe in God or not, but I find myself thinking that there must be some belief in me if I sit and think about the time when I see Owen again."

Now it was Joanne's turn to feel embarrassed. Jenny watched Joanne's neck grow blotchy. The young girl shifted uncomfortably in her chair.

"I'm sorry, I don't have a right to think such things, but I've known Owen my entire life almost," Joanne added quickly. "I..."

Stephen put the fork down and reached over to squeeze Joanne's hand. "It's okay, love. You are allowed to miss him too." He paused. "I'm glad you do."

Jenny sat watching Joanne carefully and then a tightness caught hold of her chest as she realised for the first time that Joanne had been in love with Owen. This beautiful young girl had loved her handsome son. It was something she had always wanted because she knew the pair would have made a great couple. The pleasure of the thought changed to hurt for a future that could not possibly be.

Then Jenny really looked at Joanne and she saw pain in her young face. Jenny promised herself that she would do something special for Joanne. She didn't know what yet, but she would think of something.

After dinner, Joanne followed Kirsti back upstairs. This time they walked passed Owen's room and went into Kirsti's room instead. Nothing had changed, except for the owner. Joanne studied Kirsti's profile and saw distinct changes. Her hair had lost its lustre and it fell limp and scraggy around her shoulders. Her usually healthy looking skin was blemished and sallow. Her eyes were hollow, with darkness shading them instead of the usual eye shadow. The smile Joanne had become accustomed to seeing no longer existed.

Yet the words coming from her friend suggested everything was fine—or as fine as the circumstances allowed. Joanne listened with mixed emotions as Kirsti spoke about her boss and what a terrible tyrant she thought her to be.

"...she expects me to hand out business cards at the function on Friday night. Can you believe that?" said Kirsti.

"Are you going to do it?" asked Joanne.

Kirsti looked at her and shook her head. "Of course not! She's got a cheek asking me."

Joanne agreed. "How's she treating you in general?"

Kirsti flopped back onto her pillow and looked up at the ceiling. "Oh, she makes a point of saying the right thing, but she's not sincere."

Joanne didn't know what to say to that. Did Kirsti think her concern was insincere too? As a friend, she knew she hadn't been as supportive as she should have been. Guilt tugged at her conscience. "Kirsti? If you want to talk about what happened, I hope you know you can with me. I'm a good listener."

"Yes, I know." Kirsti groaned as she sat up. "There's nothing to talk about. I'm fine."

Joanne's gut told her she had been lied to.

Tim drained the contents of the glass, immune to the burning sensation in his throat. He knew he was more than a little tipsy from the alcohol. He had consumed more than usual in the hope that it might deaden his emotions. He needed to escape reality. Even if it were for a short time while he slept the effects of the drink off.

It wasn't working.

He looked around the darkened park. No children played on the equipment at this time of night. They would be at home, snug and warm in bed. Their parents would be watching TV, feeling secure in the knowledge that their offspring were safe. They wouldn't be thinking it might be possible that their small children might become suicidal in the future.

Tim gave a loud grunt, stood, and threw the glass he was holding at a nearby brick wall. It shattered and fell in pieces to the ground. He would never be a parent. Not now. How could he believe his unborn children were safe after what had happened?

He plonked himself down again, grabbed the bottle of whisky and let more fluid slide freely down his throat.

Wednesday, 14th June

Joanne looked over her shoulder to check if Geoff was nearby. Confirming she was alone, she grabbed her mobile and quickly searched her contacts for Kirsti's number before dialling it on the surgery's landline. Geoff would only become suspicious if she made the call from her mobile phone. The number dialled, she flipped the mobile cover shut and dropped the phone into her pocket.

Kirsti's phone rang repeatedly, but there was no answer.

Joanne waited a few minutes and then pressed "redial" on the reception console. Still no answer.

What was going on? Joanne had asked herself the same question all night. She had barely slept a wink for thinking about it. Kirsti had lied to her, Joanne didn't doubt that for a moment, but why had her friend lied? What could it mean?

The door chime sounded. Joanne looked up and automatically smiled at the old woman wobbling towards her with a tan dog held lovingly in her arms. "Good morning," she said. "How can I help you?"

"Tiddles is sick," the woman said. "Can the vet see him today?"

"Of course," replied Joanne. "Take a seat and I'll let the vet know you are here."

"He's so old," said the woman. "I hope it's nothing serious. I don't know what I'd do if I lost him."

Joanne had learned long ago, never to offer reassurance in these circumstances. "The vet will do everything he can for Tiddles."

"Thank you, dear."

Joanne asked the necessary questions and typed the responses into the computer. As the old woman took a seat, Joanne pressed "save" knowing an alert would signal Geoff and tell him a patient was waiting.

As soon as the woman and Tiddles had followed Geoff into a consultation room, Joanne pressed redial on the telephone console once again.

Still no response.

Tim opened his eyes and gasped. A pair of large, round eyes stared intently at him. He lifted his head and straightened himself on the wooden bench seat.

"What are you looking at?" he asked the small boy standing in front of him.

"Are you a drunk?" the boy asked. "My sister said you're a drunken bum. She will get in trouble if Mum hears her say that word."

Tim looked at the small girl sitting on the swing a short distance away. "What would she know?"

"I'm only five, but she's eight and she knows everything," said the boy. "Are you a drunk?"

"Clear off, kid." Tim lifted his face to the warm sunshine and closed his eyes. He must have passed out. Drinking all that alcohol had worked after all.

"My sister said you probably live in the gutter. Do you?"

Tim groaned and looked around the park for the boy's mother. She sat on a bench absorbed in a magazine. "I'm not a drunk and I don't live in the gutter. Now go away!"

"Braydon! Come here immediately."

Tim looked across the park and found the boy's mother on her feet, staring at them. She took a step towards them and then another step. Her pale face and dark eyes told Tim she feared him.

"Braydon," she said after a moment, "do as you're told."

Tim looked down at Braydon. *Why is he still standing there?* "Go!"

Tim didn't mean to raise his voice, but Braydon's mother dropped the magazine and ran towards them. "Don't touch my son," she yelled at him.

The woman scooped Braydon up into her arm and held him protectively against her body. The entire time Tim felt her cold stare almost burning his skin. She turned and walked away, but she had only taken a couple of steps when Tim heard Braydon say, "You don't look like a drunk to me. Not like the one who lives under the bridge near the railway line, anyway."

The woman called her daughter to her side, picked up the discarded magazine and quickly took her children to safety.

Tim staggered in the other direction. Once he reached the footpath he stood for a moment and looked in both directions, but no one could be seen. Placing one hand on his throbbing head, he turned right and headed towards the university.

After work, Skye finally turned into the street she lived on and immediately spotted Melody's car parked out the front of her block of flats. The two girls had been spending a lot of time together over the last few weeks.

Guilt filled Skye once again. Whilst she and Melody had been hanging out more, she and Kirsti had hardly said two words to each other since the weekend. "I've been busy," Skye said to herself as she struggled out of her seat and locked the car door.

"Hey," said Melody.

"Hey to you too," replied Skye. "It's my turn to cook, so I think I'll order some Chinese food in. Do you want some?"

"Sure," replied Melody. "What happened to pizza?"

"Oh, there's only so much pizza a girl can eat. Besides, I'm over the pizza guy. I don't even know what I saw in him in the first place. There's a guy who works at the Chinese takeaway that's got my attention now instead."

Melody laughed. "I guess that means you'll be collecting the order instead of having it delivered?"

"Bloody oath!"

Skye unlocked the front door and held it open for Melody. The flat smelled a bit mouldy. Obviously, locking the windows when no one was home wasn't helping with the dampness problem they were having. She opened a couple of windows before heading down the hallway to her bedroom.

Grunting sounds came from the closest bedroom. Skye groaned. "I can't believe it. They're at it again."

"You're just jealous," said Melody, with a grin.

"Of course I am." She banged on the wall a couple of times. "Keep the noise down. This isn't a brothel, you know."

"Skye!"

"Well, it's not. Why should I have to listen to them having sex all the time?" Skye dropped her bag on her bed and kicked her shoes into a corner. "I've been thinking about Kirsti a lot today. We really need to contact her."

"I know," agreed Melody. "Actually, I tried to phone her today, but I have to admit that I was kind of happy when she didn't answer."

"Same here," said Skye, although she knew full well that she hadn't even tried to phone. What kind of a friend did that make her? But she would try, she assured herself. Tomorrow. "I feel bad. Maybe we should organise something for Saturday night?"

"Maybe."

"You don't sound too sure," said Skye.

"No. I want things to return to normal. I'm sick of feeling awkward all the time and having to watch what I say.

I've never been good at that."

"What are you saying exactly?" asked Skye.

"I'm saying that maybe it will be better if we hook up with some of our other friends on Saturday night and have a good time for a change," replied Melody, checking her reflection in the mirror. "Then we can do and say what we want without fear. We can laugh without worrying about offending Kirsti and we can have fun for once."

Skye didn't like what she had heard. "Kirsti is our friend."

"Yeah, I know that," replied Melody. She moved to stand beside the CD player. A moment later heavy metal drowned out the noises from the room next door. "I'm not saying we should dump her or anything. I'm saying we should be allowed to have a good time ... this one time. Then on Monday, we will make an extra effort to be there for Kirsti."

"I don't know," said Skye. She picked up a photograph of her and Kirsti, taken on Skye's 18th birthday, and stared at the happy, smiling faces staring back at her. "It doesn't feel right." She paused. "But I guess one night is all right."

"Sure it is," replied Melody. "How about ordering that Chinese? I'm starving."

"Jo, the movie is about to start. Are you going to watch it with me?"

Joanne heard her mother's voice clearly from the study. "Not right now, Mum." She picked up the telephone receiver and cradled it expertly between her shoulder and right ear. "I need to phone Kirsti first. I won't be long."

"Okay, dear," said her mum. "Tell Jenny that I've been thinking about her and that she should phone me if she would like to meet for a coffee and a chat."

Joanne pressed the numbers on the keypad and listened

to the ring tone. Kirsti had ignored her phone calls all day, but she wouldn't be able to ignore this phone call. Joanne would make sure of that.

"Hello?"

"Mrs Fowler, this is Joanne," she replied. "How are you?"

"Hello, Joanne," said Mrs Fowler. She sounded tired. "I'm coping. Thank you for asking."

"I'm glad." Joanne paused for a moment before continuing, not sure what else to say. She had never had difficulty talking to Mrs Fowler before. "May I speak to Kirsti if she's home?"

"Of course. I'll get her for you."

Joanne heard Mrs Fowler place the phone on the table and walk away. "Kirsti? Kirsti? Joanne's on the phone."

Joanne strained to hear Kirsti's response but heard nothing. A moment later, she heard Mrs Fowler's footsteps as she returned to the phone.

"Joanne?"

"Yes?" She was going to be given a brush off. She knew it! What excuse would be used, she wondered.

"Kirsti's on her way down," said Mrs Fowler. "When will you come over for dinner again? It was lovely having you here last night."

Kirsti was actually going to speak with her. Surprised, Joanne was caught off guard for a second.

"Joanne, are you there?"

"Oh, I'm sorry. I ... I was a million miles away," replied Joanne quickly. "Um, I'd love to come to dinner again. Soon ... whenever it's convenient. It would be a pleasure, Mrs Fowler."

"Good. I look forward to it. Well, here's Kirsti," said Mrs Fowler. "Bye for now."

"Bye." Joanne heard the phone being passed from mother to daughter before she realised she hadn't passed on her mother's message. She sighed deeply.

"That was a big sigh," said Kirsti. "What's up?"

"I forgot to pass on a message from Mum," replied Joanne. "She said she'd like to meet your mum for coffee when she feels up to it."

"I'll let Mum know," said Kirsti.

"Thanks."

There was a long pause.

"I tried to phone you today," said Joanne.

"Yeah, I know. I'm sorry. Lisa is being a real bitch about personal phone calls at work, so I put the phone on silent and forgot to change it back," replied Kirsti. "I was going to phone you tonight. You beat me to it."

Joanne doubted any of what Kirsti said was true. "No problem," she said into the receiver. "Do you want to see a movie tomorrow night?"

"I can't. Not tomorrow night," replied Kirsti. "I'm going to that function with Josh on Friday night and I need to get my hair done tomorrow after work."

"Do you want me to come with you?"

"No, that's fine. Thanks for offering though," said Kirsti. "I'll probably have the works—hair, nails and even a facial if I've got enough time. It will be boring for you."

"I don't mind."

"No, honestly. I'll be fine," said Kirsti.

Another long silence.

"Okay, well ... um ... how about meeting up on Saturday night then?" asked Joanne.

"Sure. I'll phone you on Saturday and we'll make arrangements," replied Kirsti.

Joanne stared at the desk, her temples throbbing. What was she missing? What was she doing wrong? All she wanted to do was to help her friend!

II

Light rain fell as Tim walked slowly down the hill. Behind

him, on the deserted road, was the discarded push bike which had brought him to this desolate place. The bike wasn't his; he had "borrowed" it from one of the other university students. The owner wouldn't even know it had been used. Tim was almost sure of it. No one in their right mind would ride a push bike in the early hours of the morning, without lights, in the rain! No, he was sure everything would be all right and he would return it long before first light. Besides, using his car had been out of the question. People noticed noisy things like that. And they had a habit of noticing number plates too. Tim didn't want to be noticed.

He stumbled. The ground rushed up and before he knew what had happened, he was on the ground rolling his way to the bottom where he came to a stop with a thud. The concrete retaining wall might have stopped him rolling onto the railway tracks, but it did nothing for his headache. Tim accepted the pain as punishment for his perpetual new drinking habits.

He struggled to his feet and looked around. He was scratched and damp, but he was also alone. At least he could be thankful that the people he had come to see hadn't seen his grand entrance.

The moonlight didn't make it possible for him to see anything in the pitch blackness beneath the bridge and he hesitated. If he wanted to change his mind, now was the time to do it. Was this what he really wanted? No true answer came flashing down to him, so Tim took a step forward and then another. The third step took him into the black void.

He stood still for a moment, waiting for his eyes to adjust to the lack of light. A moment later he saw movement and realised that his grand entrance had been witnessed after all. He swallowed, lifted his head and walked towards the movement he had seen.

"I'm looking for Hawk," he said with as much control of his voice as he could.

"Who's lookin'?" It was a male voice—gruff and threatening.

"Ti ... er, call me ... Fox."

"Fox?" The man laughed ... and kept laughing.

Tim felt anger stirring in his stomach. "What's so funny?"

"Listen, man, you ain't no fox," said the man. "I think a more fitting name would be Froggy."

"What you talking about?" Tim clenched his fists. He'd already had enough of this moron.

"You're wet and slimy just like a frog." Laughter burst from him again.

Tim held his tongue. He willed the anger to subside so that he could speak. He really wanted to punch the guy in the face. It would feel good to let out some of the aggression he felt inside. Instead, he took a deep breath and said, "Tell Hawk I'm here to do business and I haven't got all night to wait around while some dead shit gets his rocks off on his own jokes."

Silence.

Tim's fists were still clenched and his muscles were taut ready to react if the owner of the voice made a move towards him. *Come on! I want to bash someone's brains out. It may as well be you.*

It didn't happen. Tim felt disappointed.

The Joker moved away from him. He walked towards a huge concrete pipe and leaned into it. "Hawk, someone by the name of Froggy is here for ya."

Tim rushed forward, grabbed Joker by the scruff of the neck and slammed him back against the wall. "I said the name is Fox."

"Yeah, whatever. It's a stupid name. We all have 'em."

"Hey, Sparrow," a strange voice echoed along the pipe, "send him through."

Sparrow! "Yeah, we all have them," said Tim. "With a name like yours, I'm surprised you aren't black and blue from daily beatings."

Sparrow said nothing.

Tim shoved him to one side and stepped into the pipe. Without a sideways glance, he walked confidently along the tunnel, towards a golden light at the other end.

Hawk's "office" was nothing more than a junction in the sewer system. He had a small wooden, and mouldy, table in the middle of the space with a chair on each side facing each other. Hawk occupied one. The light source came from a gas lantern hanging on the wall behind him. Hawk was long and lanky, dressed in army camouflage. Dark, greasy hair hung limp around his ears and neck. His dark eyes never left Tim's face as his tongue played with the piercing through his bottom lip.

"So, Froggy, what is your pleasure?" asked Hawk.

Tim flinched at the name but said nothing. "What have you got?"

"The hawk has landed and he has many gems to share."

What the...? Tim felt cold. What was he doing here?

"I can see you are uncertain what gems you'd like to purchase, Froggy," said Hawk. "I'll tell you what. Seeing as you're a new customer, I'll give you a special deal."

Hawk rose from his seat and dropped a plastic bag onto the table. Tim had no idea where it had come from, but he could clearly see the tablets and powder inside.

"An introductory offer," said Hawk. "A one time offer at that."

Tim stared at the contents without saying a word.

"Three hundred," announced Hawk.

"I only have two hundred and forty," replied Tim.

"You drive a hard bargain, Froggy, my man," said Hawk. "Show me the colour of your money."

Tim pulled out the crinkled notes from his jeans pocket and dropped it on the table.

Hawk smiled. "You look like a nice kinda guy. I'll part you from that money of yours tonight, but next time ... you pay full price. And that ain't three hundred!"

Tim watched Hawk casually reach forward and take the

money. Then he turned to the pipe Tim had come through and placing several fingers into his mouth, gave a loud shrill of a whistle. A moment later, Hawk grabbed the lantern and disappeared down one of the tunnels, leaving Tim sitting in the dark.

Tim sat quietly for several minutes, half expecting Hawk's mates to jump him and beat the crap out of him, but nothing happened. Finally, Tim gingerly reached out and felt around on the table until his fingers found the plastic bag. Standing, he shoved the bag into his pocket and stumbled along the pipe. Emerging from the other end, Tim looked around for Sparrow but knew instantly that he was alone.

The hairs on his neck prickled. Tim wasted no time in finding his way back out into the moonlight, up the hill and onto the bike. With one last glance at the black void beneath the bridge, Tim turned the bike towards home and peddled as fast as he could.

Kirsti sat in her room, in the dark, after her parents went to bed. She couldn't sleep, but she pretended she did—just like she pretended a lot of things these days. She sat on the side of her bed, thinking.

Her gaze moved to the mirror above her dressing table. All she could see was a reflection of her room, but she wanted something else.

"Owen? Where are you?" she whispered. "Please visit me."

She didn't have to wait for long before the mirror image changed. Kirsti smiled, left her bed and walked across the room. "It won't be long now," she said to the Owen in the mirror. "The plans are made."

Mirror Owen turned to face her and returned her smile.

Thursday, 15th June

On Thursday morning, Jenny watched Kirsti head off to work and waited a few extra minutes before picking up her bag and walking out the front door. She ignored the garage and her car, choosing instead to walk down the street in the opposite direction to what Stephen, who had left early, and Kirsti had gone. She was in no hurry to get anywhere as she had no destination in mind.

She didn't want to be in the house alone.

Jenny walked slowly. At first, she looked at the houses and their gardens on either side of her, but she soon let her thoughts turn inward. Never in her life had she been scared to be at home alone. Never in her life had she kept secrets from those she loved. Never in her life had she felt so utterly helpless and vulnerable. Never, that is, until now.

She walked mechanically, unaware of where her feet were taking her.

After throwing the reverend out of her home on Tuesday morning, Jenny didn't know what to do with herself. Her mind was too active, yet her body felt fatigued. Maybe it was time to return to work? Jenny shook her head. She knew she wasn't ready, not while she felt this confused. Work pressures would only add to the problem. Finally, she had decided to go for a long walk and, the more distance she put between herself and the house, the more relaxed she felt. Late that afternoon, she had forced herself to return home in order to cook the evening meal for her working family, but she said nothing about her day wandering the streets to Stephen or Kirsti.

On Wednesday, she found herself roaming the streets again. The day was long, but the sun warmed her body as nothing else could.

On Thursday, Jenny was keen to walk in the sun again. But she knew something had to be done. She couldn't avoid the house forever. Could she? She certainly couldn't walk the streets every day. As she walked, she entertained the notion of returning to work again. Going to work would give her an excuse to be away from the house all day. She couldn't deny the pleasure that thought gave her. And the distraction would be good for her ... or that's what her friends kept saying. She had to admit that Kirsti didn't seem to be having much trouble coping with work pressures, and neither did Stephen, so perhaps it was time she started working toward a new normality too. Holding on to the past was unhealthy.

Jenny shook her head. No, she knew what was happening. The world was moving forward at a steady pace and she felt as if she were being dragged along with it ... and leaving Owen behind. It felt wrong and she knew she was fighting against it.

But Owen was gone. He had made a choice and now she had to learn to live with it. It hardly seemed fair or just, and she felt out of control, but she also knew that now she had to make a choice too.

She walked faster. Her steps matched the beating of her heart. She had to make a choice, but she couldn't do it. She couldn't make a decision that meant moving into the future ... and away from her son. She had failed her son once. Could this choice mean that she would fail him again?

Joanne stroked the cat's tangled fur. "Some people shouldn't have pets," she said to Geoff.

"I know," the vet replied.

"Will he survive?"

"Yes," replied Geoff. "We got this one in time. Ask Cameron to come in and assist me with the op."

Joanne sighed. "Okay."

Back at the reception desk, Joanne sat quietly pricing dog accessories and adding them to the display shelf behind the counter. She worked methodically, but her mind was elsewhere. Kirsti was in trouble. Joanne couldn't say why or how she knew this to be true, but she was sure her friend needed help. So sure, in fact, that she couldn't sleep at night worrying about it. That morning, over breakfast, Joanne had talked to her mother again about the situation.

"Darling, you need to approach Skye and Melody and tell them that they are wrong," Joanne's mother had said.

"But Skye is hard to approach, Mum."

"It doesn't matter. This isn't a silly tiff over a piece of clothing or even over a boy. This is much more important than that."

Joanne had nodded, agreeing with what her mother was saying.

"Confront her and make her see sense. I know you have it in you."

"I wish *I* knew that," replied Joanne. "I know this sounds silly, but I'm scared of her."

"You shouldn't be friends with her then."

Joanne sighed.

"What's the worst thing that can happen?" asked her mother. Before Joanne could respond, her mother continued, "She'll get offended and you won't be friends anymore. So what? Who cares? At least you tried!"

Joanne jerked back to the present. The pricing gun fell from her fingers and clattered onto the ground at her feet. Her body went cold and a shiver ran down her spine.

No, the worst thing that could happen is that Kirsti might commit suicide and I would have done nothing to try and help her.

Joanne no longer cared what Skye and Melody thought. She no longer cared if they never spoke to her again after today. All she cared about was doing the right thing for her dearest friend.

Joanne would confront Skye and Melody that afternoon ... and she would ensure they heard everything she had to say to them.

Jenny stood outside the sandstone church and stared at the cross reaching high into the clear blue sky. Her fingers touched the silver cross around her neck. Tears stung her eyes. Her gaze slowly moved downward until they rested on the open door at the top of five steps, a few paces away.

She gulped. She had already tried to find help through the church, but it hadn't worked. If she walked through those doors now, would she find Reverend McPherson on the other side? She didn't want to see him again. The man made her blood boil!

She turned to walk away but found she couldn't leave. Glancing over her shoulder at the open doorway again, she felt compelled to turn and face the place of worship. Confused, she stared at the wooden door with the old-fashioned hinges for a long time. Then something tugged at her will, nudging her to go inside. Before she could refuse the notion, Jenny took a deep breath and walked up the steps and into the church.

Inside was much lighter than Jenny had expected. High lead-light windows lined both sides of the church. The sun streamed through coloured glass. Jenny felt uplifted by the array of colour and almost smiled. Finally, her gaze rested on Jesus on a large cross, hanging above the empty pulpit.

She had never been to church. She wasn't a Christian. She had no right to be here. Yet she couldn't leave. Desperate words, seeking help and forgiveness, tumbled through her mind.

She walked slowly down the aisle, her eyes never leaving Jesus. She moved sideways and found a pew to sit on. Cradling her bag in her lap, she held the silver cross in one hand and finally closed her eyes. Warmth enveloped her. Calmness filled her. She prayed in her own misguided way.

II

Kirsti stared at the words on the pretty blue stationery pad she held. Her neat hand-writing filled the page. They were well thought out words that had taken over an hour to write. She took a sip of her coffee and cringed as the cold beverage slid down her throat.

She turned the page and continued reading. When she reached the end, she placed the pad on the table and leaned back on the wooden seat. She felt cramped and uncomfortable in the tiny booth but at least no one could peer over her shoulder to see what she was writing.

Satisfied with her words, she looked up in time to see the waitress giving her a rude look. Kirsti sighed. It was time to pay for the coffee and find another café to sit in.

Kirsti glanced over the letter one more time before carefully removing the two pages and folding them in half. She reached into a shopping bag and pulled out a small box. Opening the lid, she stared at the golden angel on a chain resting delicately on a velvet backing. Closing the lid again, Kirsti placed the necklace and the letter into a gift box and tied a length of lilac ribbon around it. On the small tag attached to the ribbon, she wrote "Joanne" before putting the gift into the shopping bag and leaving the booth to pay for the coffee.

Jenny knew she was no longer alone. She felt a nearby presence. A familiar stab of fear wrapped itself around her heart and she quickly opened her eyes. The fear subsided when she saw a man of God quietly moving around at the front of the church. He did not look at her, but she sensed he knew she was there. She wiped the dampness from her cheeks and stood to leave.

He turned to her and smiled. "Please, you don't have to leave. I can see you are upset about something. Feel free to sit in here for as long as you want." He was much younger than Reverend McPherson. His eyes were kind and his voice gentle.

"I ... I needed time ... to ... sit ... and..." Jenny didn't know what she needed and she didn't know what to say.

"You were crying before. Is there something you'd like to talk about?"

Jenny wanted him to help her. She needed it so badly. "No, I don't think you can help me."

The smile disappeared from his face. She could see concern in his eyes.

Jenny's emotions soared. She felt weary and confused. She had already discovered that the church couldn't help her, yet why had she felt compelled to come inside this church? Reverend McPherson had made all kinds of terrible accusations, so why was she allowing this man of God to talk to her? Once he heard the truth, he would look at her differently too.

The man moved his head to one side as he studied her face. "You've turned to someone for help and they've hurt you," he said.

How does he know that? A lump formed in the back of her throat. She shifted from one foot to the other. She found it difficult to hold eye contact. "I ... I'm fine."

"If you change your mind, you are always welcome here." He smiled.

The words resounded in Jenny's mind as she hurried to

the exit without even responding.

Kirsti ordered a coffee before heading for a table in the corner. She sat on the cushioned chair with her back to the wall, facing the other patrons, and looked around until her coffee was placed in front of her. She watched the waiter walk away and then she took out the blue pad and immediately started writing.

The walk from the previous coffee shop had given her enough time to think about the general contents of the letter she was writing. However, between sentences she paused and considered what words she would use next, sometimes taking a sip of her coffee at the same time.

Her words had not filled the page when she decided that she had said everything she wanted to say, and she signed her name at the bottom. She read the letter once before taking a small jewellery box from the shopping bag and holding it in her hands.

The smooth wood had been stained a reddish brown. The glass lid would allow the owner to see the rows of rings, necklaces and earrings inside. But what Kirsti especially liked about the jewellery box was the pattern of the glass. Slithers of glass were arranged in the shape of a dragon. It looked superb and Kirsti knew who she wanted to give it to as soon as she saw it.

She took another gift box from the shopping bag. Placing the letter inside the jewellery box, Kirsti packed the gift and wrapped it in lilac ribbon before writing "Skye" on the tag.

The next letter only took a few minutes to write. Words would be wasted on the recipient and Kirsti was fully aware of this fact.

The next item to be taken from the shopping bag was a DVD—The Rocky Horror Picture Show. It was a favourite, which had given many hours of enjoyment and Kirsti wanted the memories to live on. She placed the DVD and letter into another gift box and wrapped it in the lilac ribbon. She wrote "Melody" on the tag before putting the gift away.

The fourth letter she had written that day was more difficult to write as Kirsti had mixed emotions regarding the person who she addressed the letter to. She remembered the good times, but then she relived the bad times too. In truth, it was only recently that she had seen the person for who he truly was, but that didn't matter. She had things to say to him and she would say them all.

She found it difficult to get started and found herself wondering if authors of published novels felt like she did at that moment. She forced herself to write one word and then another and before she knew it, the words were tumbling out of her. Five pages later, she paused and took a deep breath. She felt exhausted.

She took a mouthful of her coffee. It was cold—again—but she hadn't expected it to be anything else.

After a few minutes of reflection, Kirsti picked up the letter and read it through. She ignored the tear smudges but corrected a few spelling mistakes as she went over what she had written. Finally, she put the letter down and took out the gift that would accompany it.

The dainty gold ring had been given to her on her sixteenth birthday. It was nothing fancy and it definitely hadn't cost much, but the ring had meant the world to her. Along with the ring she had chosen a small glass sign with the words—*Forge ahead, but don't forget the people who love you*—engraved on it. She had seen it in the window of a shop. Covered in dust, she knew it had been there for a long time, but the words jumped out at her and she knew this was the right item to buy.

She wrapped the ring in a serviette and placed it in a gift box along with the sign and the letter. Once again, she tied a lilac ribbon around it, but this time she wrote "Josh" on the tag.

"Your coffee is cold, would you like a fresh one?"

Kirsti looked up and found the waiter gazing down at her. "No, thanks. I'm leaving now."

He smiled before walking away.

Jenny stared at the path in front of her. The clip of her heels echoed in her ears, a constant reminder that she was running away. She heard grunting noises and was only vaguely aware that the noises came from her as she forced her aching legs to take her to safety. To help her escape.

Where could she go and feel safe? Would she ever feel normal and whole again? She stopped walking and stood perfectly still for a moment. Her temples thumped the side of her head. How was she meant to carry on and survive?

She screamed.

She screamed so loud and so hard that her throat felt ready to explode. She screamed so long that she finally felt a small amount of release from the sound piercing her ears and the thumping inside her head.

She stopped screaming and looked around. Everyone, in every direction, stood watching her. What was wrong with them? Did they think she was some kind of freak? No, she knew what they were thinking. They didn't bother trying to hide the fact that they thought she was crazy!

At that moment, Jenny knew the truth. She knew better than anyone what was going on inside her head. She knew, without a single doubt, that she was as crazy as they all thought she was.

And she didn't care!

But the moment past and she knew deep in her heart that she did care. She had always cared about what other people thought of her. She had always needed other people to like her, to accept her. Wasn't that the reason why she

211

had started doing charity work?

She had tried to be a good person. She had always been thoughtful of other people. She had worked hard her entire life. She had never abused her body or her children or any other living creature. She had always tried not to be judgemental. She had loved her family. She had done everything right. Or so she had always thought. But what did any of it account for? It didn't matter because none of it had kept her family safe.

And now she was being punished. Tears rolled down her face. She knew the truth. She couldn't even keep her own son alive. She deserved all the bad things that were happening to her. And she deserved worse.

"Dear?"

The soft voice sounded so strange in the darkness of her mind. Jenny turned to find a little, old lady standing near her. Her wrinkled skin and withered hands showed decades of wisdom, her bright blue eyes testified a youthful mind.

"Dear, are you all right?" asked the old woman, her head tilted to one side. "You need to calm down. Let me buy you a cup of strong tea. That always works for me."

Jenny stared at the woman as if she had never seen a human before, knowing she needed more than to be calm. "My son died." Jenny's voice was nothing more than a whisper.

The woman's gaze didn't falter. "You poor thing. Do you want to talk about it? I know I'm a stranger, but I'm a good listener."

The flood gates opened. Words tumbled from Jenny's mouth, but she would never remember what she said in the next few minutes. She felt a warm hand take hold of her elbow and steer her away from prying eyes.

"Come on, dearie, sit down over here," said the woman. "There's nothing better than a good cry when you're feeling down, you know."

Jenny allowed the stranger to take charge and guide her

to a wooden bench in a small park not far from where they were standing. She was grateful to be relieved of her duties. She didn't want to make decisions for herself.

"Cry." The woman pressed a small packet of tissues into her hand. "Let it all out."

Jenny obeyed. She cried until there was nothing left inside. When the sobbing subsided, she peered around and saw mothers and their children playing in the sunshine. It looked like a playgroup. Everyone was smiling and happy. Jenny cried some more.

"Isn't the sun warm on our backs?" asked the woman sometime later, sitting on the bench beside her. "It helps take away that empty feeling, don't you think?"

Jenny knew the woman didn't expect an answer, so she sat quietly and felt the sun warming her body for the first time that day.

"Grief is a terrible thing," said the woman. "It's like a germ that attacks the vulnerable and won't let go. When I lost my Richard after 57 years of marriage I didn't think I could go on alone. The depression I suffered in that first year was the worst experience of my life. I had survived a world war, the recession and poverty the youngsters of today wouldn't believe possible, but the passing of my beloved Richard was nearly my undoing."

The old woman fell silent whilst Jenny sat quietly digesting what she had said.

"But losing a son," she paused and patted Jenny's hand, "that is something no woman should have to endure."

Jenny swallowed the lump in her throat.

"Richard had a long life. He was almost 80 when he died. We knew it was about to happen as he had been unwell in the last few years, but it's still hard for those left behind to accept. But your son had a lot of living to do."

Another silence. Jenny could see Owen's smiling face in her mind. His life would have been good. She didn't doubt that for a minute. But he had thrown all that away and she didn't know why. She didn't know where they came from, but more tears spilled down her face.

"I don't know what happened to your son, but I can tell you that what you are feeling is normal," said the old woman. "You are not crazy. You are not going insane. You are grieving the loss of your beloved son and it will take time, a long time, before you start to heal."

Jenny felt she should say something, anything, but she couldn't force herself to speak. She dabbed her face with a handful of tissues.

"I wanted to join Richard, you know," the woman continued. "I felt my life was over without him, but a good friend of mine helped me through that phase. She gave me a book and told me that it had helped her when her mother died and she felt it would help me too. She was right, you know. It helped a lot."

Jenny turned to look at the woman sitting beside her. She looked frail. Her white hair curled neatly over her forehead. Her pink dress was old-fashioned but it suited her slim figure. She turned those blue eyes onto Jenny and smiled a radiant smile that touched Jenny's heart.

"I found comfort in the words of that book and, whilst the book isn't the reason why I chose to continue living, it did help. I'll be 90 in three months and it has been eleven years since Richard passed away. I can tell you honestly that life without Richard is different, but it's still good, and I'm glad I gave it another chance."

The two women held each other's gaze. Jenny felt understanding pass between them and for the first time in a long time, she felt as if someone really cared.

"Give it time," the woman said a moment later. "But in the meantime, be good to yourself."

Jenny nodded.

The woman patted her hand again. "How about that cup of tea?"

Jenny tried to smile. The woman had been so nice to her, so understanding. "No, thank you. I've taken up too much of your time already."

"That's all right."

"I should be running along," said Jenny, although she didn't have any errands to do.

"Are you feeling a little better?"

"Yes, I am. Thank you."

"You're welcome, dear." She stood and straightened her dress. "I'll be off then."

"Again, thank you."

The woman smiled and turned to walk away.

"Wait," said Jenny. "What was the name of that book your friend gave you?"

The woman grinned. "It was called 'When Bad Things Happen to Good People' by Harold S. Kushner, but it's an old book and I think it might be hard to find."

"I'll go to the library and see if they have a copy of it there," replied Jenny.

III

Kirsti took the CD out of the bag and smiled. It amazed her how a title of a song could bring back so many memories. *King of the Road* had been a favourite between Kirsti and her two brothers. The music was catchy and the words easy to remember. She closed her eyes and saw three youngsters miming to the song in her bedroom. Kirsti and Owen would have been seven years old, which meant Tim was nine.

Next, she took a small, metal butterfly out of her bag and stared at that. Tim had won it at a fair. He had been so proud of himself and it was the first thing that he had won on his own merits. Kirsti had fallen in love with the butterfly instantly and had badgered him to give it to her for days. Looking back, she realised that she had been mean to do that to him, but she hadn't known that at the time. Eventually, he succumbed, but he handed it over reluctantly. Tim probably thought the butterfly had been discarded years ago, but Kirsti had kept it in her little box of treasures ever since.

She placed the butterfly, CD and a letter she had written to him into a gift box and tied the familiar lilac ribbon around it. On the tag, she wrote "Tim".

Kirsti left her chair and walked up to the counter. "Excuse me," she said to the woman serving, "may I have another cup of coffee please?"

The woman smiled and nodded. "I'll bring it to your table."

"Thank you."

Seated again, she pulled the blue writing pad towards her and took a deep breath. This last letter would be the hardest to write. In this letter, she would have to explain her decision and she already felt nervous about doing that.

As she waited for the fresh coffee to arrive, she settled back against the cushions and watched the world go by. Apart from the nerves regarding the letter, she felt calm inside. The decision she had made felt right.

The coffee arrived, the waitress disappeared and Kirsti continued to sit. Half the coffee had disappeared from the cup before she picked up the blue pen she had been using all morning.

Dear Mum and Dad,
This is not an easy letter for me to write, but I want you to know that my decision to follow Owen was not made on the spur of the moment. I realise that my actions will be seen as selfish, and I know that I will not receive the same understanding as Owen did because he didn't know the pain he caused, whereas I do. The decision to end my own life is complicated. Ever since Owen's death, I have felt my own life no longer mattered. It no longer has value or meaning. I find no joy in anything I used to love. I feel a darkness taking

over my body that I never thought was possible. I want to end the confusion and pain ... and be at peace. Like Owen is.

My decision is not a reflection on my love for you, for I love you more than you can ever know. My decision is not a reflection on the way you brought me up either because my life prior to Owen's death was the best a girl could ask for and I give thanks to you for that. My decision was made because the day Owen died, part of me died too. But the part of me that lived on has somehow been corrupted and I have done and said things in these last few weeks that I am ashamed of. I have lied to everyone I love and I am truly sorry for that!

My twin brother is dead and nobody cares, apart from you. I hate the way people can't look me in the eye anymore. I feel sad by the fact that I can no longer mention Owen's name without making everyone feel uncomfortable. And I want to talk about Owen. I need to talk about him. I'm scared that if I don't then I'll forget him and I can't bear the thought of that. But I can't talk to anyone about him or about how I'm feeling, especially you guys because I can see the pain you are in and I don't want to make things worse. I never understood how bad grief can be, it's all consuming and I feel so alone and tired.

Mum and Dad, I love you so much and I'm so sorry. Please forgive me. You gave us everything and you deserve so much better than what I've done to you. But I can't stay. I tried to, for your sake, but I don't want to be here anymore. Owen has gone to a better place and I want to go there too. We'll be all right as we'll have each other. We will be your guardian angels from above. We will watch over you and take care of you. I promise.

I'm sorry for the lies, for the deception, and for causing you more pain. I wish we could have turned back
time and put things right for Owen. I wish everything
could go back to how it used to be...

But it can't.

Please place mine and Owen's ashes side by side in
the cemetery. Don't keep them in the bedrooms. It
will only make the house dark and miserable and you
don't need that. You'll never heal that way. It was our
choice to leave our bodies and I know I can speak for
Owen when I say that we don't want you burdened by
our material things.

You are not to blame for what has happened. Please
don't feel guilty about anything. Our lives were brilliant—filled with sunshine and love. You should be
proud that you loved us like you do. And it's important that you know that we love you too.

Goodbye for now. The next time we meet will be in
heaven.

With love always,
Kirsti and Owen
oxox

IV

Joanne watched Skye's car come along the road and stop
outside the block of flats. It was late afternoon and the air
was cool, a sure sign that nightfall wasn't far away. As the
car's engine went silent, she saw two sets of eyes peering
out of the window at her. She was not surprised to see
Melody sitting in the passenger's seat. These days, the two
girls were thick as thieves. It seemed the friendship between the foursome had changed dramatically and that
was the reason for Joanne's determination and willingness

to confront someone she felt nervous around. Even a little scared of.

She stood in the driveway going over her opening sentence in her mind. She had been practising it all day. She felt so worked up about this meeting that she had even asked Geoff for permission to leave work early. Nothing before this had made her feel so strongly about being heard.

"Hello, Joanne," said Skye, wearing a smart pencil skirt and white blouse. The fire in her eyes announced that she had finished a trying day at work and she wasn't in the mood for a friendly chat. "What's up?"

Melody stood silently at Skye's side.

Already feeling intimidated, Joanne forced words out of her mouth. "We have to talk. It's about Kirsti."

Melody rolled her eyes and looked at Skye as if she thought her friend would quickly put an end to the conversation so they could retreat inside.

Skye's face remained foreboding. "Well, there's no need to look so serious."

Joanne felt a moment of indecisiveness wash over her. Usually, this would be the time when she would back down, change the subject and walk away from the problem. Today was different. She couldn't afford to be weak or shy and she certainly couldn't allow herself to be scared. Not today. Knowing in her heart that the stakes were too high for her to take the safe option, she took a deep breath and tried to calm herself. The words she had rehearsed all day forgotten. "This is serious, Skye. I think Kirsti is suicidal."

"What?" Melody laughed. "Don't be stupid. She's too sensible."

Joanne looked at Melody and felt disgusted. How could she disregard something this important so easily? Anger allowed words to climb up her throat, but before she could utter them she noticed Skye turn, which stopped any retort Joanne might have given at that time. Skye's brows were drawn together in fury and her cheeks were flushed red.

"I'm sorry." Melody swallowed and lowered her gaze to the ground at their feet.

Recognising an opening, Joanne reached out and touched Skye's arm. "Skye, you know I'm right. I know you do. We have to do something to help her. Since Owen's death, we have not been there for her or offered her what she really needs ... and that is to talk. I did some research and true friends will sit and listen, without judgement, without offering advice. Just listen. We haven't done that. She's bottling up what she's feeling and it's not healthy."

"But ... but..." Skye fumbled for words.

Joanne could see her friend was clearly out of her comfort zone. It was something Joanne had never witnessed before.

"But what about Josh?" Skye finally said. "She'll be talking to him about that sort of thing."

Joanne tutted. "My God, Skye, do you really believe that? Josh is useless. He's so self-centred he wouldn't know what Kirsti was thinking or doing unless it affects him. He certainly wouldn't think to ask her. He's only interested in himself." She paused for a moment. "He didn't even go to the funeral!"

"She's right," Melody said to Skye, her voice low and her gaze immediately reverting back to the dirty concrete at their feet. "Josh wouldn't be any help to her, but her parents would. They share the same grief."

"No," said Joanne, not wanting to hear excuses. "You're wrong. I've been to the house and they don't talk. Everything is awkward and tense. They are so caught up in their own pain, they don't have room for anyone else's. The whole family's in a really bad way. They need help."

Skye and Melody looked at her as if she had all the answers.

Joanne knew she had to continue before her courage waned. "We have to show Kirsti that we really do care about her. We have to let her talk about Owen, even if it does make us feel uncomfortable—"

"But she cries and I can't stand to see her cry," said Melody.

Joanne shook her head. "It doesn't matter. Cry with her. It's what she needs."

"I don't know," replied Melody.

"More importantly, we have to encourage her to talk about that night—"

"No way!" both Skye and Melody said together.

"It will be awful to hear, but we must remember that Kirsti has to live with that memory for the rest of her life." Joanne wiped a tear from her face. "Can you imagine how that image is tormenting her?"

The three girls stood silent for several minutes.

Eventually, Joanne couldn't stand the silence a moment longer. "Skye?"

Skye looked up and Joanne saw that her eyes were moist.

"We've been selfish, haven't we?" asked Skye. The usual loudness gone from her voice.

"No, not selfish exactly," said Joanne. "Just scared, but it's not too late to change that and I think we need to act fast."

"Do you really think she's suicidal?" asked Melody, her hands beginning to shake.

"Yes, I do," replied Joanne.

"That's terrible. What should we do?" said Melody. "Isn't there someone we can phone for help?"

"We're meeting her on Saturday night," said Skye. "I think we should ask her straight out."

"We can't do that!" Melody looked horrified at the suggestion.

"We can and we will," replied Joanne.

"Shouldn't we tell someone of our suspicions?" asked Skye.

No one replied straight away. Joanne didn't have the answers. She hadn't even thought this far ahead when she was planning this meeting. Her mission for the day was to convince Skye and Melody that their friend was in trouble. She had accomplished that so now she felt confident that together they could do anything. "I think we should wait until we've spoken with her on Saturday night and then decide what to do," she said.

Tim heard the whispers that followed him down the corridor and refused to look at anyone. If he had tried hard enough he knew he would have been able to work out what they were saying about him, but he didn't care. Why should he? What difference did it make?

He slid the key into the lock and pushed against the door. At that moment, he felt a presence close behind him. He could almost feel the hot breath on his neck. He turned his head and saw black shoes. He sighed, knowing it couldn't be another student, which meant it could only be...

"Fowler, I've noticed you've been missing lectures."

Tim turned, letting the door rest heavily against his back. "Sir?"

Mr Adams peered at him from under long eyelashes and grinned. "Don't give me that innocent look, Tim. What's going on?"

Tim looked up and down the corridor. Students stood in groups discussing his meeting with the lecturer. "Nothing's going on. I'm fine."

"I know about your brother—" Mr Adams began.

"Doesn't everyone," snapped Tim. "I need time to myself. I don't intend to drop out or anything."

It was Mr Adams turn to look up and down the corridor. "How about we step inside your room so we can talk in private?"

Tim shrugged and leaned back against the door so that it opened enough to let the lecturer through. As soon as the man was clear of the door, Tim stepped to one side and let the door slam shut.

"I don't know how any of you can stand listening to that noise all day and night," said Mr Adams.

"You get used to it."

The lecturer walked along the row of benches looking at the items on each before turning to stare at Tim. "I suppose so."

Tim didn't like the man snooping at his stuff. "What do you want?"

"I'm concerned about you, Tim. The more lectures you miss the harder it will be for you to pass your exams at the end of the year."

Tim wanted to say that he didn't care about the lectures, or the exams, or passing, but he knew to say those words would only force the lecturer to do something. And Tim didn't want him to do anything. He wanted the man to leave.

"I've got it covered, Mr Adams. At the moment, I'm finding it difficult to concentrate, but that will disappear soon. I need a break and to rest up. Which I've been doing."

Mr Adams didn't look convinced.

"Besides, my mate Karl said I can read through his notes," Tim added quickly. "I'm picking them up tomorrow afternoon so that I can sit quietly and read them over the weekend."

"It's a long weekend," replied Mr Adams. "Aren't you going home?"

"Stuff at home is..." Tim felt himself starting to panic. He didn't want to talk about what was happening at home. "I'm going to stay here and read through Karl's notes. It will be much quieter." *Not to mention sane!* "I think that's the best option for me right now."

There! How could Mr Adams argue with that?

"I don't agree," said Mr Adams. "You need to be at home with your family. You need their support."

"You don't know what I need." The words left Tim's

mouth before he could stop them.

"As your lecturer, I have a duty of care and I think I need to talk to someone about your situation," said Mr Adams.

"I'm twenty-two years old, I don't need to ask anyone permission to do anything!"

"This isn't about asking permission," said Mr Adams. "This is about being responsible and I—"

"I am responsible!"

"You've misunderstood—"

"Misunderstood? Misunderstood?" Tim moved closer to Mr Adams, his clenched fists heavy at his sides. His face burning with anger. "Perhaps I've misunderstood a lot of things in my lifetime. For instance, maybe I misunderstood what the purpose of life is ... because I don't seem to know the answer to that any more. I don't seem to understand why I'm bothering to do this whole university thing when my little brother is lying dead and cold in the ground." He lifted his fists and held them a few centimetres from his lecturer's face. "And maybe I misunderstood why a perfectly happy person could take his own life. Come on; tell me Mr Know-It-All. Tell me how I misunderstood something like that."

"Tim," Mr Adams said, taking a couple of steps backwards. "You need help. I can arrange a meeting with the university's counsellor or I can give you the numbers of a few helplines if you prefer. Or I can phone your parents and ask them to come and get you if driving home is the issue."

"I don't need help!" Tim screamed into Mr Adams' face. The temptation to ram his fist into the man's face was overwhelming. "I need do-gooders like you to clear off and leave me alone."

Mr Adams inclined his head to one side. "I understand what you're going through."

"That's shit. It's bull ... shit." Tim turned away from Mr Adams and slammed his fist into the concrete wall. Spots of blood smeared the wall and he felt the warm, sticky substance on his skin. "Everyone is full of shit! You have no idea what I'm feeling or what I'm going through! Get out of my room!"

"I want to help you," said Mr Adams, his voice low and controlled.

"I don't need your help!" Tim pushed the TV set off the table. It smashed onto the floor.

"Tim?"

Tim turned to his books and with one sweeping motion of his arm, he knocked them all into the air. What he really wanted to do was rearrange Mr Adams face. But a little voice in his head refused to let him do that so, his own grunts echoing in his ears, he moved around the room and took his frustrations out on everything he owned instead.

"Tim!"

Tim grabbed his backpack and ran from the room.

"Come on, Babe," said Josh, patting the sheeted mattress beside him. "Get your gear off and get into bed."

The look he received almost dampened the mood. *She's usually quite willing*, he thought. "What's wrong with you tonight?"

Crystal spun around and glared at him. "You're an insensitive bastard."

"That never bothered you before," he replied. "What's changed tonight?"

She rushed at him.

Oh, that's more like it. Her breasts were her biggest asset and, from this angle, he could see why. She bent forward and tried to slap him, revealing cleavage that set Josh's hormones on fire again. He grabbed her hand and pulled her on top of him.

"Babe, you want it rough," he said. He swung her

around and expertly positioned himself above her. Grabbing her jaw in one hand, and a huge breast in the other, he grinned down at her. "I'm fine with rough. It's a bit of a turn on really."

"Get off me, Josh." Crystal's voice was stone cold.

What's she playing at. "You know you like it. Now stop the acting and give me some sex."

Sudden pain in the side of his head forced him to let go of Crystal. Josh felt himself falling to one side and a moment later he lay stunned on the bed. Crystal drew her legs up onto the bed and turned to face him, her face distorted with anger. Josh spotted her weapon, a stiletto, in her right hand.

"That's all I've ever been to you, isn't it?"

Josh felt ashamed at his lack of response.

"You used me for sex," she said.

"Yeah, but it was great sex. You have to admit that," replied Josh.

As soon as the words left his mouth he regretted saying them. Rage washed over Crystal's face and then the heel of her stiletto came down on his upper arm. Ignoring the pain, he sprung up and grabbed the hand holding the shoe. "Do that again, bitch, and you'll be sorry."

"You touch me again and I'll go to the police and tell them that you don't know what 'no' means. I swear I will."

Josh believed her. He let go and left the bed. "Get out. And don't bother showing your face at the gym again. You're fired!"

Crystal laughed. "You think you can threaten me?" She shook her head. "I don't think so."

What does she mean by that? "Get out!"

She picked up her bag and grabbed her other shoe. "I'm leaving and just so we're clear. I want nothing else to do with you."

She really is a dumb blond. "As if I care. You're nothing more than a slut and there are plenty of those out there for me to play with."

"I was a little worried about you when you got home from work today, Kirsti," said Jenny, her gaze watching her daughter carefully. They sat opposite each other at the dining table. Dinner was much later than normal, but no one seemed to notice or care.

Kirsti looked up. "Why?"

Jenny twirled spaghetti onto her fork casually. "Instead of coming in here and saying hello, you went straight upstairs."

"Stop fussing," said Stephen, seated to Jenny's right. "She's a big girl now."

"Thanks, Dad."

Jenny saw a slight smile crease Kirsti's lips and that one simple thing made her feel a lot better.

"I'm sorry if it seemed rude, Mum," said Kirsti. "I needed to use the bathroom and I was desperate to get changed. I felt uncomfortable in that outfit I wore today. I don't think I'll wear it again."

"The cream one?" asked Jenny. "I thought you loved that skirt."

Kirsti shrugged. "It's not comfortable."

Stephen placed his hand over hers. Jenny turned to look at him and saw that look of warning in his eyes. "Oh, it's up to you, of course," she said to Kirsti.

"What are you doing tonight, darling?" interjected Stephen in an obvious effort to change the subject.

"I thought I'd go over to Josh's," replied Kirsti. "We haven't seen much of each other lately."

"Are things okay between you two," asked Jenny, wanting to hear that they weren't. Stephen squeezed her hand again.

"I'm sorry," she said to no one in particular. "I ... I need to know that everything is all right."

Kirsti put down her fork and reached over to place her hand on top of her parent's. "I'm coping, Mum. You don't have to worry."

"I can't help but worry," said Jenny.

Kirsti pushed her chair back from the table and stood. "You don't have to worry about me." She paused. "I think the sandwich I ate at lunchtime was off. I forgot to put it in the fridge when I got to work and they had the heat so high it was overbearing. I've had a stomach ache all afternoon. Hence my need for the bathroom when I got home. I don't think I will go and see Josh tonight after all. I'm going to head off to bed instead."

"What now?" Jenny's heartbeat started to race.

Kirsti nodded. "Yes. I'll sit and read for a while before I turn the light out. I'm sleeping a lot better now, so I'll be able to catch up on some sleep. It will do me good."

Jenny looked at Stephen. She wanted him to say something wise, but he sat there looking lovingly at their daughter and nodded.

"If that's what you want," said Jenny. Something about the whole situation didn't feel right. "Do you want me to bring you up a hot cup of tea later?"

"No thanks. It will only start my stomach off again." Kirsti looked at her unfinished meal. "I'm sorry I couldn't eat more. I'm sure I'll be fine in the morning."

Jenny nodded, not sure what to say and not trusting her instincts.

"Good night."

Josh walked straight up to the bar and smiled at the waitress. "Hi, beautiful. Remember me?"

"Sure, you're the guy from the other night," the woman replied. "The one with the girlfriend."

Josh shook his head. "Nah, that's not me. You've got me

mixed up with someone else."

She laughed. "I have an excellent memory. You sat at the table over there for an hour or so with her."

"Oh, that girl," said Josh. He grinned. "That wasn't my girlfriend. My brother broke up with her and she wanted me to patch things up for her."

"Did you?"

"I tried, but he's already moved on." Josh shrugged. "Anyway, I've been thinking about you ever since and was wondering if you'd like to meet for coffee when your shift is over?"

She stared at him for the longest moment.

Josh knew the signs were good so he tried to keep that innocent look on his face. He knew the girls were suckers for it. "Go on. Don't break a guy's heart."

She smiled. "Yeah, all right. I finish at 10pm, so meet me out front then."

"I'll be there, Babe," he said. "No worries about that."

V

Kirsti climbed into bed. The room was in semi-darkness, with only a bedside lamp illuminating one corner of the room. She sat staring at herself in the wardrobe mirror, hardly recognising the dark eyes set beneath a deep frown staring back at her. Her mind worked ten to the dozen as she went through the mental list once again.

Her plan, so far, was working well. Her parents believed her story about being unwell. That untruth had given her a way out of spending the evening sitting in the lounge room with them and feeling guilty about what she had decided to do. The decision had been made and she didn't want distractions, although she would have liked to spend her last evening alive with her parents. Some things couldn't be.

She felt surprised by how calm she felt. She wasn't nervous at all, and she thought she would be. In fact, she felt a weight had been lifted from her shoulders. She looked at the mirror and silently wished that Owen would visit her one last time, but all she could see was her own pale face.

She turned her attention back to the list.

The letters and gifts had been hidden in the back of the wardrobe. In a shopping bag beside the gifts was a coil of rope she had purchased earlier in the day. A knot grabbed at her stomach when she thought about the rope, but a lengthy internet search that afternoon, from an internet café, had given her the information she needed to ensure she didn't suffer for any longer than necessary. With those items ticked off, there was only one more thing left to do.

Find the garage key!

She would have to wait until her parents went to sleep before she could search the house.

Tim walked up to a swing, dropped his backpack on to the ground, and sat on the black curved plastic that represented a seat. He pushed back and then lifted his feet off the ground, immediately forgetting his immediate surroundings.

Tim felt confused.

His mind rushed in every direction, thinking about too many things at once. He felt alone and lonely yet didn't want people around. His grief weighed him down, but he didn't want anyone to take that weight away from him. He cared about the rest of his family, but he didn't want to see them because he couldn't handle seeing the pain in their eyes. He missed his little brother something bad, but...

He forced the swing to stop by grinding his feet onto the ground. Grabbing the backpack, he walked slowly to what was becoming his favourite bench. Once seated, he put his hand into the opening of his backpack and took out the plastic bag he had purchased the previous night.

Unopened, the bag felt light considering how much he had paid for it. His thumbs gently moved the contents around the small space. Tim stared at the powder and tablets and wondered what he had bought exactly. As long as it stilled his mind, did it really matter?

I could take the lot right now, he thought. Part of him was tempted, but that small rational part of his brain that had not succumbed to the grief dismissed the thought immediately. He didn't want to end it, he reminded himself. All he wanted was a few hours of peace.

He tugged the bag open and looked inside. He would have a tablet. Just one. It was probably ecstasy and he knew that people could have a bad reaction to them. Some people even died from using them, but he was prepared to take the risk if it meant finding some peace and quiet for his anxious mind.

He took one from the bag and held it in the palm of his hand. In the moonlight, it looked grey but he knew it was white. What if...? He shrugged and lifted his hand to his mouth.

"Tim?"

Tim felt his face flush as he quickly dropped the tablet back in the bag and scrunched the bag into his pocket. Why couldn't people leave him alone?

"May I sit down?"

Tim looked up to find Kate standing before him. She wore hip-hugging jeans and a top that didn't quite cover her belly. He could see the glint of a belly ring. He forced his gaze up to her face and shrugged. "Told you before, I can't stop you."

"I'll take that as a yes," she said before sitting beside him. "What was in the bag?"

"What bag?"

"The bag you stashed into your pocket."

Tim didn't want to lie to her. "None of your damn business."

"Thought so." She folded her arms across her chest and shivered. "It's cold out here."

"Go home then."

"Come with me back to Atchison Street," she said. "We can talk there."

"I don't want to talk," he replied. "I want to be left alone."

"So that you can overdose," said Kate. "I don't think so."

Tim sprang to his feet and turned to face her. Kate sat motionless on the bench, her face not betraying what she felt.

"What would you know? How dare you judge me. You don't even know me," said Tim.

"I know enough," she replied. "I know you have a bag full of drugs. By what I saw, you could be arrested for possession and the police would think you're trafficking. I know you attacked a teacher today—"

"I didn't touch him. He's lying if he said I did." The anger resurfaced. He wanted to hurt someone. He was desperate to cause pain.

Kate stood. "I know how you feel."

Tim grabbed Kate by the arms and squeezed. "It really pisses me off when everyone thinks they know how I feel. No one can possibly know what I'm feeling. Half the time, *I* don't even know."

Kate didn't look away. She didn't look scared. When she spoke her voice remained calm. "I know because someone in my family suicided too."

For a brief moment, Tim felt something touch his heart. At that moment he felt a little better. But the moment passed quickly and before he knew what was happening, he had shoved Kate away from him and she fell backwards onto the bench.

"You need to talk about it, Tim," she said immediately. "Sit down and talk to me."

Tim slammed his fist into the bench. Over and over again, his knuckled met the wood. He felt no pain in his hand because the rage inside him was eating him alive. Punch. Punch. Punch. Each punch was harder than the last. Each punch forced a guttural grunt from his stomach. Each punch made Tim feel that much better.

He continued to punch the seat until his energy was depleted and his brain acknowledged the agony he caused himself. Once that realisation found him, he became aware of Kate's pleading voice.

"Please stop, Tim! Please!"

He straightened. His breathing came in short gasps. He stared at the blood and broken flesh for only a second before turning to Kate. The tears rolling down her cheeks were the last straw. Tim sank to his knees and sobbed.

The night air washed over Tim's cold skin, making him shiver. Unaware of the passing of time, Tim felt the presence beside him. Kate had let him cry like a girl without saying a word. Now that he sat quietly wiping the wetness from his face and nursing his ego, he felt her hand squeeze his shoulder.

"Tim, don't feel ashamed," she said, almost as if she had been reading his mind. "Come and sit on the bench and talk to me."

He couldn't look at her, but he did as she asked and moved to the bench. He became aware that Kate was shivering from the cold and felt guilty, so he quickly reached into his bag and pulled out a sloppy joe. "Here, put this on," he said, shoving the garment into her lap.

"Thanks. I needed that," she replied after pulling it on.

Tim watched her as she returned to the seat beside him, their shoulders touching.

"Let me look at your hand," said Kate after a moment's silence.

He lifted his hand and was surprised to see blood and skin mangled together. As soon as he saw it, the pain started.

"That needs attention," said Kate. "You might find you've broken something in there." She pressed gently on the back of his hand and around his knuckles.

Tim refused to react. He deserved the pain.

"It will be swollen tomorrow and probably bruised. You might have even broken something and need treatment," she added.

She fell silent again and they stared across the park at the lights of the houses. *An evening as normal for them,* thought Tim, doubting he would ever know what normal meant again.

"Why are you angry?" asked Kate.

Tim turned to look at her. "What do you mean? I'm not angry."

She smiled. "Yes, you are. I can hear it in your voice and I certainly can see it in your actions."

Heat rose to Tim's face. "People say stupid things."

"What things?"

"I don't know," said Tim, the coldness in the air retreating as his body temperature rose. "Things about stuff that isn't important. Their priorities are wrong. They have no idea."

"You are annoyed because people in general talk about things that are not important to you?" she asked.

She makes me sound selfish. "Not exactly."

She grinned at him. "I'm not attacking you, Tim. I know what the problem is and I'm trying to help *you* see what it is too."

Tim didn't feel like playing games. "Can't you tell me?"

She shook her head. "That wouldn't be helpful. You have to say it yourself."

He stared at her, knowing that if anyone else had said that to him he would have flown off the handle again and stormed away. But Kate was different. He didn't know why.

"Why are you angry?" she asked again.

"I'm angry because I haven't slept, I can't concentrate, I don't want to be around people, I feel confused—" Tim abruptly stood and walked away from Kate and the bench. He felt the anger turning physical again and he would not risk hurting Kate again.

But she kept pressing him. "Why are you angry, Tim?"

"Leave me alone, Kate," he warned.

"No. Why are you angry?"

He spun around. "I'm angry because people pretend to know what I'm feeling when they haven't got a clue." He shouted into Kate's face, but she didn't flinch. "I'm angry because people can't look me in the eye anymore when they speak to me. I'm angry because nobody really cares. Not really. They say they do, but life goes on for them and they expect me to keep up. How am I supposed to do that?"

"That's better," said Kate. "But you haven't told me why you are angry?"

"Shit, Kate," he yelled, his throat hoarse from the unusually high pitch of his voice. "Why do you think I'm angry? My brother is dead!"

"And?"

"And..." He broke eye contact and backed away from her. Every part of his body felt tense and painful. He needed to release the anger.

"Say it!" This time Kate was yelling. "Say it, Tim!"

"And I'm angry ... at him. Okay, are you satisfied? I'm angry at my brother for killing himself and leaving us in this mess." He turned around so that his back was to Kate and he lifted his face to the heavens. "Did you hear that, Owen? I'm bloody angry at you for doing this. You broke our hearts and didn't even tell us why! I'm your bro, I would have done anything to help you. You should have come to me, Owen. Why didn't you come to me?"

More tears flowed down his face. He couldn't stop them and no longer cared who saw them. He loved his brother and had not wanted to admit his anger, but now that he had, he felt the pressure evaporating.

"Talk to me, Tim."

"When Owen died, I had to sit back and watch my mother fall apart. I've never felt so utterly helpless in my life. And then they started looking at me differently and I knew they thought I'd do the same thing. I mean, why would I? Isn't that the most selfish thing you can imagine?" He stared at the stars for a second. "My parents will never utter a bad word about what has happened. They will defend Owen's actions to their death. My sister thinks Owen can do no wrong. And I ... I feel betrayed." He closed his eyes and felt the breeze cooling him down again. "Don't get me wrong. I love my little brother. But I think it could have been different. He had options and none of them included us, his family."

"Anger is a normal part of grief," said Kate. "And you're right, we all have options. Maybe Owen's options weren't clear to him."

"Maybe," replied Tim. "I guess I'm angry because he didn't give me the chance to help him. I want to turn back the clock and change the outcome, and I'm also angry because I don't have that option."

"Concentrate on the options you do have," said Kate. "Because up to this point you've been opting for the self-destruct mode and I think it might be time to look at what else is available to you."

Tim sighed. He knew she was right.

He felt her hand on his arm. "Will you come back to Atchison Street with me?" she asked. "It's freezing out here. Most of the boys have taken off for the long weekend, so it will be quiet at the house and we can talk."

"Yeah, all right."

Kirsti closed the bedroom door behind her as she stepped out onto the landing. The house was in darkness and had been for several hours. She looked quickly at her parent's closed door before turning and creeping past Owen's bedroom and down the stairs.

Aware of the possibility of disturbing her parents, Kirsti's stood still for a moment and let her breathing return to normal. She had spent two hours sitting in the dark after her parents went to bed at midnight, waiting for the house to settle into the night and thinking about the places they might have hidden the garage key. Her first thought was the study. Only her parents used the room, so it seemed a good place to start her search.

She walked briskly towards the study and pushed the door open. Turning the light on, she stood and looked around the room. She could not deny that what she was about to do was wrong and the thought made her hesitate for a second. She shook her head. She needed to find the key, so she forced herself into action.

She opened drawers, patted under the desktop, looked inside the filing cabinet and even pulled the bag out of the bin and looked inside. She flipped through several books before pulling all the books out of the bookcase, one shelf at a time. She lifted the throw rug, checked on top of the door and window frames then shifted the computer tower. She looked inside the pen holder, under the computer keyboard and checked behind the printer. She stood on the swivel chair and gingerly checked the overhead fan. Finally, she stood in the centre of the room and sighed. The key was not in the study.

Kirsti quickly put everything back as she had found it and turned the light out as she left the room. For a moment, she stood in blackness again. Waiting for her eyes to adjust, she thought about the next place she intended to search—the kitchen. Her hopes had already diminished, but sometimes the best place to hide something was in plain sight.

She walked through the lounge room, hoping she wouldn't have to search it later. In the dining room, she paused for a moment before deciding to turn on the light. She had planned to open the blinds and use the moonlight to search by, but it would mean she might miss the small object she was looking for and that made her take risks.

She tried to be quiet but searching through pots and pans and other cooking utensils made that difficult. Several times she paused and listened for movement above her, but hearing nothing she continued with what she was doing.

She searched all the cupboards and drawers. Again, she pulled the garbage bag out of the bin and looked inside. She picked up the telephone and checked to see if the key was taped underneath it. She pulled the curtains back and searched the gap between the fridge and benchtop. She knelt down and pulled the fake kickboard off, knowing it was an excellent place to hide things because she had used it several times to hide Christmas presents there herself. Nothing.

In the dining room, she peered under the table and all the chairs. She looked through the wooden dresser where her mum displayed expensive china. She took the painting off the wall and checked behind that too. Still nothing.

She stepped into the lounge room and sighed. In her heart, she knew the key would not be hidden anywhere in this room. It was the most used room in the house and her parents would have worried that the key would have been discovered. But Kirsti dropped to her knees and pulling the cushions off the sofa anyway. She found a few coins where her father usually sat, but no key. She went through the magazines and books on the coffee table. She looked through the photo albums. She picked up every photo frame in the room and checked it for signs that it might have been recently dismantled. She looked behind the curtains, behind the stereo system and behind the huge collection of CD's the family owned. She searched the cabinets and inside and under ornaments. She looked in every corner and inspected every item before she threw herself on the sofa with a groan.

"Where else could it be?" she whispered to herself. Her gaze lifted to the ceiling. "Crap. Their bedroom."

Kirsti returned to the dining room to switch off the light,

but before doing so she checked her watch. Three o'clock. Did she have the guts to walk directly into her parent's room and remove the key while they were asleep in bed? She felt hot and bothered just thinking about it. No, she would have to wait until first thing in the morning.

Tim turned over on the lumpy mattress and listened to the murmur of voices in the next room. Kate and Karl had not stopped talking since he had agreed to try and get some sleep a couple of hours beforehand. Thing is, he couldn't sleep. His mind wouldn't shut down. He thought about the bag of drugs in his backpack and quickly pushed the thought aside.

Drugs weren't the answer. He had always known that. All they would do was numb the problem and he needed a permanent fix. He didn't have a clue what that fix might be.

He wasted no time thinking about it either. Instead, he thought about how he had felt when he walked through the front door of Atchison Street and saw Karl sitting in the lounge room. He shouldn't have been surprised to see him here of course, because the guy was the principal tenant. It was his name on the lease. But for some reason when Kate asked him to come back here with her, Tim had thought they would be alone. Not that he would have tried anything. He knew that was out of the question, even if he was in the right frame of mind, which he wasn't. He had not forgotten that Kate and Karl were an item, but he supposed that he had tried to think that things were different.

The second surprise was how jealous he felt whilst watching them together. Tim had always prided himself for being a cool dude, not the jealous type who wanted to grab Karl every time he looked at Kate and bash his head in. These were emotions he couldn't handle on top of everything else. But none of that seemed to be noticed by the couple. They greeted each other warmly and it was obvious they felt comfortable together. It was obvious to Tim that they shared a good relationship.

Kate had announced that she and Tim would be spending the night. Karl didn't even ask why they were together. They spent the next hour passing the Playstation joystick backwards and forwards. Tim even surprised himself when he genuinely laughed out loud.

Finally, Kate told Tim he was to sleep in the front bedroom. Tim agreed only because she had made the suggestion. He found himself ushered into the room, the bed made up and Kate telling him that if he needed anything he only had to call out to her.

For two hours he had lain on that bed thinking about her. He was obsessed with what she and Karl might be doing in the other room. He was tempted to walk out unexpectedly, but couldn't make himself do it because he really didn't want to see them doing anything intimate. So he laid and listened to the murmur of their voices instead.

He heard the springs of Karl's old sofa squeak and shot up in bed. Perhaps he should get himself a drink. It would mean he would have to walk through the lounge and disturb them, but he couldn't help that. He shook his head. They were a couple. He had no right to interrupt and it was none of his business what they were doing.

He turned over again and squeezed his eyes shut.

"Do you think he's asleep?"

Kate was standing outside the bedroom door. Tim was sure of it.

"Yes," said Karl. "He's had a bad day. He must be exhausted."

"Well, I can't rest unless I know for sure he's all right," replied Kate.

There were some shuffling sounds.

"Careful, the door squeaks. Don't wake him up!" said Karl.

"Shh!"

Tim heard the door squeak open and footsteps come in-to the room.

"Right, are you satisfied now?" asked Karl, in a low whisper.

"Yes," whispered Kate. "Can you keep watch? I need to get some sleep."

"Okay," replied Karl. "I'll wake you in a couple of hours and then we'll swap."

"Can I sleep in your bed?" asked Kate.

"Sure."

"Come on," said Kate. "But leave the door ajar and keep checking on him. He's vulnerable right now and we have to keep him safe."

He heard them return to the hallway. It went quiet and Tim's imagination took over for a moment, teasing him with images of the pair kissing passionately outside his door. And then he heard Kate murmur something he couldn't quite catch and Tim knew she had gone to bed.

He rolled over onto his back and opened his eyes. They were keeping watch over him. What did they expect him to do? Commit suicide? Anger burned in his stomach, but so did something else. He could only say it was relief, or may-be even gratitude, that someone cared enough to try and keep him alive.

Friday, 16th June

Kirsti had been awake all night. In the morning, she listened to her parent's chatter as they left their room and went downstairs. She could hear the vague sounds of movement in the kitchen. It wasn't until she heard her father start his car and pull out of the drive that she left the bed and walked to the door.

On the landing, she listened intently to the movements of her mother. Satisfied that she wouldn't be interrupted, Kirsti pushed open her parent's bedroom door and peered into the room. Everything was in order. The bed was already made and nothing was out of place.

With one last check on her mother, Kirsti moved further into the room and started opening drawers and wardrobe doors. She checked suit pockets. She made sure the key wasn't hanging from a hanger—used or otherwise. She checked inside shoes, under clothes, behind boxes. She pulled out the wedding album and looked inside. She rummaged through trinket boxes on her mothers dressing table. She even went into the ensuite and carefully checked every possible hiding place in there.

Several minutes later, Kirsti sighed and quickly made her way to the door. She hadn't found the key.

"Kirsti?"

She jumped and looked towards the stairs guiltily. Her mum was nowhere to be seen, but Kirsti knew she was standing in the hallway downstairs.

"Yes?" replied Kirsti.

"Breakfast is ready, darling."

"Okay. I'll only be a minute," replied Kirsti.

She listened to her mother walk away and quickly turned to pull the door closed. It was then that she saw her mother's handbag. It was sacrilege, but Kirsti knew exactly where the key would be.

Before her conscience could tell her otherwise, she ran across the room and grabbed the handbag. Unzipping the top, her fingers felt inside for a second zipper and pulled it open.

"There!" she said aloud. "I should have known all alone."

Securing the bag, she put it back where she had found it and left the room—the key cold in her sweaty palm.

Minutes later, she raced into the kitchen. "I'm sorry, Mum, I'm running late."

"What about breakfast?" asked Jenny, standing at the kitchen sink.

"I'll buy something from the café down the road from work," replied Kirsti, avoiding her mother's gaze. "I forgot that we have an early meeting, so I have to get there a bit earlier today."

"Well, that's not right. They shouldn't expect you to go in early for a meeting. Especially if it means you miss eating breakfast," said her mother. She stopped wiping dishes and looked at Kirsti. "I didn't hear the shower, did you have one?"

"Of course!" Another lie! Kirsti turned and raced across the lounge room. "I have to go."

"Make sure you leave to come home on time," called her mum. "You've got that benefit to go to tonight."

"Yes, I know." Kirsti opened the front door. "Bye."

"See you tonight, love."

Kirsti drove away from the house before being able to breathe a sigh of relief. Everything was going to plan. She had the presents, the notes and now the key. Now she had to occupy herself on the last day of her life.

She took a right at the next intersection and headed towards the local lookout.

Jenny locked the front door and started walking. The library book was packed neatly into her bag, the leather bookmark tucked carefully into the page she had been reading the night before.

The old woman was right. The author of the book had suffered a terrible loss and for that reason alone Jenny felt a connection with the man, but more importantly, she was compelled to read his words. Not wanting to be in the house alone, Jenny had decided that she would return to the park. Sitting in the sunshine, surrounded by laughing children and smiling faces, whilst she read the book would surely do her the world of good.

She moved quietly along the streets, her gaze focused on the pavement in front of her. She didn't look about. She didn't look at people. She didn't listen to what was happening around her. She tried not to think. She just walked.

When she looked up sometime later, instead of finding herself standing on the outskirts of a park, she stood in the shadows of a church. The same church she had entered the day before.

Her throat constricted. She stared at the cross at the top of the building. Her grip on the bag in her hand tightened.

She stared at the church for a long time. Why had she returned to this place? Her heart felt confused. She didn't want to make a decision.

And she didn't have to.

"Hello."

Jenny turned to find a man with a white collar standing beside her. She instantly recognised him from the day before.

"Hello," she replied.

He smiled. "I didn't mean to scare you away yesterday."

Jenny felt the colour touch her face. She looked at the ground between their feet. "It was rude of me to run off like that. I'm sorry."

"Not at all," replied the man. "You had your reasons."

She wanted to share her burden. She needed to desperately. Her gaze caught his.

"Can I help you?" he asked, concerned.

Tell him. The words seemed to stick in her throat. But she really wanted to release some of the burden. "My son..." she stammered.

He waited for a moment. "What about your son?" he prompted.

"He took his own life," she whispered. "I feel so lost and empty. I don't know what to do."

"Come inside. We can talk privately in there," he said, taking a step towards the church.

"No!" Her voice cracked. She couldn't move. "I'm sorry. I'm not a Christian and it's hypocritical of me to even be here." She looked at the church and felt a yearning to believe in something. "I always believed that dead is dead, but I'm not finding that thought particularly comforting at the moment and I want to believe that I'll see my son again. I need to believe that," she lowered her gaze, "but something is happening to me and I'm scared."

"It's all right. If you feel more comfortable, we can stand right here. No one's around anyway," he replied. "What are you scared of?"

Tears spilled down Jenny's face. Although she was accustomed to the wetness, she hated herself for not being able to control it anymore and all she did these days was cry. "I'm scared to go home. Something evil is there."

Jenny saw the man's eyes narrow.

Heat rose to Jenny's cheeks. "And before you jump to the wrong conclusion, my husband isn't abusive and I haven't tried to harm myself."

The man cocked his head to one side and observed her thoughtfully.

She shrugged and ignored the urge to be defensive. "I've never been scared to be home alone before. I don't know what to do. I'm scared to be awake and I'm too scared to sleep ... because of the nightmares I'm having. I have a deep fear for my other two children as well and that is tearing me apart. I'm so confused and I can't concentrate. My mind is racing all the time and I feel so exhausted. Can you help me?"

Jenny stared into his hazel eyes looking for the tell-tale sign that would confirm he thought she was crazy. But she didn't see what she expected. Instead, she saw understanding. Then she noticed that he was nodding.

"Yes, I can help you," he said. "I can give you phone numbers so that you and your family can receive counselling. You all need to talk about your feelings and even the closest of families need help at times. Grief is different for all of us and often family members don't want to burden each other with the little things so they keep them hidden, which isn't healthy and can cause long term suffering. Talking to a third party allows you to say whatever is in your heart. For you, counselling could give the answer to why you are having nightmares. The confusion and lack of concentration are normal. You shouldn't worry about those things."

"But what about the oppression I feel in the garage?" asked Jenny.

"Did your son take his life there?"

Jenny wiped tears from her cheeks. "Yes."

"It's understandable that you feel the oppression there. Your family is vulnerable and things like this happen. If you want, I can visit your home. I'll lay some flowers where your son passed away and will recite some passages from the bible. None of your family needs to be present when I do this. Knowing it has happened will help."

Jenny felt lighter just hearing him telling her that he'd do it.

He reached into his jacket pocket and pulled out a small

card. "My name is Philip Knight. Go home and talk to your husband. If he agrees then phone me at home tonight and I'll come around to see you tomorrow."

She took the card and peered at the neat printing on it. "It's Saturday and, besides, it's a long weekend. Do you mind?"

"Of course not," he replied with a genuine smile. "I believe it is important for your family and my wife will agree, so she will not mind either. Besides, it won't take long."

Jenny smiled through her tears. "Thank you. Thank you so much." She turned to walk away, clutching the card tightly against her chest, but quickly looked back and added, "My name is Jennifer Fowler."

Kirsti sat on the embankment and looked at the town below. The lookout had always been a joke to the locals, as there was nothing of interest to see. It was mainly used by young lovers looking for some privacy.

Today, however, Kirsti sat alone in the sunshine staring at the place where she had lived her entire life. She looked at the buildings below, knowing their history and who might be found in the vicinity of each.

The largest building was the taxation office. It was ludicrous that the people who took from the working classes had the largest building of all. To her, it said everything, but she didn't want to waste her last hours pondering on it now.

The library was an old haunt of hers. She and her friends had used the place as a social gathering spot as much as a place to study. When those days had come to an end and there were no excuses for meeting there anymore, they had been upset. Now the place would be occupied by the next generation. Kirsti laughed. At twenty, she couldn't be called old, but to the people in that building right now she might as well be a hundred!

At opposite ends of the town, two church steeples shone white in the sun. It was something she had never really noticed before, being a non-religious person. She had been in both churches at some time in her life, but never for a regular Sunday service. However, since the death of her brother she had found herself asking questions that she didn't know the answers to. Did anyone know the answers? She wouldn't be around long enough to find out, but she suspected not.

The shopping centre would be packed with people. People she had known all her life, as well as complete strangers. She thought back to when she was fourteen and fifteen. Many of her classmates joined "the walk" on a Thursday night. All students—males and females—walked around the interior showing off their wares. Their wares, of course, being themselves. For the girls, it was a look but don't touch exercise and the boys were eager to look. There was no doubt about that. Kirsti felt embarrassed thinking about it now, but everyone did it and she thought it was fun at the time.

Trees blocked the view of her home and, in fact, the entire street, so she leaned forward and searched for another building instead. It took a while to find, but eventually, she saw the pink sign out the front and knew she had the right place. Naturally, she was too far away to read the sign, but she knew the wording—Steve's Auto Repairs—because she had helped her father paint it. Hence the colour pink.

She stared at the winding roads and rooftops spread out before her. Who would have guessed at any of those times that Owen would now be dead and she was soon to follow?

Her mobile beeped, telling her a text message had been received. She pressed a few buttons.

Sorry for not being there for you recently. That will change, I promise. Luv u, Jo.

Kirsti lowered herself onto her back, letting the phone drop onto her stomach, and stared up at the cloudless, blue sky.

Tim woke to the sounds of laughter. He sat up in bed and looked around, feeling a little disorientated. Then he remembered what had happened the night before and flopped back down. He didn't want to witness the happiness he heard from Kate and Karl. But he knew it was unavoidable.

He sat up again and quickly checked his watch. 11.30am. He had slept after all. And now it was time to find out how many bridges he had burned.

The kitchen was bright and airy and smelled of bacon. Kate and Karl sat at the table. They didn't look like they had been awake all night. In fact, they looked so cheery that it made Tim feel uncomfortable because he knew he would ruin their day by being present.

As soon as he walked into the room, Kate left her chair and rushed over to him. "Tim, you're awake. Are you hungry? I made some bacon and eggs for you too."

He wasn't hungry ... when he got up, but the smell made him so. "Sure. I could eat something."

She pushed him gently towards the table and went to the stove. "Sit down. I only just dished ours out, so yours is still hot."

Tim sat and Karl smiled at him.

"How ya feeling, mate?" asked Karl, before stuffing half a rasher of bacon covered in the yolk of an egg into his mouth.

Tim shrugged. "I'll eat and then I'll get out of your way."

"No ... don't be silly," said Karl, juices running down his chin. "We want you to stay."

Kate appeared at Tim's side. She placed a plate of food in front of him. "That's right. You're not going anywhere."

Tim took the knife and fork offered to him and broke the egg yolk. "I've caused you enough trouble."

"Eat your breakfast and then we'll have a chat," replied Kate.

The three of them sat quietly while they ate. It was the first meal Tim had eaten in ... well, he really couldn't remember. Everything tasted so *real* and he enjoyed every mouthful. When he was offered more toast, he was quick to say yes.

When breakfast was over, Karl stood. "I'll wash up while you two talk."

Karl was given them space to talk and it should have been the other way round. Tim felt his face redden, but he didn't object.

He thought he and Kate might wander off for their "chat", but Kate was quite content to stay where she was and say what needed to be said in front of Karl. After everything that had happened, Tim didn't feel he could object to that either, so he sat quietly waiting for her to start the conversation.

"You look heaps better this morning, Tim," she said after taking a mouthful of orange juice. "We were really worried about you last night, you know."

"I'm sorry." Tim didn't know what else to say.

Her hand covered his and he found himself looking over his shoulder at Karl, expecting the other male to show anger at the touch. But Karl either didn't notice or didn't care because he continued with the washing up in silence.

"You're a friend and we don't care about anything except your safety," said Kate. "To be honest, I thought you might try something stupid."

"What do you mean?" asked Tim, pulling his hand out from under hers.

"Are you suicidal?"

It wasn't a question he expected, but he understood why

she asked it. Tim shook his head. "No."

She stared into his eyes as if by doing so she would see the truth. After a moment or two, she leaned back in her chair. "All right. I believe you."

Tim breathed a sigh of relief. "I'm not suicidal. Never have been, but you helped me realise that I'm angry."

"Who with? Yourself? Your brother? Your family?" she asked.

"All of the above," said Tim. He lowered his gaze. He didn't realise how much anger he had bottled up until now. "I'm angry at myself for not knowing and not doing something about it. I'm angry at my folks for the same reason. But most of all I'm angry at Owen." There, he had said it.

"Why?"

"Because he didn't think of us." Tim swallowed the lump in his throat. "He didn't write a note and tell us why he did it. I need to know. I've gone over everything that we did and said, thinking that maybe I'm to blame. I need to know why he did it. He should have at least given us an explanation."

"As you know, Tim and I have lost someone to suicide," said Kate.

He felt his face colouring again. For a moment, Tim didn't know what to say. He had forgotten, but he knew she had known someone who had suicided and he could vaguely remember Karl saying his father had suicided too. He had been so caught up in his own grief that he had discarded this news without a moments thought. He realised that he had believed his family was the only people affected by this type of tragedy. Naturally, he had seen things on TV and in magazines, but he had never really associated it with real life. Now he found himself wondering how common suicide was.

"I can't speak for Karl because everyone is different, but I feel that no matter what the reason for your brother taking his own life, that reason might well be something minor." She paused for a moment and Tim could see that she was thinking back to another time. "I have to believe that my father didn't think of us because his problems were so huge that he couldn't think of anything else. It had nothing to do with love. I know that. And I believe that if I had the opportunity to ask him about it now, he would regret what he did to us ... and himself."

Tim found himself wondering if Owen regretted his decision.

"But I also know that Mum and the rest of my family were not responsible," she continued. "We all say and do things that we regret, but mostly everyone gets over those things. If you remember a negative between you and your brother then discard it and remember the positives instead. You didn't make Owen hang himself. No one made him do that. It was his choice and only his choice."

He knew she was right. "But he could have made it easier by telling us why."

"My father left a suicide note," replied Kate. "The reason he gave was stupid and that made me angry at him for years. Owen didn't leave a note and that is making you angry at him." She reached for his hand again. "Tim, don't waste months and months being angry. Knowing the reason would not change things so don't waste energy on trying to figure it out. You will come to accept what has happened and you will learn to live with the grief. Your brother made his choice and now you must make yours."

"I told you, I'm not suicidal!"

"I know," she said, her voice soft and calming. It almost sounded as if she were talking to an injured animal. "I'm not talking about that."

"Oh. What are you talking about then?" he asked.

"You've already made the decision to live. We have established that," she said. "Now you have to decide if you're going to let the anger take control and ruin your life." She paused for a moment and stared at him. "Or, are you going to decide to take back control of your life."

Tim remained silent, but his brain was working feverishly. He understood what she was saying. He didn't like the Tim that had been hanging around campus for the last few weeks. He preferred to find the old Tim or maybe a new Tim with as many of the old values as possible now that he had suffered a great loss.

Kate squeezed his hand and Tim jumped when Karl placed his hand on his shoulder.

"We both have experienced similar emotions to what you're going through now," said Karl.

"Go home, Tim." Kate's voice sounded high pitched and emotional. "Go home to your family and talk to them. Forgive them if you have to, but talk to them. It will make all the difference."

"For you and for them," added Karl. "It's important to communicate."

"It's a long weekend. Your family will love to see you. Will you go home?" asked Kate.

"I—"

"We'll drive you there today and bring you back on Sunday if you want," offered Karl.

"That's an excellent idea. Thank you, Karl," said Kate.

"No, it's all right. I can drive myself," replied Tim.

"So you'll go? Today?" asked Kate.

Tim nodded. "Yes, I'll go home for the weekend and I'll be open and honest with my folks. Actually, I think I'll stay for a week because there's a lot to talk about and do."

"Brilliant!" Kate sprang from her chair and hugged him.

II

Kirsti stared at herself in the mirror. Normally, for an occasion like this, she would have spent the afternoon at the hairdressers ensuring she looked her best. But tonight, although she had washed her hair because not to do so would have raised suspicion, she didn't even wear her hair up.

Her hair fell on to her bare shoulders, brushing gently against the straps of her elegant dress. Josh had instructed her to wear a certain dress, but she ignored him. Sapphire blue in colour, the material shimmered whenever she moved. She had always loved the effect and she had chosen this dress especially for this evening.

She didn't want to go to the function. She didn't want to see Josh. But she knew she had to do both. Her gaze roamed the entire mirror, looking for something other than what she could see. Why hadn't Owen visited her this week? She needed to see him.

"Kirsti darling, may I come in?"

No! I don't want to see you. Her entire body locked up, except for her mouth. She almost groaned as she heard herself say calmly, "Come in, Mum."

The door opened and instead of one pair of eyes, there were four. Kirsti turned back to the mirror and hoped her feelings of dread didn't show on her face. Joanne, Skye and Melody followed Jenny into the room and sighs of admiration began.

"You look beautiful," said Jenny.

Kirsti couldn't watch the tears welling in her mother's eyes, so she turned shyly to face her friends. Their smiles were too much, so she quickly moved away from them and made as if she were looking for something in her clutch bag.

This wasn't part of the plan, so why had they shown up tonight? She had deliberately made plans with the girls so that this wouldn't happen. It never did in the past so what had changed now.

Kirsti heard the sigh escape her lips and quickly looked at the faces staring silently at her. None of them seemed aware of her awkwardness and then Joanne stepped forward.

"Kirsti, there's something I have to say to you," the girl said looking shyly at the other occupants in the room.

Kirsti got the feeling that Joanne would have preferred

to say whatever it was she was about to say without an audience, but that wasn't going to stop her.

"I feel as if I've let you down since Owen's death," said Joanne. "I'm sorry. We all are." She indicated the other two girls, who nodded their agreeance. "None of us knew what to say to you or how to act—"

"I wanted you to be yourselves," said Kirsti, her gaze on her mum.

"We know that now," said Joanne, with a quick glance at Jenny. "And from now on we will be."

"It can't be the same," added Skye, "because with Owen gone, it can't be, but we are your friends and we love you."

"We want to help you," said Melody. "Not like the bungled job we've made of it up till now. I mean really help you."

"We want you to talk to us. We can listen to everything you have to share. We can cry together. We can remember and preserve Owen's memory," said Joanne, tears freely flowing down her cheeks.

Jenny caught a sob and Joanne turned to look at her. Kirsti felt uncomfortable with the entire situation. None of this was supposed to happen.

"Mrs Fowler, I loved Owen," Joanne blurted out. "I've loved him since we were children. He was the only person, except for Kirsti, who really touched my heart. He meant the world to me."

The room fell into silence. Joanne and her mum faced each other and sobbed. Kirsti felt surprised by Joanne's admission, but a part of her looked at the mirror behind her mother and yearned for total release. For a split second, she thought she saw Owen standing there, holding out his hand to her. Kirsti felt the tug on her heart as well as her mind, but the moment was shattered by her mother reaching to grab Joanne's shoulders and drawing the sobbing girl into her arms.

"I had ... always ... hoped that ... you ... and Owen ... would get ... together," said Jenny.

Skye stepped forward and gently rubbed Joanne's back. "We've all made terrible mistakes, Mrs Fowler, but we want to fix those mistakes."

Kirsti noticed Melody's black make-up smudging as she dabbed her eyes with a tissue. And then she heard Josh's car horn sound out on the road. She hadn't been eager to see him, but the sound was like music to her ears.

"I have to go," she said, not knowing if anyone heard her.

Her mum stepped away from Joanne. They all wiped their hands across wet faces and turned to look at Kirsti, the only person dry faced.

"You look incredible," said Skye, taking charge of the situation. "And that tool out in the car doesn't deserve you, but I've told you that how many times already. Tomorrow night we are going out, the four of us, and we're going to find you a new boyfriend. Someone worthy."

Kirsti smiled. It felt alien, but in some way right. "Okay."

Her mum leaned forward and looked out of the window. "Do you mean to tell me that Josh isn't even going to get out of the car and knock on the door?" She shook her head, her dark eyes drawn together in obvious disgust. "That's plain rude!"

Kirsti felt strange. Her plans had not included this either. She had wanted to go to the benefit with minimum fuss. She couldn't afford to let herself be distracted. She hadn't wanted to confront her friends. She didn't need to witness her mother's tears ... or disgust. All she wanted was an end to the confusion and to see Owen again.

Josh tooted his horn again. Kirsti groaned. "Well, I have to go," she said again before moving towards the door, towards her final escape.

She swept through the door and down the stairs, faintly aware of another sound outside. And then she saw headlights flash through the glass beside the front door. Had Josh changed his mind and driven into the driveway after all. Her step quickened. She didn't want confrontation. Not now. She didn't want her mother's last memory of her daughter tainted by feelings of guilt.

Kirsti pulled the door open and gasped. Walking up the steps was not Josh, but her brother, Tim. She heard a sob come from her mother, who stood behind her. And she heard the tiny whisper of his name and knew instantly that this was something her mum had wished for.

Before anyone could react, Tim beamed at Kirsti. "Sis, you look fabulous. I think I'll have to escort you to the benefit in order to keep the boys of this town away from you."

Melody laughed.

"It's about time you noticed you've got a beautiful sister, Tim," said Skye confidently.

"Hey, I always knew that. How could a good looking dude like me have an ugly sister?"

Now Skye joined in the laughter.

Kirsti stood rigid in front of her brother, terrified that he might see something the others didn't.

Their gaze locked and then he stepped towards her and hugged her. "I'm sorry for everything, little sis," he whispered in her ear. "I've been a dog, but I think I'm back on track now."

Kirsti was painfully aware of their mother. She felt her hand on her shoulder, squeezing lovingly, and knew the other was doing the same to Tim. When Tim released her and stepped towards her mum, Kirsti saw more tears streaming down her mum's pale face.

"I love you," Tim said to his mum. "I'm sorry for making you worry."

"Are you home for the weekend?" asked Jenny, her eyes alight for the first time in weeks.

"No. I'm home for a week," replied Tim with a grin. He took his mother's hand and then Kirsti's. "This family has some issues we need to sort out."

The words alone struck her, but it was her mother's reaction to those words that cut into her heart. Jenny fell against Tim and sobbed like she hadn't done since finding out about Owen.

Kirsti swallowed and blinked several times, trying to force back tears. She needed to distance herself from what was happening. She needed to break free. She looked at Josh, still sitting in the car. He glared at her and tapped his watch as if to say they were in a desperate hurry. She knew that wasn't the case, but the action broke the spell and allowed her to take back control.

"I'm sorry, Mum, I really do have to go," she said for the third time.

"Of course, darling," said Jenny. "Have a lovely evening."

Kirsti wasn't sure if Tim and her mother stepped away or if her friends crowded in around her, but a second later she was confronted with three pairs of eyes admiring her again.

"I wish I could be there with you," said Skye. "It would be so much fun."

"I love that dress," said Melody, which was a real compliment coming from a goth.

"Have fun," said Joanne. "I can't wait for tomorrow night."

"Yeah, it's going to be fantastic!" said Skye.

Kirsti turned and walked down the steps towards the car, her focus on Josh. He leaned across the passenger seat and opened the door for her. Skye groaned but said nothing.

At the car, Kirsti turned back to the house. She looked at the home she had always loved, then she smiled weakly at her mum and brother and waved, mouthing the words *I love you*. Finally, she looked at each of her friends. She touched their hands, one at a time, before stepping into the car. She couldn't say what she wanted to say, but it didn't matter, her letters would say it for her.

She wound the window half-way down. "Bye."

"Bye," they all waved and smiled as they watched her and Josh drive away.

III

"Frigging hell, Kirsti," said Josh. "What was all that about?"

Kirsti felt tense.

"We're going to be late now," he continued, and she realised he wasn't concerned in the slightest about her or her family, so she relaxed again. "You know how important this is for me," he added.

"I do," she said, her voice calm, "and that's why I wore this dress. It will draw attention to us all night."

She glanced sideways at him and saw him grin.

The benefit was being held in the community hall attached to the council building. Being the largest venue in town, the event spoke high finance and influential people. Yet none of this impressed Kirsti. To her, it was another occasion where people kissed arse in order to move up the ladder. She despised everything about it.

When the car was parked, she didn't bother waiting for Josh to open the door for her. He had done so in the past, mainly to impress onlookers, but Owen's death had brought out the worse in him and she didn't feel like the embarrassment of waiting for something that wasn't going to happen. She couldn't believe how he was acting these days and she was amazed how quickly her love for him had evaporated.

Without a word, they walked towards the entrance. People milled about, watching arrivals, waiting to pounce on the important people. No one pounced on them.

As they walked up the steps, Josh spoke. "Don't make a fool of me tonight."

It was a threat if ever she'd heard one. Starting in the pit of her stomach, anger welled inside her. She shot him a sideways glance and, for the first time, saw the real person beneath the mask, but she said nothing. She decided to embrace the anger and use it to her advantage. Tonight would be the last night for many things, including her life, but she would make it worth remembering—especially for Josh. He wouldn't forget her in a hurry!

The noise inside was a little overwhelming. They stopped and looked about.

Long posters, suspended in the air, by almost invisible fishing line, moved gently to a breeze she couldn't feel. Streamers, mostly pink and silver, joined the motion as they stretched across the room. Below the decorations gathered people of all ages, all smiling and drinking. Mr Shimizu moved slowly around the room, expertly separating people and their cash—Kirsti imagined he would be successful even if it was in the form of a promise to write a cheque later. Donations would be high as Mr Shimizu knew how to approach people, she could see that, and he knew what to say. Besides, everyone knew someone who had died of cancer or who were currently battling the disease, so they were more than willing to support the cause.

The patrons wore their best evening wear. The women looked elegant in long flowing dresses, with their hair pulled away from made-up faces, and fake jewellery glittering around the necks. Even the men looked dashing in their tailored suits. It was rare that the community looked so ... toffee-nosed! The thought made Kirsti gasp. She looked around again and the brightness dimmed and the noise diminished. Everyone was pretending to be something they were not. Including her.

It was the underlying reason for being at the function that Kirsti objected to.

"There's Mr Shimizu," said Josh. "Smile and look pretty, but leave the talking to me."

Kirsti checked her watch as they moved down the stairs and towards Mr Shimizu. Almost eight o'clock. She had three hours.

Mr Shimizu gave Kirsti more than a passing glance. He stared at her openly, letting his gaze wander over her entire body. It made Kirsti feel uncomfortable, to say the least, but she remained silent and smiled sweetly.

"Mr Shimizu," said Josh, holding out his hand. "It's good to see you again. I was hoping we might take a few minutes later to go over a few details."

Mr Shimizu accepted Josh's handshake, but not his enthusiasm about talking later. "This is a benefit for charity, Mr Edwards," said Mr Shimizu in broken English. "I do not speak business when at a benefit. The two should be kept separate. That principle has served me well."

Josh nodded, but Kirsti doubted he understood the businessman. "Yeah, sure. Whatever you say. Give the signal if you change your mind."

"Signal?" repeated Mr Shimizu.

"Yeah." Josh grinned from ear to ear and turned to Kirsti. "Come on, let's mingle."

Josh led her onto the dance floor. He turned to face her and instantly started to strut his stuff. He did nothing he hadn't always done, but previously his crazy moves amused her. He had always enjoyed being the centre of attention. This time, however, the embarrassment started deep within before burning her skin from the top of her head right down to her little toe. She didn't know where to look but was more than a little conscious of the way people were looking at them. Were they laughing at them? Had they always laughed and she hadn't noticed? She looked at his feet and felt the anger surface again. The embarrassment evaporated and, once again, she felt in control.

She stopped moving her body to the music and walked away from him. She wasn't here to endure his pathetic attention-getting antics, she was here for another reason and it was time to focus on that.

"Hey, what the hell are you doing?" Josh grabbed her arm and swung her around to face him.

She glared at him before leaning close to his ear. "Careful, Josh, Mr Shimizu might see that you're not the person you pretend to be."

"What the hell does that mean," said Josh, pushing her

away from him. "What's wrong with you?"

"My brother's dead," she whispered. "What could possibly be wrong with me?"

"You're frigging looney!"

For a moment she believed him. This wasn't her. She would never set someone up for a fall. People liked hanging out with her because she was fun to be with. She wasn't crazy. She laughed at silly things, but she wasn't looney. So why was she having these weird thoughts?

"Jerk!" The word left her mouth in a strangled sob. She pushed passed Josh and made her way quickly to the ladies, where he wouldn't be able to follow. Once there, she found an empty cubicle and locked herself inside. Leaning against the door, she closed her eyes and fought to hold back the tears.

Why are you crying? she asked herself. *What are you doing here tonight?*

"Hey, are you all right in there?"

Kirsti's eyes snapped open and she moved away from the door. "Yeah, I'm fine."

There was no response from the woman on the other side of the door, but Kirsti watched the shadow on the floor and sighed with relief when it disappeared. She turned and closed the toilet lid before she sat. *What is up with you, Kirsti?*

She shook her head and then reached for the toilet roll to dab at her face. But as her fingers brushed against the paper, an image appeared in the silver dispenser. A blurry image. A face smiling at her. Owen. She held her breath for a moment. Their gaze met and he smiled at her. At her!

"Owen?" she whispered.

She saw his hand come into the small space and he beckoned to her. *Come.*

"I am," she said. "Tonight."

Come to me. Happy.

Tears spilled down her face and this time she did nothing to try and stop them. "It's all planned," she said and looked at her watch. "A couple of hours and I'll be with you."

Waiting.

A buzzing noise sounded in her silver purse. Opening the zipper, she pulled out her pink phone and looked at the screen. Joanne.

Flipping open the top, she pressed the mobile to her ear. "Hello."

"Hi, Kirsti. It's Joanne. I wanted to tell you that your mum invited me to stay tomorrow night. Is that okay?"

"Sure," replied Kirsti.

"I have a scrapbooking album I made in memory of Owen and I'd like to bring it over and show you. Is that okay?" asked Joanne.

Owen. Kirsti leaned sideways against the cubicle wall. "I'd like that."

"I meant what I said to your mum, Kirsti," said Joanne. "And I want to make up for my lack of support in your time of grief. We can sit and go through the scrapbook and remember old times. We can talk about the crazy things we used to do and we can cry together. We should have done it ages ago."

Remember. Talk. Cry. Kirsti heard the awkward sentences and sighed. She had wanted these things so badly. They would have helped her. But now it was too late because tomorrow Kirsti Fowler would be another suicide statistic.

"Kirsti?"

"I'm here," replied Kirsti. "I have to go, but I'll see you tomorrow."

"Bye."

She pushed the mobile into the opening of her bag and turned her attention back to the dispenser. Nothing. Owen was gone. She sighed again.

Kirsti sat quietly in the cubicle for a long time. Finally, she decided that her plans for this evening were not right. She wasn't mean spirited and could only guess that her plan to ruin Josh was a remnant of some underlying stress. Maybe it was the grief. Whatever it was, she wouldn't go through with it. She didn't want to cause her family more pain than she had to. She would forget this evening, she would go home, and she would end her life. Simple.

Kirsti left the cubicle and washed her hands. Vaguely aware of movement around her, she glanced in the mirror and seeing herself, turned and left the restroom. The brightness and noise in the hall overwhelmed her for a moment. She stood quietly and took in everything with one slow sweep of the room.

They said life was short. Being only twenty, Kirsti had never agreed with the statement as she had a long, exciting life ahead of her. But now she thought differently. Life didn't necessarily mean we would live until we were old and crotchety. It was a mistake to think that was true. Life could end in an instant, next week or tomorrow or in a moment from now. No one knew for sure when their time on earth would be up ... except for those who took control of their own lives, like Owen.

The future looked bleak, yet the people surrounding her selfishly put their own needs first and were using the function, a benefit for raising money for the terminally ill, to better themselves. Josh was somewhere in the crowd trying to convince Mr Shimizu to invest in his scheme for the new gym. Her ex-boss, Lisa, had wanted Kirsti to hand out business cards to important people so her business would climb the social ladder. How many other people were prostituting themselves openly in public? It made Kirsti feel sick to the stomach.

She was happy believing the world was good and it upset her to think that her innocence had died when she lost her brother. She could no longer see the positives around her. All she could see was greed and selfishness, and she wanted no part of it.

Kirsti's gaze found the entrance and she moved quickly across the hall towards it. Three-quarters of the way there a hand grabbed her arm and spun her around.

Josh glared at her. "Where in the hell have you been?"

"I'm not feeling well. I'm going home," said Kirsti.

"You look fine to me," he replied, his eyebrows narrowing. "I've been watching Mr Shimizu and he seems focused on the ladies, so I want you to use your charm and get his attention." His eyes roamed over her dress. "Flirt with him. Bat your eyelids. Do whatever it is girls do to draw a man in. Yes, that should work."

"I'm not a piece of meat and I am not a slut," said Kirsti. "And I don't take orders from you. If you want to talk to Mr Shimizu get in line and wait your turn, like everyone else."

"He's only talking to women!"

Kirsti glanced at the banners above them. "Maybe that has something to do with why he's here. You know, breast cancer."

"Stuff breast cancer. I'm only interested in getting my gym financed!"

Kirsti noticed the silence first. When she looked around it seemed everyone in the hall was staring at them. She swallowed and looked at Josh. His face shone with embarrassment and then the colour was gone as his gaze settled on Mr Shimizu.

"I didn't mean it the way it sounded," said Josh, his voice little more than a squeak. He looked about and then turned to Kirsti. "Tell them what I meant."

He stepped towards her, smiling. His arm went around her and he laughed. To Kirsti, the laugh was forced and desperate. She couldn't imagine anyone else mistaking the laugh for anything else.

"I ... I..." he stammered.

Mr Shimizu now stood a few feet away glaring at them. *You managed to get his attention, Josh,* thought Kirsti.

Kirsti stepped away from Josh.

"Kirsti?" Josh's confidence had plummeted. She didn't like to see him like this, but she knew he deserved it. "Help me?"

Kirsti shook her head. "This is what you wanted, Josh. It's always about what you want, but I never saw that until recently. I'm going home."

She turned and left.

IV

Kirsti walked home. She expected someone to come after her to ensure she was all right and she was prepared to deal with that. But no one bothered. Telling herself that she hadn't wanted anyone to follow her anyway, she still couldn't shake the isolated feeling of being alone. Was this what the rest of her life would have been like? The thought made her cringe. Although she had always been independent, she missed the security of a loving home and caring friends. She felt as if everything she treasured had been taken from her in one moment.

She walked faster—the clip of her heels sounding loud in the crisp evening. Looking around and feeling alone made goosebumps crawl along her arms and down her back. What if someone grabbed her before she reached the garage? What if she were raped or murdered? Kicking her shoes off, she continued walking, not bothering to pick them up. She would not need them after tonight anyway, but she didn't want someone else to be in control of her life ... and death. The choice had to be hers and hers alone.

The two storey house she lived in with her parents was quiet, only the downstairs lights were on. Her parents would be sitting in the lounge room with Tim. They might be talking or maybe they were enjoying the quiet as they watched a movie.

Kirsti walked barefoot to her car. She had deliberately left it unlocked for her own convenience. She opened the passenger side door and reached in and grabbed the bag she had hidden behind the seat.

Leaving the car door open, she glanced at the house and moved silently to the garage. Her heart pounded in her chest as nerves kicked in. Taking the key from the bag, she pushed it into the lock and twisted it to one side. The garage lifted a touch, coldness swirled around her feet and she gasped.

Her fingers fumbled on the ledge and then she lifted the roller door, knowing it would make a noise if she let it go too high. She ducked underneath and closed it quickly before turning to stand in the darkness.

Her body reacted differently to what she had imagined. She started to tremble. Her head throbbed with anxiety. She pulled a torch out of the bag and quickly turned it on. The dim light did nothing to ease her nervousness. The circular glow moved slowly around the workshop and then up to the beam where Owen had ended his life.

"Well, this is it," she said aloud. She didn't know what she expected, but the loneliness tore at her heart. "I'll be with you soon, Owen. Please ... give me courage."

At that moment, she numbed and mechanically set her plans into motion. The bag with the letters and gifts were placed in plain view. Her clutch bag rested gently against the gift bag, its contents unimportant now. She reached for the rope she had purchased a few days beforehand. After removing the packaging, she cut a long length of rope and moved to stand beneath the beam. She looked up at the beam for only a second and then she dragged a petrol can closer and stood on it.

The rope fitted between the beam and the tin roof easily. She tied a knot to hold it in place and then she made a noose. Her fingers moved quickly, but her body felt cold. She didn't realise she was crying until a tear dripped onto her hand. She quickly wiped it away.

Realising she needed to be higher off the ground, Kirsti stepped off the can and grabbed a bucket. Placing it on top of the can she turned to face the roller door before climbing up onto the bucket, which was placed precariously on top of the petrol can. The bucket threatened to break under her weight, but she didn't care. *It might make my job easier,* she thought.

Kirsti looked up at the rope and that's when she saw the tiny wooden cross. It couldn't be seen from the roller door side of the beam, but it was in plain sight now. She stared at it for a long moment, the noose in her hand. *Who stuck that there?* she wondered. *Stay focused. It doesn't matter anymore.*

She pulled the noose over her head, resting the knot against her right ear.

All I have to do is kick the bucket out from under me and I'll be with Owen, she thought. She ignored the tears rolling down her face. She ignored the beating of her heart, hammering against cold, shaking flesh. *What did Owen think about when he was standing here? Was he scared too? What if it doesn't work? What if I end up a quadriplegic?*

She shook her head and the bucket wobbled. A sharp gasp escaped her lips and she grabbed the beam to steady herself.

I wish I knew why!
Does it matter now?
What if I don't die?
Of course, you will.
I'm scared of the pain.
Do it!
What about Mum and Dad?
They don't care about you.
Yes, they do! Don't say that.
They only care about Owen. It's always Owen this and Owen that.
That's not true!
You know it's true. Do it!
I miss Owen.
He's waiting for you.
How do I know that for sure?

Push the bucket out from under your feet and you'll be with him.

But...

There is no but.

The bucket moved beneath her. Kirsti cried out in horror. She grabbed the rope and held it tightly, her gaze returning to the little wooden cross.

Our Father, who art in heaven, hallowed be thy name, thy kingdom come, thy will be done, on earth as it is in heaven...

The bucket broke and she jolted downwards, the rope tightening around her neck.

V

No! I don't want to die!

The tips of the toes of her left foot touched the petrol can. Kirsti reached for the beam, straining with her fingers to get a hold and pull herself upwards.

Heat ran in waves through her body. Her sweaty fingers swelled. No thoughts ran through her brain, except ones of survival. The can jolted under her movements. She panicked. If the can toppled over, she would be dead in seconds. She had done her research. She knew what to expect. But she didn't want death now. She knew that with certainty. Today would not be ... the end!

The fingers of one hand wrapped tightly around the rope, the other hand barely holding the beam above her, Kirsti brought up the leg that was not touching the can and placed it heavily on the bonnet of her father's car. With strength she didn't know existed, she pulled her entire weight up onto the car, releasing the tension around her neck. With one quick, determined movement she pulled her head out of the noose and fell off the car's bonnet, landing on the cement beside the petrol can with a thud.

She breathed deep gulps of air, relishing the fumes of petrol and sweat because she figured that meant she was alive. Her fingers rubbed her throat. Her tears mingled with the dust on the floor.

"Give us this day our daily bread. And forgive us our trespasses, as we forgive those who trespass against us. And lead us not into temptation, but deliver us from evil. For thine is the kingdom, the power and the glory, for ever and ever. Amen."

Kirsti didn't move for several minutes. Her body ached. Her throat was sore. She continued to tremble violently. Having planned her death, she realised in those last seconds that she desperately wanted to live. What if Owen had a similar realisation, but didn't manage to save himself? She cried some more.

Sometime later, Kirsti struggled to her feet. Looking at the huge dent in her father bonnet, she shrugged inwardly. It didn't matter. Her gaze went upwards to the noose and then the cross above it. How had she allowed life to get this bad? Why hadn't she been able to admit that she was suicidal? She didn't care about the damage. She knew there were more important things to do right now. Leaving everything as it was, she walked through the door into the storage room and unlocked the door into the backyard.

As she had expected, the back door was unlocked. Wasting no time and not caring how she looked, Kirsti walked through the dining room and into the lounge room where her parents and brother were watching TV.

Before they could react to her appearance, she said, "I'm suicidal and I need help."

VI

The moment Kirsti walked into the lounge room, time seemed to slow down. Every emotion Jenny had felt over the last couple of months came to the surface in a rush, causing her to feel dizzy. When Kirsti announced she needed help, Jenny didn't think it was possible for the feelings to intensify, but they did. Beside her, Stephen and Tim sat silent and motionless and she knew they were as stunned as she felt.

Jenny looked intently at Kirsti. Her beautiful dress was dirty and torn and Jenny was only vaguely aware of her daughter's bare feet. What had happened to her shoes and where was her bag? Had she been raped? The grip on her heart tightened. Her gaze went to Kirsti's face. Her long hair hung in knots around a face, which was smeared with dirt. What was happening? What had Kirsti said? The words had tumbled out of her mouth so quickly Jenny had no time to absorb them.

Makeup ran down her daughter's cheeks, amidst a river of tears. But that wasn't what finally got through to Jenny. The thing that alarmed her the most, and made her hold her breath, was the fresh bruise around Kirsti's neck. The sight of it broke the spell and, finally, Jenny sprang into action.

"My God! What happened?" Jenny rose from the sofa. "Who did this to you?"

"I did it to myself," replied Kirsti.

"What? Why?" Jenny pulled her daughter into her arms and tried to squeeze love into Kirsti's fragile body.

"Mum..." Kirsti pulled away from her. "...I told you. I'm suicidal and have been for weeks. I tried to hang myself, but at the last minute, I realised I didn't really want to die. But at the same time, I don't feel as if I really want to live either. I'm so confused."

Shock. Pain. Disbelief. What was happening to her family? Jenny didn't know what to say or do. She found it hard to think.

"It was almost too late," continued Kirsti in a flurry of words. "I was already choking, but I managed to free myself in time. Owen took everything when he suicided.

Everything. My ability to reason. My sense of security. My happiness. I don't know what to think or feel. I don't care about the things I once loved because nothing is important anymore. I know nothing will ever be the same again. How can it be when I feel so different inside? Life is too hard!"

Kirsti spoke words that struck a chord with Jenny. She understood everything her daughter said. She felt the same way. Jenny glanced at Stephen, needing help and support, and found him holding Tim's shoulder firmly, but knowing the confusion in his eyes probably mirrored her own. She wasn't surprised to find her husband and son nodding in agreement.

"My friends act as if I'm a leper. Josh ... well, I've been blind there," said Kirsti. "And that relationship is over." She paused. "I ... I've lied to everyone. I've quit my job. I see Owen everywhere. I want to be with him. I need answers. I feel as if nothing can ever be normal again. Will it?" The look of desperation on Kirsti's face dug deep into Jenny's heart. "Will it?" Kirsti asked again.

Jenny heard the agony in Kirsti's voice and shuddered. What could she possibly say to make things right, to make her daughter feel better? She didn't know the answers to her questions. She didn't believe they could return to their previous lives, as they had moved too far away from them. Besides, without Owen, it couldn't possibly be the same.

The seconds ticked by slowly. The family stood as if frozen in time. Desperately wanting to hear and be heard. This moment in time would never leave them. It would bind them together, always etched into their memories, but never wholly complete in details.

At last, Stephen stepped forward and took control. "I have already failed one of my children." His voice quivered and it made Jenny want to scream in pain. "I will not fail this family again," he continued. "We need to talk and, more importantly, we all need professional help. We've been too caught up in our own individual grief to realise it."

Jenny pushed the wetness from her own face with her hands. Her husband was right. She couldn't live with the fear any longer. It would destroy her if she let it, and she refused to let that happen. She had known for a while that she had to make a choice and Kirsti's actions made that choice clear and easy.

She chose to live!

Something had to be done. Today! Now! She chose to move forward and find the path that would lead them all to something better, something concrete ... maybe even something that reminded them of the normal lives they once shared. Reaching into her pocket, she took out the card Philip Knight had given her. It was late, but this was an emergency, and she knew he would understand. With one glance at her devastated family, she moved quickly to the telephone and dialled the number on the card.

It happened so suddenly, so unexpectedly. One minute he was sitting quietly with his parents and the next minute a bedraggled Kirsti was standing before him with rope marks around her neck. Tim wanted to vomit. He actually felt himself gagging when his father had placed a firm hand on his shoulder and squeezed it. His dad would never know how that one action had given him something he needed at that moment. Strength. Tim felt the burden lessen.

He listened to Kirsti's words and nodded. She was talking about him. She had to be. Then he realised she was telling them how *she* felt and it was identical to his feelings. He wasn't alone and that was another realisation that did wonders for him. He could tell by the looks on his parent's faces that they understood too, and that they also felt the mixed emotions he felt. He would have smiled at that moment, except his little sister had tried to commit suicide.

His dad stepped forward and drew the family close. Tim knew that the confusion of the last two months would end because his parents had finally seen passed their own grief and were reaching out to them. If Tim were a religious man, he would have thanked God at that moment. But he wasn't a religious man. He would, however, allow his parents to take control and they would move forward together. A third realisation hit him. This was what he wanted the most. Direction. Hope. Stability.

It was after 10pm, but his mother made a phone call regardless. The call was short and the look of achievement on her face, when she put the phone down, warmed him from the inside. The healing process was starting to happen. He could feel it. He rejoiced in it.

His mother reached out and took her husband's hand. "Something evil has attached itself to our family. Owen's death made us vulnerable. I have been walking the streets during the day because I'm scared to be home alone. I asked a minister to come over tomorrow and pray for us ... and for Owen. I think it's important."

His mother wasn't religious either, but he could see she needed the minister's visit. He approved for her sake, but for his own as well ... and Kirsti's. Something was happening in this house and it wasn't anything good.

"I'll make enquiries tomorrow and will organise counselling for all of us," announced his dad. "Individually and as a group. We can't hold our emotions in any longer."

Good. Tim knew he needed to talk about his feelings. He needed to be honest. A group session would open communications between the family again, which will allow them to sit down and talk when they are at home, but there were some things he didn't want to share with them, but would be comfortable talking to someone else—a stranger—about.

His mobile rang. He looked at the screen. Karl. "Hello."

"Tim, I'm sorry to phone so late," said Karl. "Kate has been worried about you. She needed to know that you're okay, mate."

Was he okay? He looked at his bruised sister, and then his gaze went to his parents. "Yes, I'm going to be okay."

There was a short pause and he heard Karl whisper something to Kate and she murmured her reply, but he couldn't make out the words. "That's great. We're pleased."

"I'm sorry for the hassle I've been to you," replied Tim. "You and Kate don't have to worry about me any more. Go out for a romantic dinner or something now that I'm out of your hair."

Karl laughed before whispering something to Kate again. "Tim, I think you've gotten the wrong idea."

"What do you mean?"

"Do you think me and Kate are ... an item?" asked Karl.

Tim clearly heard Kate's gasp. "Well, yes, aren't you?"

"He thinks you're my girlfriend," Karl said to Kate.

"Gross!" said Kate.

"Kate's my sister, knucklehead," said Karl. "We thought you knew that. She's been waiting for you to ask for her mobile number."

"Has she?" The flicker of hope strengthened. "Well, you'd better give it to me then."

Kirsti felt exhausted—mentally and physically. So much had happened in such a short time. But she also felt as if she had instigated a change within her family. She had reached out and opened a door, and they had all stepped through it together.

Her family understood. After her attempted suicide and confessions, she had expected anger and shouting, but she was wrong. Totally wrong! And it wasn't the only thing she had been wrong about either. Not everything had been taken away from her at the moment of Owen's death. Love remained. True, it had been hidden beneath the grief, barely visible, but they had managed to find it again. And now she also had hope to add to it. Love and hope would make a good foundation to build on. The future already looked more positive.

They didn't know why Owen had chosen to die. They would always speculate, of that Kirsti had no doubt, but they would never know for sure. And whilst she knew the reason did matter and always would, she also knew that knowing or not knowing made no difference to the outcome. Her brother was gone. Forever. Permanently. And it was something she didn't want for herself. She knew that now. She had chosen to live because she wanted to experience all things life had to offer—romance, love, marriage, children, grandchildren, multiple jobs, friends she hadn't yet met, overseas holidays and many other things she didn't have a clue about yet. She understood that future experiences wouldn't all be good, but that was life. She accepted that.

Having been in Owen's shoes, however, Kirsti understood now how quickly a healthy brain could become confused and how quickly depression could take hold. She also knew those feelings had affected everything in her life—all her senses, the way she interacted with people, the way she thought. Of course, not sleeping or eating didn't help. Her body and mind were unhealthy and she reacted to things that may not have been there—she glanced at the small mirror on the wall, knowing nothing would be there. Thankful all she saw was the room and her family.

Owen would never guide her to death. She knew that with a clarity that surprised her. It was a pity she hadn't realised that well before now. Was it an evil spirit, like her mother seemed to be suggesting? Did grief and lack of sleep cause her to hallucinate? Was it something else? She didn't know. She did know, however, that with her parent's help, she would be given the tools to beat it. And she would beat it because she had made a choice and she was going to live her life to the fullest.

All she ever had to do was ask for help.

Afterword

Thank you for reading the Fowler's tragic story. Some readers have asked why the reason for Owen's suicide was not disclosed. Was it an oversight? No, it wasn't. I never intended for a reason to be given. Firstly, why Owen took his own life was not important to the story. The effects of his decision was the main motivator for writing this novel. And secondly, some families never know why their loved ones make a decision so final as suicide. They are left to speculate *why* for the rest of their lives.

As a mother of someone who took his own life, I can confirm that the Fowler family might come across as wallowing in self-pity, but in reality, their pain and suffering would last much longer than two months. My family suffered for at least two years. But even today, whilst we have discovered a new normal, we sometimes slip back into an all-consuming depression. However, the difficult days happen less often and for shorter periods of time before the sun shines for us once again.

The effects of suicide are different for each individual family; as are the emotions and reactions associated with suicide. It's important to remember that you are not alone, the feelings of grief vary and it will take a long time before things start feeling manageable, let alone normal again. This is typical of grief, but I urge you to seek professional help and to be kind to yourself.

"Time heals all wounds." I don't know who said that, but in my case, it is true. Of course, my son is still gone and I still grieve for him, but I have learned to live with the missing part inside me. I have accepted his decision and have made my own. And because of that, I am coping. It took time, a long time, and there will always be a visible scar; but time did help me. If you have lost someone too, I sincerely hope time helps you as well.

Bonus

Read the quick facts that follow and become suicide aware.

Suicide Statistics in Australia

Since I live in Australia, I feel the Australian statistics are important. So here they are:

1. More than 41,000 Australians died by suicide between 1979 and 1998.
2. In 2006, there were 1,799 suicides recorded in Australia – 1,398 were males and 401 were females.
3. In 2016, there were 2,866 deaths by suicide in Australia – 2,151 were males and 715 were females.
4. Consistently over the past 10 years, the number of suicide deaths was approximately three times higher in males than females. In 2016, 75.1% of people who died by suicide were male.
5. Over a five year period from 2012 to 2016, the average number of suicide deaths per year was 2,795.
6. In 2016, preliminary data showed an average of approximately 8 deaths by suicide in Australia each day.
7. For every person who dies by suicide, it is estimated 30 people attempt suicide. That is approximately 63,600 suicide attempts each year.
8. Generally, suicidal people give some warning prior to attempting or completely the incident. However, the warnings are usually only realised in hindsight for a family with no understanding of the warning signs.
9. A person who attempts suicide is usually suffering from strong negative thoughts and feelings. These people need your help, not your judgement.
10. The suicide rate for Aboriginal and or Torres Strait Islander People in 2016 (23.8 per 100,000) is approximately twice as high as non-indigenous people (11.4 per 100,000).
11. While many people who take their own lives have a

mental disorder, a person doesn't have to have a mental illness to be suicidal.

12. Drug and alcohol abuse is closely related to suicidal behaviour.

13. Depression doesn't necessarily lead to suicide, but it means the person has a higher risk of getting there.

14. Suicide was the leading cause of death among people aged 15 to 44 years.

Sources:

Australian Institute of Health and Welfare (AIHW): Harrison JE, Pointer S and Elnour AA 2009. A review of suicide statistics in Australia. Injury research and statistics series no. 49. Cat. no. INJCAT 121. Adelaide: AIHW.

Australian Bureau of Statistics (2010). Causes of Death, Australia, Suicides 2008. ABS Catalogue No. 3303.0.

Australian Bureau of Statistics. (2017). Causes of Death, Australia, 2016. Catalogue No. 3303.0.

SANE Australia (2005). Facts and Figures about Mental Illness. Fact sheet 14 – Suicidal behaviour and self-harm.

Suicide Around the World

The World Health Organization (WHO) estimate that approximately 800,000 people die by suicide each year and for each person who died by suicide there may have been more than 20 others attempting suicide worldwide. This represents a global mortality rate of one death every forty seconds and one attempt every three seconds.

Suicide accounted for 1.4% of all deaths worldwide, making it the 17th leading cause of death in 2015.

The highest suicide rates, for both men and women, are recorded by the countries in Northern Europe, India and some African countries.

The Eastern Mediterranean Region and Central Asia republics have the lowest suicide rates.

The American Foundation for Suicide Prevention website states that approximately 45,000 Americans die by suicide each year (on average about 123 suicides per day) and for every suicide, there are 25 attempts. Suicide by males is about three and a half times more often than females. Suicide is the 10th leading cause of death in the US.

The UK National Statistics states that in the UK, there were 3.6% fewer suicides registered in 2016 than in 2015; this equates to 5,965 in 2016, a decrease from 6,188 deaths in 2015. Of these, the Welsh and Northern Ireland rates have both fallen slightly, but the Scottish rate has risen a small amount. Three-quarters of these suicides were male.

Sources:

World Health Organization (WHO) website—http://www.who.int/en/

American Foundation for Suicide Prevention website—
https://afsp.org/about-suicide/suicide-statistics/

UK National Statistics website—http://www.statistics.gov.uk/hub/

What are the Causes of Suicide?

There are many factors that increase the risk of suicide in teenagers. Some include:

- depression, bipolar and other psychological disorders
- feelings of hopelessness and worthlessness brought about by repeatedly failing at school, abuse at home or isolation from peers
- marital or relationship breakdown
- loss of employment
- financial hardship
- the recent loss of a loved one
- previous suicide attempts
- family history of depression and suicide
- dealing with homosexuality in an unsupportive family, school or community
- physical and sexual abuse
- drug and alcohol abuse

A combination of the above often triggers suicidal thoughts. Males are more likely to complete suicide, although statistics show females have a higher attempt rate.

Warning Signs

Suicide can be impulsive or a well thought out plan. While it is true that some people who die by suicide do not show any suicide warning signs, most do exhibit several of the warning signs listed below.

- sudden change in behaviour
- changes in sleep patterns and eating habits
- start to neglect hygiene and no longer take pride in how they look
- finds it hard to concentrate
- becomes irritable, angry and hostile
- distances themselves from family and friends
- gives treasured items away or throws them out
- loss of interest in activities previously enjoyed
- negative attitude towards life
- feelings of worthlessness and guilt
- thinks and talks about suicide and death
- starts saying things like, "I'm better off dead" or "There's no way out"
- sudden abuse of alcohol and drugs
- depression, sadness and lots of crying
- availability of weapons

About 80% of youths who die by suicide told someone what they were planning. If you or someone you know exhibits several of these signs, **take immediate action!**

Myths and Facts

Myth: Talking about suicide with someone who is at risk will put the idea into their head.
Fact: Asking someone if they are having suicidal thoughts opens up communication. It shows you care about them and it gives them permission to talk about their feelings. This lowers the risk of an impulsive act.

Myth: People who attempt suicide are weak or selfish.
Fact: People who attempt suicide are often experiencing strong negative feelings and a loss of hope. They may believe there is no other solution. They need support, not judgement.

Myth: Suicidal people want to die.
Fact: Suicidal people just want the emotional turmoil/pain to end. They often believe ending their life is the only option available to them.

Myth: People who talk about suicide don't do it.
Fact: Most people who have died by suicide told someone of their intentions.

Myth: If someone makes a quick recovery after a very long downtime, I can stop worrying.
Fact: A sudden behavioural swing can mean a decision has been made to end their life. The decision makes them seem happier and more peaceful.

Drugs and Alcohol

Statistics also show that about 34% of people had drugs or alcohol in their system at the time of their death. However, drugs and alcohol are not the primary cause of suicide.

It is true that some may use these substances to boost their courage. Some may allow impulsive decisions to rule them while their thought processors are impaired. Yet the true cause of suicide usually goes much deeper.

Suicidal people turn to drugs and alcohol as a way to escape the negative feelings and pain they are experiencing. During the use of drugs and alcohol, everything may seem brighter for a while, but this false sense of hope never lasts for long. Eventually, the person starts thinking of a more permanent solution to their problem. Suicide.

Whilst it is important to educate young adults of the dangers of drug and alcohol abuse, it is also important for friends and family of those at risk of suicide to look deeper and find real solutions to the root problems causing the abuse in the first place.

Source:

Australian Bureau of Statistics 2009, Causes of Death, Australia, 2009, cat. no. 3303.0, ABS, Canberra.

Helping a Friend through Loss

Suicide affects family and friends in many ways and to varying degrees. If a person does not receive the support they need, they may become suicidal themselves.

Don't let discomfort prevent you from reaching out and helping someone who is grieving. It is important they know they have your love and support. You might not know what to do or say, but that is okay. You may not have answers or feel qualified to give advice, but that doesn't matter either. The most important thing you can do for a grieving friend is to simply be there. Your presence will help them cope with the pain and begin to heal.

Coping with grief is more difficult when there is no one to talk to, so be prepared to sit and listen. Encourage them to tell you stories about their loved one. Offer your own memories. Ask them how and what they are feeling. Allow the person to cry and don't be afraid to cry with them.

Don't tell the person how they should feel. Don't make remarks like "Time heals all wounds" because wounds never heal completely, but the person will learn to live with the loss. Don't blame or judge. Don't compare their loss with someone else's.

While you may feel helpless, remember all you need to do is be there. Listening is the best gift you can give a grieving person. Just let the person tell their story over and over again. Offer support and assistance and your friend will know they are loved and not alone.

How to Help Someone at Risk of Suicide

by beyondblue

It's distressing to realise that someone close to you may be thinking about taking their own life. It's often difficult to know what to say and do, and how to make sure the person is safe. Most people who feel suicidal recover from these intense feelings. Family, friends and health professionals can make a big difference in helping people stay safe and to find positive reasons for living.

Act straight away, take warning signs seriously and ask the person if they are considering suicide and if they have any plans. This won't put the idea into their head but will encourage them to talk about their feelings. The person's safety is your main concern and you need to do whatever it takes to get them the help and support they need.

The tips in the next section, "What You Can Do to Keep Yourself Safe", can help you to work out some practical things you can do to help – for example, don't leave the person alone, and remove any means of suicide available (weapons, medications, alcohol and other drugs and access to a car). Encourage the person to get support from a health professional. Try to give them hope.

Ask him/her to promise that they will reach out and tell someone if suicidal thoughts return. And remember to look after yourself in this difficult and emotionally draining time.

It's not always possible to intervene. In some people, the warning signs of suicide are not obvious and even the most skilled health professionals may miss them.

What You Can Do to Keep Yourself Safe

by beyondblue

It's possible to get through tough times by creating your own 'tool kit' of coping strategies, which you can use when you're feeling suicidal or when things feel hopeless. It's vital to sort out the underlying problem—whether it's depression, an anxiety disorder or something else.

Postpone Any Decision to End Your Life

Keep a list of things you can do to distract yourself and use it when the feeling starts to surface. Give yourself time to get the support you need.

Talk to Someone

Reach out to others who might help you to see alternative ways of solving or thinking about a problem, and help you to have a more positive outlook.

If you're having trouble talking to people you know, phone a crisis line (e.g. Kids Help Line, Lifeline or the Suicide Callback Service).

Avoid Being Alone

Have someone stay with you, especially at night, until your thoughts of suicide decrease.

Write a Safety Plan

Come up with a plan you can put into action anytime – such as organising that you will ring a friend or family member when you feel overwhelmed or upset.

Write Down Your Feelings
Writing down your feelings, or keeping a journal, can be a great way to understand your feelings, your situation, and think about alternative solutions to problems.

Set Small Goals
Try to set goals that are achievable for you, even if it's on a day-by-day, or hour-by-hour, basis. And remember to reward yourself too.

Stay Healthy
Exercise and eating well can help you to feel better and manage difficult things in your life. Start by doing something small a couple of times a week (e.g. a 15-minute walk or two or three laps of a pool).

Avoid Drugs and Alcohol
Alcohol and other drugs are depressants that make you feel worse. They don't help to solve your problems and they can make you do things you wouldn't normally do.

See a Mental Health Professional
Psychologists, psychiatrists, counsellors and other health professionals are trained to deal with issues relating to suicide, mental illness and well-being. Ask your General Practitioner (GP) or contact a crisis line for information.

Where to Get Help

If a life is in immediate danger call Emergency Services immediately.

Australia — 000
Canada — 911
United Kingdom — 999 and 112
United States — 911

Suicide crisis lines can be found in most countries worldwide. Go to Wikipedia and search for "list of suicide crisis lines" and then search for your country for more details, including helplines, information and counselling.

Disclaimer:

The above information was correct at the time of publication.

Disclaimer

The information contained in the Bonus Suicide Awareness section of this ebook is general in nature and not intended to replace professional advice. While every effort has been taken to ensure the information is accurate, I make no claim and cannot be held responsible for information that is not complete, current, reliable or suitable for any purpose.

Links and contact phone numbers are given for convenience only and are not an endorsement of the products and or services provided.

About the Author

Born within the sound of the Bow bells in London, Karen Lee Field was seven when her parents decided to move to the "Lucky Country" and settle in Sydney, Australia. Apart from enjoying time with her family and pets, Karen loves escaping to fantasy worlds—places where her sometimes ordinary life is transformed into an exciting adventure and her imagination is set free. She writes novels for children and adults in various genres and her short stories appear in several anthologies. She currently lives on the south coast of NSW.

Connect with the Author

Would you like to be the first to hear my latest news? Please head over to my website to sign up to my author newsletter. I'll send them out whenever I have important news (once every two months or so). They will include new release announcements, and free and discounted book offers.

Website: http://www.karenleefield.com
Twitter: http://twitter.com/karenleefield
Facebook: http://facebook.com/karenleefield
Or search for "Karen Lee Field" on Goodreads

Did you enjoy reading
Domino Effect?

Authors love reviews. They are important, especially for independent authors. They bring credibility to the author and make books more discoverable for other readers.

Please consider leaving a short review online at the bookstore's website where you purchased this book, on Goodreads website or your own website if you have one.

Thank you.